One Little Secret

ELIZA LENTZSKI

ISBN-13: 9781074016609
Imprint: Independently published

OTHER WORKS BY ELIZA LENTZSKI

Don't Call Me Hero Series

Don't Call Me Hero

Damaged Goods

Cold Blooded Lover

One Little Secret

+ + +

Winter Jacket Series

Winter Jacket

Winter Jacket 2: New Beginnings

Winter Jacket 3: Finding Home

Winter Jacket 4: All In

Hunter

http://www.elizalentzski.com

Standalones

Sunscreen & Coconuts

The Final Rose

Bittersweet Homecoming

Fragmented

Apophis: Love Story for the End of the World

Second Chances

Date Night

Love, Lust, & Other Mistakes

Diary of a Human

+ + +

Works as E.L. Blaisdell

Drained: The Lucid (with Nica Curt)

CONTENTS

DEDICATION

To C

WAGER

I have been the victim of creative suffering. I know what it feels like to put your faith in someone, only for them to let you down.

I felt, rather than saw, Julia's hand brush at the hair closest to my temple.

"You're giving yourself frown lines, dear."

I waved her hands away in irritation and leaned forward on the couch.

I'd been here before with the same stupid optimism despite how many times I'd been hurt. I should have known better. Experience told me it would end like this, but I'd naively believed that this time would be different. I should have known it wouldn't last.

Her steady, rational voice tried to reach me: "It's only a game."

"Tell that to my heart," I bitterly replied.

The Minnesota Vikings had been coming up with new and creative ways to break my heart ever since I was a kid. The string of heartache had begun years before my birth. In 1988, running back Darrin Nelson bungled a pass on the goal line, which would have beat Washington. Gary Anderson in 1999 hadn't missed a kick all year—a perfect 35 of 35. So, of course, he missed a 38-yard field goal. 2001 had been a total embarrassment of a game when we lost 41-0 to the Giants. A Brett Favre pass was intercepted in 2010 with 15 seconds left to play. And more recently, Blair Walsh had missed a 27-yard chip shot in the 2016 Wild Card game.

"You shouldn't give up on them," she told me.

I pressed my lips together, feeling empty and disappointed. We trailed, 23-24 with ten seconds remaining in the game. No time outs. The ball was placed on our own 39-yard line. We were 61 yards away from the end zone, and our quarterback didn't have that kind of arm.

I rubbed my hands over my face. "I can guarantee they're not going to win this one."

"Wanna bet?"

I turned away from the television, briefly. "What'd you have in mind?"

Her features were impassive. "Vikings win, I get what I want. Saints win, you win."

"And what do you want?" I asked.

She didn't hesitate. "You in my bed. However I want you."

I swallowed thickly. "And if the Saints win?"

She raised a perfect eyebrow. "What do you want, dear?"

I didn't have to think on it. "Same."

A ghost of a smile played on her lips. "Do you want to shake on it?"

There was no time for such formalities. The home crowd roared as the center hiked the football.

Case Keenum dropped back and then stepped up into the pocket. The ball released from his hand and traveled 25-yards down the field.

I leaned forward on the couch, my hands clasped together.

Stefon Diggs leapt into the air and came down with the ball. A white-shirted opponent lunged for his body to make the game-ending tackle.

He missed.

There was no one between Diggs and the end zone.

"Oh my God," I muttered in complete disbelief.

The television announcers began to yell as Diggs raced down the field. 30 yards. 20. 10. No one was going to catch him.

"Oh my God."

Stefon Diggs stood in the purple end zone. Game over. The Vikings had won.

"Oh my God." My brain had broken.

The couch cushions shifted beside me as Julia pulled herself to her feet. She took a few steps before finally addressing me. "Bedroom," she commanded. "And bring your jersey."

Julia's bedroom was completely dark, with the exception of pale moonlight that slithered through the slats of the window blinds.

"On the bed," she instructed with a curt nod. "And take off your clothes."

I pulled my jersey over my head. My ponytail caught on the neckline and nearly tugged free from its rubber band. "Not wasting any time, eh?"

"I don't believe I asked for any comments from you." Her tone was cool and indifferent.

I dropped my jersey to the bedroom floor without another syllable. I wouldn't be needing any of my clothes; the chill in her attitude had made me hot all over. I'd actually come to love losing these bets.

I struggled with the nylon knot that held up my old sweatpants. I probably should have donated or thrown them away. The elastic waistband had long ago given up and the screen-printed 'Marines' along the left leg was cracked and peeling.

"I don't have all night, Miss Miller," she snapped.

Her impatience belied what was to follow. I knew she was going to take her time with me. She was going to make me unravel. She was going to make me come undone, again and again, but deny my orgasm until I was a liquid pool of desperation.

I abandoned the challenge of untying my sweatpants and wiggled them past my hips instead. The waistband dropped to my knees, and I inelegantly pulled my feet and ankles free of the offending item. I knew Julia was carefully studying my every move, but she remained silent while I struggled with the elementary task of undressing.

Only a white tank top remained, which I wore as a barrier between my skin and the scratchy material of the football jersey. My erratic tug of the shirt over my head simultaneously freed my hair from the rubber band that had formerly contained its wavy chaos in a slightly less chaotic ponytail.

"Bed," Julia sternly commanded, as if I'd forgotten the purpose of our being there.

Another bratty retort danced at the end of my tongue, but I suppressed the urge to further annoy my girlfriend. Her tongue could be far more pleasant than mine.

I crawled onto our shared mattress. I still thought of the apartment and its furniture as Julia's, but it was beginning to feel more like ours instead of only hers. My hands and knees disturbed the tautness of the duvet cover as I traveled to the center of the bed. When I had lived on my own, I had never bothered to make my bed. It had probably been a micro-aggression against the rigidity of military life when I'd been inspected for the crispness of my hospital corners to the cleanliness of my fingernails. Cohabitating with Julia came with its own regulations—dirty dishes in the sink, cleaning my hair out of the shower drain, coasters under my beer bottles—but the rewards of picking up after myself far outweighed the inconvenience.

I tossed a look over my shoulder, even though I had no doubt that Julia continued to inspect me. Our eyes briefly locked before her gaze raked over my naked form like hot coals. Her voice may have exuded icy control, but her wild eyes were an inferno.

I knew what she saw. The fine muscles of my triceps as I held myself up. The length of slender calves. The swell of my backside. The gap between my thighs. The scars across my back from a dirty bomb. The streaming moonlight felt like a spotlight on my imperfections.

I shifted my position with the intention of getting off of my hands and knees, but a single-worded command had me freezing in place.

"Stay," Julia demanded.

I remained in the vulnerable position, feeling a little like livestock on the auction block. Objectively, I knew my body was attractive and fit. I religiously worked out, but no amount of running or swimming could ever wipe clean the canvas. Because of those scars I doubted I would ever feel completely at ease in my skin, even in front of Julia.

Julia's steps were silent on the bedroom carpeting; I could neither hear nor see her approach. I visibly shivered at the sensation of a single finger tracing the length of my spinal column. Her touch was fluid and light; she took her time from the base of my neck to just above my tailbone. She was the only non-medical personnel to have touched my back since Afghanistan.

Despite my discomfort, a quiet sigh escaped my lungs.

"On your back, Miss Miller." Gone was the previous sharpness. In its place, Julia's tone had softened, rounded, and warmed. The gentle command surrounded me like a blanket.

I maneuvered on the mattress until I was on my back with my head toward the headboard. Julia's caramel gaze meandered from my face to my feet. She drank in every inch of my naked flesh, entirely on display for her. I watched the tip of her tongue travel from one corner of her mouth to the other. I should have withered under her pointed stare, but the open desire with which she looked at me only heightened my arousal.

"Can I trust you to keep your hands where I want them?" she asked.

"Probably not," I retorted.

My tone probably held too much cheekiness for her liking. I watched her nostrils slightly flare and her eyes narrow in displeasure.

"That's a pity," she clucked. "We'll have to do something about that, otherwise I'm afraid you might spoil my plans for you."

Julia silently stalked to her clothing bureau and opened the top drawer. Her hands disappeared from my view before producing a number of colorful patterned neck scarves. I primarily associated them with Julia hiding bite marks. On those occasions she would chastise my over eagerness, claiming she was too old for hickies—or at least those that were publicly visible.

Julia floated two scarves in my direction. They landed beside me on the mattress. "Tie one around either wrist, and then tie yourself to the bed frame."

I passed the woven silk through my hands before securing the material around my wrists. I had hoped that Julia would have restrained me herself, but there was also something exciting about doing it to myself. I knew she would be displeased if the knots came undone, so I focused on doing a good job. The silk scarves were slippery, but I managed a tight knot around each wrist. I was only able to tie my left hand to the bed frame, however. Julia would have to complete the job.

When I looked up for further instructions, my breath caught in my throat. In the time it had taken me to bind my wrists and semi-tie myself to the bed, Julia had slipped out of her t-shirt and yoga pants and into my football jersey. From the look of it, she was *only* wearing the jersey. Her arms swam in the abundant material, and the bottom hem stopped just above her upper thighs. The shirt was too large for her lithe frame, but it had never looked so good.

"You're lucky I'm over here," I throatily warned. I tugged at my constraints for added effect.

Julia's lips twisted into a wry smile. "That would be a violation of the terms of our agreement," she remarked.

"I don't remember signing a contract, Counselor."

Julia's hard gaze put me in my place. Her hands rested on her hips, causing the jersey material to creep up her exposed thighs.

"Why do you insist on defying me, Miss Miller? I thought we had an agreement."

"I'm sorry," came my meek apology.

She dropped her hands to her sides. "No touching," she told me. "Or I'll really give you something to be sorry about."

I nearly asked what I wasn't supposed to touch until she joined me on the mattress. Her naked thighs brushed against my legs. She lightly perched across my bare abdomen, her thighs straddling my torso. I was tempted to reach out and touch her with my one free hand, but I instead remained still and permitted her to tie the scarf attached to my right hand to the bedframe.

I tested the strength of the knots by flexing my forearms and tugging at my bonds. I pulled at my ties until the bedframe groaned. Julia's headboard was perfectly designed for these kinds of activities. The dark wood was of sturdy construction, so I didn't worry about snapping the wooden slats.

"I'll ask you not to ruin those scarves," Julia interrupted my experiment. "They're vintage and very expensive."

"Then why use them?" I challenged.

Julia curled her lip. "Because I don't do cheap, my dear."

I had a self-depreciating comment at the ready, but I smartly left it alone.

She rested her weight more solidly on my abdomen. I hissed when I realized she wore no underwear beneath my purple and yellow jersey. Her naked skin came in contact with my stomach.

A needy whine ripped through my lips. "God, you're such a tease."

"And you're always impatient," she darkly returned. "I thought you might have learned some willpower by now."

I bucked up against her, but with no real desire to break free. Losing had never felt so good.

She dragged her manicured nails down the valley of my naked breasts. "I'll pay attention to you in time, my dear, but first I should be rewarded for winning this bet."

An inquiry about the nature of her reward was on my lips, but she answered my unspoken question with her body. The mattress dipped on either side of me as she scooted up closer to the headboard. She held onto the top of the headboard and slowly lowered herself onto my waiting mouth.

I heard her quiet grunt when my tongue made first contact with her naked sex. She raised herself up again so she hovered just above my outstretched tongue. She lowered herself, only slightly, so I could barely get a taste.

I held my tongue rigid while she raised herself up and down. Up and down. My tongue slipped in and out of her clenching pussy. She ground her clit against my mouth in wide and loose circles.

If my hands had been free, I would have clamped tight to her twitching thighs and pulled her down to me. Instead, I had no choice but to grip the spindles of the headboard. I frantically moved my tongue and lips, but I was under no disillusionment; she was in complete control. She controlled the pace, the angle, the pressure.

The stiff mesh material of the football jersey scratched against my nose. I loved it when she wore my clothes, but at that moment, I needed the football jersey to be gone. I wanted to see her naked body floating above me. I wanted to watch the bounce of her naked breasts as she ground her clit into my mouth. Instead, I focused on her parted lips and upturned nose and dark, flashing eyes.

She gasped when I thrust my tongue up as far as I could reach. I moaned for more at the slight tang of her arousal.

Julia dropped the headboard and held onto my breasts for leverage. My aching nipples were starved for attention, but this wasn't about me. I lapped hungrily at her seeping slit. My saliva combined with her arousal, and I could feel the wetness spreading across my face. There was nothing dainty or delicate about this. It was sloppy and messy—everything Julia was not beyond the bedroom doors.

Her breathing became erratic and her movements against my mouth were more deliberate. God, I wanted to rip through those damn vintage scarves that held me prisoner, flip her onto her back, and fuck her into the mattress until she screamed my name. I hated this useless, helpless feeling, but I also knew I didn't have a choice. Julia had won our wager, and I would have to play by her rules.

"There," she panted. "Right. There."

I clenched the wooden spindles of the headboard and heard them creak from the pressure. The scarves bit into my wrists. I licked harder against her clit and hummed into her pussy.

She gripped my breasts tighter and ground her lower body more solidly against my mouth. I heard her quiet curse and felt her body shudder: "Fuck, Cassidy."

Her movements gradually slowed as she rode out her orgasm. I could feel her body tense and twitch from sensitivity when I continued to lick against her.

"Enough, enough," she begged off.

"What? That was too easy; I can do this all night," I insisted. I opened my mouth wide and stretched out my jaw, which had started to become sore. But I would never admit that to her.

She patted her hand against my collarbone. "At ease, soldier," she murmured. "Let me catch my breath."

Julia dismounted me, one long leg at a time, and rolled onto her side to lie beside me on the bed. One hand rested in the now-sweaty valley between my breasts and the other tangled itself in my hair. She pressed the entire length of her body against mine, and I smiled when I heard her deeply contented sigh.

My eyes fluttered shut and I loudly exhaled, appreciating being able to take a full breath again now that my mouth wasn't otherwise occupied.

"Whoops."

I cracked one eye open. "Whoops?" I curiously repeated.

"I seem to have mangled your, uh, breasts," she said, amusement in her tone.

Still tied to the bed, I lifted my head as best as I could to see to what she was referring. The normally pale skin of my breasts were flushed an angry red. Her grip on my breasts had been tight, but in the heat of the moment, I hadn't realized how hard she'd been holding onto me. I could practically see her fingerprints inlaid into my skin.

"What did you do to me?" I squeaked. "I'm disfigured!"

"Oh, hush," she chastised. "It's not that bad."

"But I bruise easily!" I complained.

She nuzzled her nose against the side of my face. "Yes, but just think of how pleasant those memories will be, dear, when you see those bruises."

Her fingers began to work loose the knots at my wrists. All of my tensing and pulling had managed to tighten them even more, threatening to cut off my circulation. I was surprised my hands weren't the same color as my Vikings jersey.

When Julia finally removed the scarves at my wrists, I rubbed at the tender skin.

"Loyalty, darling," she purred into my ear. "Let that be a lesson."

I'd never been a strong pupil in school, but it was one lesson I wasn't going to forget anytime soon.

CHAPTER ONE

The morning paper called it the Minneapolis Miracle. It was probably a moment I would always remember, but less for the last-second heroics on the football field and more for what had followed in Julia's bedroom. I wasn't a religious person, and I didn't necessarily believe in concepts like 'Fate' or 'Meant to Be,' but I considered my relationship with Julia nothing less than a miracle.

She was out of my league—anyone with working eyes could see that. But the timing of it all felt like some force, some guiding principle, had designed the circumstances surrounding us ever meeting. The spilled drinks at the Minneapolis bar. The job opportunity in the tiny, remote town of Embarrass, Minnesota. When I'd been cursing my bad luck, frying beneath the unforgiving desert sun, lips blistered and cracked, there was no way I could have predicted how my story would take a turn. If I'd never suffered from PTSD, if I'd never gone to Afghanistan, if I'd never joined the Marines—all of those circumstances and pathways had led me to meeting and falling in love with Julia Desjardin.

"Are you done with that?"

Stanley Harris' voice snapped me from uncharacteristically deep thoughts.

I hadn't yet touched the daily paper on my desk, but Stanley's question was part of the morning routine. I skimmed the front page before separated the sports section and comics for myself, leaving the serious bits for my Cold Case partner.

Stanley Harris was more gnome than man. His full, bushy beard typically held clues to whatever he'd eaten earlier in the day. His awkward sense of humor was out of place everywhere except for the basement of the Fourth Precinct. Our entire division was a haphazard, motley crew of misfits who didn't quite belong anywhere else within the city police department.

I didn't quite have an office of my own. We all shared a communal space with the exception of our supervisor, Captain Forrester. He was a seasoned veteran, disenchanted with police work. From the moment I'd met him I knew we wouldn't get along. He was biding his time until he could collect his pension and social security, and I was a young cop looking to cut my teeth and make a name for myself somewhere.

"Yeah, man. It's all yours."

Stanley took the newspaper and folded it in half. He rocked back on his heels. "If anyone calls," he began.

"No one ever calls," Sarah Conrad piped in. She sat at her desk, eyes focused on her computer screen. I wondered if she'd broken her top score in Solitaire yet.

Besides Stanley Harris, Captain Forrester, and myself, the last member of the Cold Case division was a woman by the name of Sarah Conrad. She split her time between our office in the basement of the Fourth Police Precinct and a Victim's Advocate office across town. Whereas Stanley and I worked to solve unresolved crimes or put criminals behind bars, Sarah's role was to assist the victims, or in our case, typically the victim's family. If I wasn't already head-over-heels in love with another woman, Sarah's beauty probably would have made me nervous. Even then, she was a challenge to be around. Dark hair, long eyelashes, a perpetually painted, red pouty lip. She had a penchant for scoop and v-neck shirts that showed off her prominent cleavage. She was also dry, sarcastic, and a terrible flirt.

"Well … if they do." Stanley clucked his tongue on the roof of his mouth.

"Don't worry; I won't tell them you're in the can," I promised with a grin.

Stanley produced a tense smile before leaving the office, newspaper tucked under his arm.

"Does anyone else find it morbid that he reads the obituaries in the bathroom?" Sarah announced when Stanley had left the office.

"My grandma would cross names out of the phonebook while she read the obits," I noted.

Sarah wrinkled her nose. "Okay. That's morbid on a whole new level."

"Or practical," I supplied in my grandmother's defense.

The squeak of tennis shoes on aging linoleum drew my attention to the perpetually open door of our shared office. A red-faced and out-of-breath Stanley Harris stood in the threshold.

"That was fast," Sarah observed. "I hope you washed your hands."

"I found a person of interest from an old case in the newspaper," Stanley panted, ignoring Sarah's unorthodox humor.

"Oh yeah? Which case?" I asked. I was starting to feel more comfortable with our case load, but I was nowhere near as versed as Stanley. The guy must have had a photographic memory the way he could recall the tiniest details.

"About three years back, a group of local high school kids were partying after their graduation. Someone at the party got shot and later died in the hospital. No one fessed up to firing the gun, and the case went cold."

"What's our person of interest in the paper for?" Sarah asked.

"She's dead."

+ + +

When a cadaver is discovered, standard operating procedure varies depending on the cause of death. When the death appears to have resulted from natural causes, a medical examiner or licensed physician signs a death certificate before the body is released to the deceased's next-of-kin. If foul play is suspected, however, an entirely different chain of events—like a complicated dance—is evoked.

In the hospital morgue, bodies slide in and out on metal trays, just like on TV. But instead of paper tags attached to big toes, plastic bracelets around an ankle identify a name and a date of birth. Weight and height are recorded. Identifying marks like scars or tattoos are observed. The body is photographed, and forensic evidence is collected—scrapings under the fingernails, clothing is removed and bagged, pelvic exams are conducted for signs of trauma. Not all bodies are given an autopsy, however; some causes of death are more obvious than others.

"Kennedy Petersik. 20 years old."

I stood in a hospital morgue with Stanley and a forensic pathologist who'd simply introduced himself as Gary. We all wore surgical masks, not so much to prevent contamination, but to counter the stale smell of formaldehyde that hung in the air.

Gary had a full head of grey hair. His face was long and drawn with wide-set blue eyes. I didn't really know if we were supposed to be there. Cold Case typically didn't gain access to recent deaths, but Stanley had called ahead; he apparently knew Gary from when they'd been in college together. Stanley had originally gone to school to become a medical examiner, but his path had deviated to Cold Case.

Kennedy Petersik's eyes were closed. Her long, blonde hair was fanned out behind her on the metal trolley. Everything but her head and neck were blanketed with a cheap, crinkly sheet that hospitals insist on using in life as well as in death. I was used to photos of dead bodies, but it had been a while since I'd been in front of an actual cadaver. I don't think anyone really gets comfortable with death, unless it's their job. I hoped I wouldn't embarrass myself in front of these two veteran men, but even Stanley looked a little paler and more uncomfortable than usual.

Gary sighed wistfully as we collectively gazed upon the body. "These ones don't get any easier. I mean, Christ, she was just a kid."

I'd been ankle-deep in Afghan sand when I was twenty. I hadn't felt like a kid then. But I kept those sentiments to myself.

I cleared my throat. "Cause of death?"

Gary consulted a clipboard and flipped to the second page. "Single gunshot wound to the abdomen. Slightly downward, right-to-left internal bullet path."

I visibly winced when Gary pulled back the sheet that had been covering the body. Kennedy Petersik was naked. Her skin was pale, almost light blue. The Y-shaped autopsy incision stretched across her chest, connected at the sternum, and continued down to her pelvic bone. I wanted to yank the thin blanket out of Gary's hands and shield her body; this young woman been through enough without having to be on display in a room of strangers.

"Gunshots to the stomach are tricky," Gary remarked. "The death can be quick and painless, slow and messy, or not fatal at all. It all depends on what the bullet hits as it makes its way through the body. She was lucky. The bullet could have severed her spinal cord and paralyzed, but not kill her. If it had hit her intestines, which are full of bacteria, it would have been a slow, painful death by infection."

I didn't know how 'lucky,' death was, but I saw no reason to interject.

Instead of moving closer to get a better look at the star-shaped bullet hole in the woman's midsection, Stanley took a step back. I observed him out of the corner of my eye. It was hard to read his emotions because of the surgical mask that covered most of his face, but something had him thrown. He wasn't naturally gregarious or outgoing, but he seemed to have become more withdrawn in the morgue, even more than was usual for him.

In the absence of his assistance, I stepped up.

"What are we thinking? Homicide? Suicide? Accident?" I proposed.

"There was only one gunshot; multiple shots typically indicate homicide." Gary ran a gloved finger around the skin that surrounded the tidy, single bullet hole in Kennedy Petersik's abdomen. "But we also have to consider the distance of the gun from body. Suicide shots are at contact or near contact range. It causes a burn mark around the wound, just like this," he said, tapping the taunt skin, "and it leaves behind gunfire residue, or GSR."

"Was GSR present on our victim's hands, too?" I asked.

Gary nodded. "But we also have to consider that the gun went off inside a contained environment—in this case, inside the victim's car. We found GSR on just about everything. This also goes back to our contact range wound," he continued. "At contact range the gunshot wound tends to form a star-shaped entry wound, like what you see here."

"But someone could have just as easily pressed the gun against her stomach and shot, right?" I proposed.

"True," Gary conceded. "But there's no signs of struggle—no other scratches or bruises that suggests she fought back. You would expect to see those if her attacker was in such close proximity when the gun went off."

"What about these marks?" I didn't touch the body, but I motioned towards the insides of the young woman's arms where I could just see small, pale, horizontal lines, slightly raised in comparison to the rest of the surrounding skin.

Gary didn't show the same restraint as me. He gripped the woman's wrist and twisted the arm awkwardly so the neat lines were more visible.

"Old scars," he said. "I'd guess she was probably into self-harm. We found little lines on her inner thighs as well. Typically in cases like this, the cuts start out hidden, then they become more visible, like a cry for help that becomes progressively louder."

Gary, thankfully, returned the white sheet to its previous position and covered up Kennedy Petersik's nakedness.

"If it was suicide, the method used strikes me as unusual," he noted as he covered the body back up. "Men tend to choose more violent suicide methods like guns or hanging; women are more likely to overdose on medications. They go to sleep and never wake up."

I heard Stanley's sharp intake of air. When I looked in his direction, he tried to cover up his reaction with a cough.

I had more questions for Gary, but I was growing concerned about Stanley's well-being. I watched him rapidly swallowing as if trying to force down the rising bile in his throat. He hadn't spoken a word since we'd arrived. I'd thought death and decay didn't rattle him, but maybe I'd been wrong.

"Gary, thanks for seeing us on such notice," I said in earnest. "I'll be in touch if we have other questions."

"The pleasure's all mine, Detective," he said, nodding his head obligingly. He looked around the room at our somber surroundings. "Feel free to drop by anytime; it gets a little lonely down here."

+ + +

The door of my beat-up Crown Vic slammed noisily behind me. I hadn't used much force, but the old cop car seemed to rattle on its axles.

The small parking lot was mostly empty, which made Julia's black Mercedes more obvious than usual. I hadn't memorized the vehicles of Julia's co-workers, but then again, I'd never met any of them with the exception of Alice, the cute and capable office manager. It made me question if my girlfriend was the only one who actually did any case work.

New that day was a silver Mercedes coupe, a style newer and slightly flashier than Julia's sedan. Parked beside the two luxury cars, my police-issued vehicle looked more embarrassing than usual. Cold Case was like the estranged third-cousin of the Minneapolis police department. Our resources, like my patrol car, tended to be hand-me-downs.

I reached the front door of the public defender office at the same moment that someone was leaving. I instinctively yanked the door wide open and held it for the woman exiting. I smiled and made eye contact as she breezed past without so much as a thank you. I froze, forgetting my annoyance at the woman's lack of courtesy, when I realized I knew who she was.

She didn't give me a second look, however, no sign of recognition. Melissa Ferdet unlocked her silver sports car from afar. The fancy vehicle chirped before she opened the driver's side door and stepped inside, one long leg after the other. Her tailored pantsuit accentuated the long, lean lines of her figure. I couldn't imagine what business the high-profile criminal lawyer would have had at a public defender's office, but I immediately suspected the worst.

I stood on the concrete stoop of Julia's law office and watched Melissa Ferdet drive away. A peculiar, uneasy feeling settled in my chest. I was instantly transported back to the bar where Julia and I had originally run into the woman, but more so than the visualization, I remembered how it had felt. In her shock at seeing her old acquaintance, Julia had ignored me—failed to introduce or involve me. All of those same feelings of inadequacy bubbled to the surface.

The front lobby area of the legal aid office was empty. I hovered near the front reception desk and waited for Alice, the fresh-faced legal assistant, to make an appearance, but she never appeared.

Instead of waiting in the lobby, I walked down the short hallway that led to Julia's office. Her door was slightly ajar. The mostly-closed barrier between us caused the feeling in my chest to grow heavier. What would I find on the other side of the door? My girlfriend working diligently behind her desk? Or a disheveled Julia, cleaning up the signs of indiscretion. I shut my eyes as a wave of what I can only describe as extreme nausea cascaded over me.

Stop being a coward, Marine. Open the door and get it over with.

I nudged the door open with the toe of my heavy black boot. It swung noiselessly open and stopped just before it could connect with the wall behind it. It was the same motion I might make if I was searching a house for a wanted felon.

Julia stood behind her desk, eyes cast down.

She hadn't noticed my silent arrival. I did a quick scan of the room. The file folders and books on her desk were intact, not flung to the floor in a fit of passion. Her hair was carefully tucked behind one ear, not sweaty or in disarray, and her bright red lipstick was in place, not smudged or kissed entirely off.

The hemline of her pencil skirt was straight, the white Oxford shirt carefully tucked in. Her shirt was crisply pressed, unbuttoned to that damn third button, straining but not obscene.

Her pale neck and collarbone were unblemished, untouched, no scratches or love bites, no flush to her apple cheekbones.

I heard her heavy sigh. The force of her breath rustled the loose papers on her desk. Her body language revealed fatigue.

"Hi." The one-word greeting got caught in my throat.

Julia's head snapped up. "Jesus, Cassidy," she exclaimed. "Where'd you come from?"

It was a rhetorical question and not meant to be answered. I shifted my weight from one foot to the other. "Sorry. I didn't mean to scare you."

Julia walked around her desk. In her high heels, she was slightly taller than me. Her fingers touched the collar of my button-up shirt and she instinctively re-arranged the material. "It's okay; I didn't know to expect you."

"I was in the neighborhood," I told her. "I had an unplanned trip to a hospital morgue."

"Oh?" Her eyebrows arched in interest. "Anyone we know?"

"A local girl got shot. It might be connected to an old cold case." I wasn't forthcoming with the details, but only because something else had taken residency in my thoughts. "What was your ex-girlfriend doing here?" I blurted out.

Julia's caramel eyes perceptively narrowed. "I would hardly call Melissa Ferdet an ex," she resisted.

"What would you call her, then?" I challenged, although my tone held neither malice nor heat.

"We were both interns at the same law firm during law school."

"Yeah, but you guys have *history*."

"History?" she repeated with an incredulous laugh. "We made out *once* at a company Christmas party."

I nearly choked. "You did *what?*"

Julia pursed her lips. "Let's not be naïve, darling. We both were with other people before we found each other."

"I know that," I scowled, "I just never expected to actually *meet* any of your exes."

"I told you—Melissa Ferdet isn't an ex-girlfriend. It was a one-time thing. I can assure you that it went no further than the women's bathroom."

I nearly hyperventilated. "You made out in a public bathroom?"

Julia rolled her eyes. "It was the company bathroom of a powerful criminal law firm, not a port-a-potty, Cassidy."

"What was she doing here?" I asked. A new misgiving crept into my brain. "How did she even find you?"

"It's called Google, dear. I never told her where I worked, if you'll remember. Apparently, she made an innocent comment to someone at her firm about running into me, and they asked her to follow up."

"For what?"

"For a job," she clipped. "I'm being head hunted."

"Why?"

"Why are you asking so many questions?" she deflected.

"I'm a detective. It's what I do," I responded.

"Well there's nothing you have to *detect* from me."

I watched her work the back muscles of her jaw. "Why are you getting so mad?"

"I don't know," she practically growled. "Maybe it's because Melissa Ferdet just barged into my office with her vintage Gucci suit and Jimmy Cho heels and Louis Vuitton bag."

"You look fine," I naïvely remarked.

Julia struck her hand against the top of her desk. "That's not the point."

The hamster that worked the giant wheel of my brain slowly caught up with our conversation. "It's because you're a public defender. And your office always smells like burnt coffee. And she's going to be partner at some high-profile criminal defense firm."

Julia shuttered her eyes and her shoulders drooped forward. She didn't verbally confirm my revelation, but she didn't need to.

I dropped my blind jealousy and wrapped my arms around her. When I realized she was silently shaking, I tightened my hold. "Shhh," I hushed into her ear. "Baby, it's okay," I tried to sooth.

"It's so juvenile. It's so pathetic. *I'm* pathetic. This shouldn't be a contest. I like the work I do; it's challenging and rewarding like nothing else I've done."

"And yet ..." I started for her.

"And yet ... why do I let the Melissa Ferdets of the world make me feel ashamed of where I am?"

Surprisingly, I could relate to Julia's frustration. I'd joined the military to escape St. Cloud. I'd become a police officer because it was the most logical transition from the Marines. But being a Cold Case detective had never been part of the plan—not that I'd ever been good at setting out personal career goals for myself.

When she'd been in law school or studying for the bar exam, I was sure Julia had never imagined this career for herself. The stains on the worn carpeting. The peeling wallpaper. The outdated furniture. They were much more than ugly interior design elements; they were a microcosm for how far she'd fallen, from small-town city prosecutor to indigent public defender. The work she was doing was important—so important—but in the day-to-day monotonous grind, it was easy for the bigger picture to get lost.

"I feel like some of my insecurity is rubbing off on you," I muttered guiltily.

Julia brushed at the hair that had fallen across her eyes. "Don't try to shoulder the burden here, Hero," she mumbled. "I've got to get out of my own way and out of my head."

"Good luck with that," I said cheekily. "It's a pretty big head."

Julia's mouth fell open and an offended noise rattled up from her throat.

"But it's only big because of that big old brain in there," I quickly backpedaled. "I don't know how your neck doesn't get tired from holding it up all the time."

A small smile played on Julia's painted lips. She shook her head. "You're normally so charming. What happened?"

"I guess I must be a little rusty," I shrugged. "Why don't you get your friend back in here, and I can practice on her?"

The air suddenly felt like it had been sucked out of the room. Julia flicked the tip of her tongue against the fine, pale scar at the edge of her lip. She stood perfectly still, like a rattlesnake coiling unobtrusively in the moments before it lashed out at its unsuspecting prey.

But I wasn't unsuspecting. I knew exactly what I was doing. I might not have had the consoling and reassuring words to pull Julia out of her Melissa Ferdet-induced funk, but I knew how to make her mad. Jealous. Angry. Fiery. There would be no room in that big brain of hers for self-doubt if she had me bent over her office desk. My lower abdomen warmed at the simple imagery.

"That won't be necessary," she said. Her tone was even and measured.

I raised my eyebrows. "No?" I questioned with faux innocence.

"Is Alice still out there?" she questioned.

I grinned and rocked back on my heels. "Nope." I let my lips emphasize the second half of the word. "It's just you and me."

Julia's normally erect posture visibly sagged. "I'm sorry. I don't feel like doing this here."

My cocky façade fell away. "Wait. What?"

Julia's features lost some of their sharpness and heat. "I've been in this office for long enough today, Cassidy," she sighed. "Can we continue this conversation at home?"

I nodded and cleared my throat of the disappointment that had lodged itself there. "Yeah. Sure. Of course."

I followed the red taillights of Julia's black Mercedes back to her St. Paul apartment. Too many conflicting thoughts and emotions ricocheted around in my head. My brain hollered louder than the in-car radio. I had expected to be slammed against an office wall. Julia would have made quick work of my belt and the front fastenings of my dress pants before jamming her fingers down the front of my underwear with the same intensity with which she threw my willing body against the back of her office door. I could practically feel the phantom lingering of her teeth in my neck and her fingers twisting and pulling at my nipples.

Fuck. What had gone wrong? Where had I messed up?

I worried that my teasing may have gone too far. Julia clearly had strong opinions about this Melissa woman. Maybe I'd unintentionally stepped over a boundary with her.

I entered the apartment with a ready apology. "Julia, I—." But before I could say anymore, a body crushed against mine.

Eager teeth nipped at the sensitive flesh of my neck. The bottom of my shirt was unceremoniously yanked out of my pants. It normally wasn't smart to ambush a police officer who also happened to be a formerly enlisted Marine, but I leaned into the attack when Julia's sandalwood musk overwhelmed my senses.

"I-I thought you were pissed at me?" I managed to gasp. Fingers wiggled under my shirt and polished nails scratched across my bare torso.

Julia cocked her head to the side. "Why would I be mad at you, dear? I only wanted to fuck you from the comfort of our bed and not on an office floor. It's hard on my body; I'm not as young and pliable as I used to be."

"No more public bathroom make out sessions for you, huh?" I teased.

I watched the previous fire from her law office return. Flames practically flickered behind her caramel irises.

"Not another word from you, Miss Miller," she sternly commanded, "unless it's my name."

I swallowed hard and nodded.

CHAPTER TWO

The Fourth Precinct was a large building—one of the largest police stations in the city—yet it wasn't big enough to house all of the physical evidence related to the unsolved missing persons, homicides, and general crimes that we oversaw in the Cold Case division.

I was crammed into the passenger side of Stanley's hybrid car on the way to the warehouse we referred to as the Freezer. It had been Stanley who had unironically come up with the nickname; we worked for Cold Case and the storage facility was kept at a consistently chilly temperature to preserve the integrity of the evidence stored inside. I had only been to the evidence warehouse a few times, but Stanley split his time between our basement office in the Fourth Precinct and the Freezer.

Our task that day was to retrieve the evidence boxes connected to the investigation of the death of a young man named Michael Bloom. He had been shot at a post-high school graduation party, and later died at an area hospital from gunshot wounds. The case had gone cold when none of the teenagers were forthcoming about what they had or hadn't witnessed that night, and everything related to the teen's death had been boxed up and sent to the Freezer until new information was discovered that might warrant a second look.

The dead girl at the morgue, Kennedy Petersik, had been present at the house party where Bloom had been shot. The coincidence itself, of course, wasn't enough to re-open the Bloom case. Ideally, we would need the bullets retrieved from both shootings to match— to have come from the same gun. It was a long shot, but the more time I spent on the Cold Case team, the more I recognized that we existed solely for these long shots.

Stanley stared straight ahead at the road in front of us. His hands gripped the steering wheel at 10 and 2. "Did you know that Vincent van Gogh died from a gunshot wound to the abdomen?"

"The painter?" I asked.

"It was the early morning of July 29th, 1890," he recited. "He died in his room at the Auberge Ravoux in the village of Auvers-sur-Oise in northern France. To this day, it's still debated if it was suicide or murder. They never found the gun, and eyewitness accounts kept changing. Most people at the time assumed that he'd killed himself, but I mean, who shoots themselves in the stomach?"

"Maybe the kind of person who cuts off his own ear?" I proposed.

I'd noticed a change in my co-worker ever since our visit to the hospital morgue. Stanley had never been a chatterbox, but he'd become more reserved over the past few days. I'd also caught him talking to himself on a number of occasions. Something was off, but I didn't know how to ask.

"Stanley—do you have a photographic memory?"

"A little bit, but it's not textbook," he stated. "It's never been clinically documented, at least."

"How did you remember Kennedy Petersik was a person of interest in an old cold case?" I inquired. "We have hundreds of unsolved cases. Maybe thousands."

"I didn't—not really." His lips thinned momentarily before he began again. "We went to the same high school. Not at the same time, though. I graduated eons ago."

Stanley didn't look much older than myself, but he wasn't fishing for compliments about his youthful appearance. He was only stating facts.

"Kennedy and I were recipients of the same academic scholarship at Pius High School," he continued. "It goes to disadvantaged youth who show academic potential. I'm on the board now that reviews applications for who gets the scholarship each year. We also have a mentor program to help the recipients through their first year. It can be hard being the Scholarship Kid at a private high school," he remarked in his matter-of-fact style. "We all wore the same khaki pants and polo shirt uniform, but you still stuck out like a sore thumb."

Stanley's tone wasn't wistful or melancholy, yet my stomach sank uncomfortably. "Were you Kennedy Petersik's mentor, Stanley?"

He didn't provide me with an immediate response. He cleared his throat and his grip tightened on the steering wheel of his hybrid car. His non-answer was telling.

"I'm sorry." My apology stuck in my throat.

Stanley wiped at his nose with the back of his hand. "I am, too."

+ + +

I stood in front of a giant whiteboard with eight names written to one side. A series of numbers were located next to the names, giving it the appearance of a scoreboard, but I didn't know the game. The Homicide division was located on the ground floor of the Fourth Precinct building. I'd walked past the area countless times, but I'd never had a reason to actually visit.

"That's the clearance board," a nearing voice informed me. "The Sergeant keeps track of open, closed, and pending cases on it. All of those numbers represent a dead person."

I looked to my right to see a man in a fitted suit standing beside me. His badge hung on a chain around his neck, just like I'd been doing until Julia had convinced me to wear my badge on my belt. She'd been right about the look—the man looked like he was attending an IT conference or worked at a big box store rather than being a police officer.

The man stuck his hands in his pants pockets and rocked on his heels in expensive-looking loafers. "Did you know that if you're murdered in America," he continued, "there's only a one in three chance of finding the killer? The national clearance rate is under 60 percent. Back in the 1960s, it was as high as 90 percent."

"Why so low?" I questioned. "I would have thought the reverse considering new technology, like DNA testing."

"The standards for charging are too fucking high," he grumbled. "These goddamned prosecutors are only willing to charge someone if they've got an open-and-shut case." He removed his right hand from his pocket and thrust it in my direction. "Detective Jason Ryan," he introduced himself. "Homicide."

Jason Ryan was young—maybe even younger than myself. Excitable blue eyes that bounced around the room as if he was always looking for the next best thing. Brown hair trimmed on the sides and a little longer on top. He used an unnecessary amount of hair product to keep the top hair slicked back. His stubble looked purposeful—highly manicured, not the result of being too lazy to shave his face that morning. Non-uniformed police could do whatever they wanted to do with their facial hair—within reason—since they didn't have to worry about riot gear making a tight seal against their jawline.

His navy blue suit was too fitted for a police officer. The men I knew in the department wore boxy dress pants, white collared shirts, and ties they'd gotten for Father's Day or as a birthday present. Detective Ryan's pants were skinnier than mine.

His youth and wardrobe set off a warning flag. Typical homicide detectives had spent a lifetime in the department as they slowly worked their way up the food chain, one grueling promotion after the next. I was an anomaly at the rank of detective—damaged goods not fit for a patrol car, but too much time as a police officer to be discarded entirely. It made me wonder what Detective Jason Ryan's situation was. He could have annoyed people along the way and gotten shuffled from one department to the next. It took a lot to fire someone who'd made it through the academy.

"Detective Cassidy Miller," I eventually returned, shaking his hand. "Cold Case."

Detective Ryan's eyebrows furrowed. "Cold Case? What are you doing up here? I thought you all hung out in the basement."

"We have a mutual interest in the death of Kennedy Petersik."

"Petersik. Petersik." He chanted the name as if it was somehow familiar, but he couldn't recall why.

"Caucasian. Female. Twenty years old. Single gunshot wound to the abdomen," I recited.

Detective Ryan snapped his fingers. "Petersik! Damn it. I should have remembered. Her parents call us nearly every day to see if there's new leads on her homicide."

"You're ruling it foul play already?" My surprise showed on my face and in my voice. "I didn't know the forensics was conclusive."

His eyes narrowed slightly. "What do you know about it?"

"I went down to the morgue and saw the body."

Ryan's upper lip curled. "Are you some kind of overachiever? Betting that we won't solve this thing, so you're getting a head start?"

"No, of course not. She was a person of interest in one of our files."

"And now that she's dead you think there's a connection?" he posed.

I shrugged. "Could be. We think it's worth checking out, at least."

I noticed, then, that one of the names on the clearance board was Ryan's own. The number thirty-five was written in bright red marker next to his last name.

"This number," I said, pointing at the thirty-five, "is that Kennedy Petersik?"

He nodded.

"Where was she found?" I asked.

"State trooper found her after investigating an abandoned car on the shoulder of a county road. She was in the driver's seat, still buckled in."

"Was the weapon still there, too?" I asked.

"A 9 millimeter was found by her feet," he noted. "The bullet extracted from the body matched the gun."

"Prints?"

"Hers," Ryan confirmed. "We lifted a separate print off the cartridge, but nothing came back."

"Did her family know anything about the gun?" I asked.

"Nothing. And they were adamant about it. They never kept guns in the house, so they had no idea where it might have come from."

"Anything else in the car?"

"It was pretty clean. No wrappers or trash."

"I mean other prints or DNA," I sighed with annoyance.

Ryan flashed me what I'm sure he thought was a charming smile. "I know. The car was clean. No fibers, prints, or blood that shouldn't have been there."

"And yet you still think it was homicide?" I challenged.

"Didn't find a suicide note," he reasoned. "Her parents say she was quite the writer—seems like something a writer would do if she wanted to off herself."

I curled my lip at the casualness with which he spoke about another human life. But he wasn't the first cop to act that way and he wouldn't be the last.

"I need you to sign off on this request." I didn't frame my statement as an actual request, although technically I needed permission from someone in Homicide to do anything with evidence that wasn't mine. "We're hoping to get an analysis on the bullet from our cold case and compare it to the one retrieved from Kennedy Petersik," I explained. "I've got the old bullet in our materials, but I need access to the active file."

"Sure. Knock yourself out," Ryan breezed. He grabbed the written request form I held in my hand and scribbled his name at the bottom. "I'm sure you don't have much else to do in Cold Case; might as well keep yourself busy."

Stanley was alone in the Cold Case office when I returned from upstairs. The evidence boxes and case files we'd retrieved from the Freezer related to the death of Michael Bloom were spread out on one of the large work tables.

I briefly scanned the items that Stanley had pulled out of the evidence boxes. Numerous paper files and small cassette tapes filled with witness testimonies, I suspected. The work table was littered with blown up images of the scene of the crime—a grassy field a few yards from a massive house—and photographs of our teenaged victim.

"Did you get the bullet from the Petersik case?" Stanley asked.

I held up the plastic baggie that contained the irreplaceable evidence. "Got it," I confirmed. "Some guy in Homicide really made me work for it though. Cops are such pricks."

Beyond our estranged supervisor, I was the only badge in our Division. My weak attempt at a joke didn't register with Stanley, however.

"So, fill me in on this cold case," I prodded. "A high school graduation party, right? And Kennedy was there?"

Stanley nodded. "I never got the chance to ask her about it though. By the time it was handed off to Cold Case, she was already gone to college."

"What happened?"

"Every year, the seniors rent a big house on a lake after graduation. It's a tradition at Pius that predates even me. Some of the parents put up the money for the house to make sure the kids aren't drinking and driving."

"Do they put up money for the booze, too?" I questioned.

Stanley's fair skin flushed. "Uh, well …"

"It doesn't matter," I dismissed. "Continue. Please."

"I didn't actually go the year I graduated, so I don't know much else," he admitted. "I didn't have a lot in common with the kids that went to those kinds of things. And there was probably an *X-Files* marathon on that night that I didn't want to miss."

Despite talking about an unsolved death, I smiled at the mental imagery of Stanley in high school. I wondered if he'd had the long beard yet. I imagined he probably had a bit of a baby face without the facial hair and kept it to look older.

"What do you know about the victim?" I asked.

"Michael Bloom. 18 years old. He was an academic scholarship kid like Kennedy. And me," he added.

"But he, apparently, went to his post-graduation party." I picked up one of the photographs of the victim. Michael Bloom's eyes were closed. His dark hair was slicked back away from his youthful face. A large blood stain spread across the front of his t-shirt.

I squinted my eyes as if to see the wound better. "Shot in the stomach, too?" I guessed.

"Uh huh," Stanley confirmed. "But the wound variations are different. Kennedy was shot at close range. Michael was shot from a distance, maybe thirty feet or more. Both from a similar handgun though."

"You really think there could be a connection between their deaths?"

"Maybe I'm seeing connections where there are none," Stanley conceded, "But two deaths from the same small, graduating class and in the same way? That seems like too much of a coincidence. Plus, they never found the gun at the graduation party. Police found a bunch of hunting rifles at the house, all locked up, but nothing matching the caliber from Michael Bloom's gun wound."

"What about gunpowder residue?"

Stanley shook his head. "The first responders didn't think to test any of the kids for residue. It was a bit of a screw up."

"Sounds like a mega screw up," I remarked. I dropped the photograph back onto the table. "And I'm sure these kids' parents' money had nothing to do with the case going cold, either."

Stanley looked uncomfortable for a second time. I knew I was being critical of a school—an institution—that continued to play a large role in his life. But I also knew that wasn't exactly his world.

"I'm sure there was pressure on Homicide for this to go away," he acknowledged. "Their parents probably framed it as high school graduates with their whole lives ahead of them, only a few months away from going off to college. Why ruin their lives over one random accident?"

"Except for Michael Bloom's parents," I gravely observed. "Do you think it's worthwhile talking to them yet?"

"I would hold off for now," Stanley said, "at least until we know if the bullets match. Otherwise we might get their hopes up for no reason."

"So we wait," I sighed.

Stanley made a good point, but I was anxious to have something tangible to do—something to get me out of the office. Patience was a big element to this job. Being a beat cop could be monotonous, patrolling the same city streets day after day, but at least I constantly had something to do. Most days I reported directly to the basement and sat behind a computer screen. The only variety came in the form of what donuts were available in the breakroom upstairs.

"Hey, uh, if you're free this weekend, I mean if you're not doing anything else," Stanley verbally stumbled, "the Petersiks are having a memorial service for Kennedy. There won't be a body—she's still at the morgue until Homicide decides to call it homicide or suicide—but the family needs some kind of ceremony for closure. Which I totally get; it seems to me like a memorial service is even more important when you have a situation like this."

My lips curved up at Stanley's bumbling. He'd been so withdrawn since seeing Kennedy Petersik's obituary in the newspaper, it was nice to see him beginning to act like his awkward self again. "Is there a question in there, Stanley?"

He loudly exhaled. "Yeah. Yes. Do you want to go to the memorial with me? As a friend," he hastily added, "not a date."

My stomach twisted. I was free that weekend, but no one actually volunteered to go to a funeral—body or not—if they could help it.

And yet from his bumbled request, it was clear that Stanley didn't have a lot of people in his life who could support him and attend that kind of event with him.

I didn't want to go, but I needed to. For Stanley.

"Sure thing," I agreed with a gentle smile. "Not a date."

CHAPTER THREE

Stanley said he knew the way, so he volunteered to drive. I knew the neighborhood, but only by reputation. Single-family homes and duplexes. Small yards, but mature trees. The residents were predominantly white and working class. The driveways were long and narrow, wide enough for only one compact car. Oversized pickup trucks straddled the paved driveway with two wheels on the grass and two on blacktop.

Neither Stanley nor I were religious, so we'd skipped the church service earlier in the day. The Petersiks had invited folks over to their house for a post-funeral lunch. I wasn't going to know a single person there, so I stuck close to Stanley.

Before we did anything else, Stanley first offered his condolences to Kennedy Petersik's parents. They were both respectfully dressed in black, Mr. Petersik in a suit and tie and his wife in a dress and shawl that covered her shoulders. They spoke in hushed tones while I hovered in the background, wanting to give them some privacy for their conversation but also feeling out of place.

While I waited for Stanley to make his rounds around the living room, I studied family portraits set atop an upright piano. Three smiling faces stared back at me from behind their various picture frames. A family vacation to Disney World. First communion. High school graduation. Kennedy Petersik was positioned at the center of each photograph—the epicenter of her parents' world.

Stanley returned after a while. "I hope you're hungry."

"Starved," I confirmed.

The spread on the white tablecloth nearly brought tears to my eyes. Casserole dishes as far as the eye could see. Tater tot hotdish, crockpots filled with steaming Swedish meatballs, hot ham and rolls, green Jell-O salad with shredded carrot suspended in time and space. The unwillingness to talk about grief or other hard emotions manifested itself in an outpouring of potluck dishes. Midwesterners don't know how to discuss trauma, but we sure know how to make comfort food.

Stanley grabbed a Styrofoam plate from a stack and handed it to me. "Eat," he told me.

After piling our plates high with potluck supper food, Stanley and I moved to one corner of the living room. We ate standing up, balancing our plates and plastic utensils. I hadn't spoken to anyone besides my colleague since arriving, so I felt a little guilty to be eating their food.

"Do you know a lot of people here?" I asked.

Stanley made a noise as he took a large bite of a cold noodle salad. "Mostly teachers from Pius," he said around the mouthful. "Some members of the Board of Trustees."

"Board of Trustees?"

"Pius has a Board of Trustees instead of a School Board."

"Geez, Stanley," I quietly chuckled. "You private school kids are way too fancy for me."

A slender man in a dark suit appeared at my hip. He held a small notebook, flipped open to a blank page. "How did you know the deceased?"

His question caused me to draw back.

"Who wants to know?" I bristled.

"Detective Jason Ryan, MPD." It was then I realized I knew the man in the finely tailored suit. He was the homicide detective who'd been so obstinate a few days before.

"Dude, that's tacky," I admonished. "You shouldn't be taking statements at a funeral."

Detective Ryan snapped shut his notebook and tucked it into a hidden inner pocket in his suit jacket. "Who are you, the etiquette police?"

"No. I'm police, too. We've met, remember? Cassidy Miller. Cold Case."

"Cold Case. That's right." His eyes narrowed in scrutiny. "You look different with your hair down."

I absently touched my fingers to my head. I typically wore my hair in a bun at work. I didn't have an expansive wardrobe, so I'd worn the same dark suit I'd worn to Geoff Reilly's funeral.

"What are you doing here?" he questioned. "Still trying to steal my case?"

"No. I'm here to support my friend," I said, gesturing to Stanley. I turned the question back on Detective Ryan. "What are *you* doing here?"

"I told you—taking statements. People are more talkative in a setting like this than at a police station. Plus, it's a well-known fact that murderers get a perverse thrill out of attending the funeral of the people they killed."

"It's still tacky," I opined.

"Whatever," Ryan sniffed. "Just don't get in my way." He stiffly buttoned up his suit jacket and stalked away.

I turned to Stanley who had remained silent during my interaction with Jason Ryan. "Do you know that guy? He apparently works in Homicide."

Stanley carefully nibbled on a wavy carrot stick. It looked like a crinkle fry, but in vegetable form. "We don't play well with Homicide."

"Aren't we on the same team?" As soon as the words slipped out, I recognized my own naivety.

"Cold Case only exists because Homicide can't close cases," he reminded me. "We're like a physical manifestation of their failures. And it makes them look even worse when we clear a case they were unable to."

I nodded distractedly while I observed Detective Ryan continue to work the Petersiks' living room. With that dumb little notebook in hand, he approached individuals just as they were mid-bite. He had the timing of a restaurant server checking on a table to make sure everything was all right with their meal.

One by one, polite Midwesterners put their grief on pause to address the man with the badge. He asked what were, no doubt, intrusive questions, and they patiently humored him. The longer I stared, the angrier I became. Inconsiderate, tactless, narcissists like Jason Ryan added on to the mountain of reasons to not like police.

"I gotta pee," I abruptly announced.

Stanley gave my pronouncement a curious look. "It's probably down that hallway," he guessed.

I escaped the front living room down the long hallway to which Stanley had motioned. Not knowing the layout of the ranch-style house, I peered experimentally into each room I passed, on the lookout for a toilet. I didn't actually have to use the bathroom, but I needed a distraction; I didn't trust myself to not go off on Detective Jason Ryan in a house full of mourning strangers.

I stuck my head into one room and paused. Sunlight shone brightly through the single window into a decidedly feminine-presenting bedroom. A light pink comforter covered a twin-sized mattress. The headboard was stacked high with stuffed animals. I would have mistaken the room as belonging to a child if not for the plaques and ribbons that adorned the pink walls. A dark blue graduation cap with a yellow tassel hung from a bulletin board. Next to it hung a gold medal attached to a dark blue ribbon.

The voice directly behind me was unexpected: "Last person in the world to have committed suicide if you ask me."

I tensed at the unanticipated voice, but I thankfully didn't let loose any number of profanities that danced on the tip of my tongue.

The voice and the wistful statement about Kennedy Petersik belonged to an older woman. Permed dirty blonde hair. Heavy eye makeup. Fake tan. Her black dress hung on a shapeless body.

"Are you a friend from school?" she asked me.

"Oh, uh, no, ma'am," I stumbled. "I came to support my friend Stanley Harris. He knew Kennedy. They both went to Pius."

She looked bored before I'd even finished my explanation. "Kennedy was such a good girl," she clucked. "So bright. Maybe too bright. All those brains, all that thinking. It can't be good to do so much thinking."

She held out a limp wrist and pressed her hand into mine. "I'm her Aunt Jo. It's short for Josephine."

"So you don't think Kennedy killed herself?" I pressed. I didn't want to turn into Jason Ryan, but I couldn't help my question.

"Seemed to me the girl had too much to live for. But I suppose we never truly know what's going on in a person's mind," she philosophized.

I nodded at her words. "I should, uh, get back to my friend." I hadn't intended to linger in the deceased girl's childhood bedroom, and even though he knew people at the gathering, I regretted leaving Stanley on his own.

A sharp shout, coming from the direction of the living room, interrupted my thoughts. Instinct kicked in, and I rushed past Kennedy Petersik's aunt in the direction of the loud voices. A crowd of onlookers had gathered to form a tight circle around the source of the shouting. I had to restrain myself from barging through bodies to get to the epicenter of the circle. Instead, I stood on my tiptoes to peer past the heads that obstructed my view.

Two young men stood center stage in the living room, like boxers in the ring. They looked to be about the same age, height, and build. Both wore suits, one ill-fitting and the other obviously tailored.

"Better watch yourself." The young man in the fitted suit pushed at the other boy's chest. The second man stumbled back several feet, too many, I thought, for a simple push. He nearly collided with the upright piano I'd been hovering around earlier.

The boy in the more expensive suit waved his hand in front of his nose and made a face. "You should lay off the booze, man. Wouldn't want you injuring your other knee."

The young man in the loose suit steadied himself and scowled. "Wouldn't want you injuring that pretty face," he countered.

"Landon, honey, I think it's time for you to go home." Kennedy's mom appeared from among the crowd of bystanders. She rested her hand on the young man's shoulder. He twitched, ready for a fight, until he recognized to whom the gesture belonged.

He didn't offer up a verbal response; his eyes shut and his head drooped forward.

I watched the man wade unsteadily through the crowd that had gathered in the living room. He was clearly having a hard time walking in a straight line. No one spoke to him on his way out the front door. Only the slam of the screen door announced his swift departure.

I followed the boy's slumped figure via the front picture window. He'd obviously been drinking, and I worried he might try to get behind the wheel of a car, but he only shuffled to the adjacent yard and let himself into the neighboring house.

"Who wants cake?" A woman whom I didn't know cut through the discomfort that lingered despite the young man's removal. The living room's occupants seemed to collectively exhale and everyone returned to their previous activities.

I didn't have to wonder long about how the intoxicated man fit into the picture. Kennedy's aunt remained by my side like an omnipresent narrator: "That was Landon Tauer. He grew up in the house next door. After graduation, he played Junior hockey in Canada, but he got injured, so now he's back. I heard he's been working at the shoe factory over in Red Wing."

"And the other boy?" I asked.

I trained my eyes on the clean-shaven blond man who'd pushed Landon Tauer. A collection of admirers had gathered around him after the confrontation. I hadn't noticed him before, but now I observed his movements and mannerisms. His suit was too tailored and his posture was too perfect to belong to that of a college-aged boy. One look at him, and I could tell he came from money.

"Chase Trask," Aunt Jo supplied. "He and Kennedy dated in high school. They split after graduation though. His dad got him into a college on the East Coast, and I'm sure he didn't want to be tied down to a girl from back home."

"Who's his dad?" I wondered.

"State Senator Robert Trask," Stanley supplied. I hadn't realized he'd been listening to our conversation. "Rumor has it, he's considering running for governor next election cycle."

I hadn't been back in the States long enough to be interested in politics. We had absentee voting on our military bases, but I had never really cared enough to cast my ballot. As far as I was concerned, both political parties had sent us to war and neither seemed too eager to bring us back.

"How much longer do you want to stick around?" I asked.

Stanley looked around the room. "We can go now," he decided.

"We can stay as long as you want to," I insisted. "I was only asking."

"No, I'm good. I need to go home and feed Einstein and Sabin anyways."

"Are those your cats?" I guessed.

"Parakeets."

"A bird man, huh," I mused. "I'm learning all kinds of new things about you, Stanley."

I waited near the front door while Stanley said his goodbyes to Kennedy's parents. My attention drifted from their farewells and mutual well wishes to the house next door. Only a few feet of grass separated the driveways between houses.

Landon Tauer was standing on the concrete stoop of his parents' neighboring house. He still wore the too-baggy dress pants, but he'd abandoned the black jacket and white button-up shirt and stood outside in only a white undershirt. His head was tilted towards the grey-blue sky; a cigarette dangled from his lips. He looked once in the direction of the Petersik's house before tossing his half-finished cigarette into the lawn and disappearing inside.

+ + +

The muffled sounds of the city outside filtered into the bedroom. It was a warm night—one of the last of the season, perhaps—and the windows were cracked open. A light rain struck against the window panes, and a few stories on the streets below, tires rolled across damp pavement.

I exhaled.

Julia's graveled voice cut through the night: "Problems sleeping, dear?"

I grimaced; I hadn't meant to wake her up.

"Not for the usual reasons," I promised.

My journal in the end table beside my side of the bed was filled with re-imagined results of my time in Afghanistan. My therapist, Dr. Susan Warren, had me write out my trauma from my time abroad, but create alternative—and better—endings. Each night before I went to sleep I tried to come up with a new way to save the lives of every man in my unit. Pensacola didn't lose his legs to a dirty bomb, and I never had to kill an insurgent at point-blank range.

It was a simple assignment, but it worked. My nights weren't entirely terror free, but I no longer dreaded sleep like I had just a year ago. But I also accredited the woman who slept beside me as a major reason why the nightmares had lessened in frequency and intensity.

Julia rolled over to face me. "What's wrong?"

I continued to stare at the ceiling. "I can't shut off my brain," I told her. "I keep thinking about this new potential case."

Julia shifted on the bed and scooted her body closer. She wiggled her hands between my back and the mattress. My shirt had ridden up in the night, and a high-pitched yelp pushed past my lips when her skin made contact with mine. Her hands were like blocks of ice.

"Jesus, you're freezing!" I exclaimed.

"Mmm, so warm," she purred. Her speech was slightly slurred from sleep.

Her feet rustled under the sheets and came to rest against the side of my leg. I could feel her frozen toes through the material of my sweatpants.

"Are you trying to kill me, woman?" I declared.

"No, just steal your body heat."

"How are you this cold?" I wondered aloud.

Her body continued to wiggle against me in a futile attempt to get warm. "Go back to telling me about your case. It'll take your mind off of it."

"It's not my case yet," I corrected. "And it won't be mine unless the bullets from both deaths are from the same gun."

"When will you know that?" she asked.

"I don't know. The crime lab confirmed they received them, so it's just a matter of them processing the bullets and doing the comparison."

I was growing agitated with nothing else to occupy my time. I hoped the wait from the crime lab wouldn't be much longer. Even if the bullets didn't turn out to be a match, at least then I could move on to something else.

"And to make matters worse, the homicide detective who's actually assigned to the case is a total asshole," I cursed. "Dude had the balls to show up at the girl's memorial service and started interrogating everybody there. It's like, Jesus, give the family some space."

"Talk to his boss," Julia suggested. "His supervising officer or whatever. I'm sure they'd appreciate knowing how he's been representing the department in the community."

"You don't go over people's heads," I rejected. "That's not how things work in cop world."

"So you'll just steal his clothes in the locker room and spray him down with a fire hose instead?" Despite the darkness in the room, I could tell she was smiling.

"We're not *that* bad," I defended.

In truth, she wasn't that far off. There was definitely a juvenile hazing component to my sphere. And I had enough buddies upstairs in the Fourth Precinct who could make Detective Ryan's life hell.

I remained silent while I waited for Julia's response; she didn't have an immediate opinion. Eventually, I heard her quiet, even breaths in the darkness. She'd fallen back asleep.

I gingerly moved her hands, which she had pinned beneath my lower back. I brushed the hair away from her unlined forehead and pressed my lips against her brow. My heart seized with how much I loved this woman—ice feet and all.

"Sweet dreams," I whispered.

CHAPTER FOUR

I arrived to work the next day overly tired and overly annoyed. Stanley was babysitting the Freezer and Sarah was about to beat her top score on Minesweeper, but I had nothing so tedious to occupy my time. Instead of spending the day bouncing off the walls, I grabbed the keys to my second-hand patrol car and drove to the opposite side of town. I didn't need to look up the address for Kennedy Petersik's home. I'd already been there once.

A woman answered the front door, and I lifted my badge to eye level. "Detective Cassidy Miller, ma'am."

Mrs. Petersik's eyes widened. "Has there been a break in the case? I called this morning, but the Detective I talked to said they didn't have anything new."

"No, ma'am. I can't speak to that. But I was wondering if I could talk to you and your husband about Michael Bloom."

I wasn't technically assigned to the Petersik case, so I had no authority to go poking around for information regarding the young woman's death. But that didn't mean I couldn't speak to Kennedy's parents about Michael Bloom's death. And if I discovered a connection between the two deaths along the way, so be it. All I knew is I couldn't continue to sit passively in our basement office.

Mrs. Petersik seemed to take a step backwards into the protection of her home. "Bloom? You mean that boy who was shot a few years back?"

I nodded. I didn't explain the possible connection since it was such a long shot. I was sure Mrs. Petersik had enough on her plate.

"I don't, well, I don't know how I could be any help," she floundered. "It was so long ago and I really don't know much about the details."

"Just a few minutes of your time, ma'am," I promised.

Mrs. Petersik nodded tightly and opened the door wider for me.

The Petersik home was empty and quiet, with the exception of a television program playing quietly in the background. The crowds of mourners were gone, along with their many casserole dishes and crockpots. Mrs. Petersik's black dress and shawl had been replaced with a sweatshirt and jeans.

"My husband, Frank, is at work," she seemed to apologize as she shut the front door. "Can I get you something to drink? Coffee? Tea?"

I waved off her hospitality. "No thank you, ma'am. I don't want to be a burden."

"Oh, it's no trouble at all," she insisted.

She hustled off in another direction before I could double down on my refusal. She disappeared behind a swinging half door, like something straight out of an Old West movie.

I remained on my own in the living room while Mrs. Petersik clanked around in the kitchen. I took a step toward the swinging doors, but I stopped when a flash of movement caught my eye. A little girl sat on a blanket in the middle of the living room, surrounded by wooden blocks and plastic toys. She wore tiny blue jeans and a tiny pink t-shirt. Her wispy blonde hair was just long enough for a tiny ponytail that plumed up from the top of her head.

I crouched down to the little girl's level. "Hey there. What's your name?"

Clear blue orbs stared back at me. She didn't respond, but I wasn't surprised. She was a toddler, only one or two years old, if I had had to guess.

"Oh, I see you've met."

I turned away from the little girl to see that Mrs. Petersik had returned. Her hands were empty.

"Just barely," I said, standing up. "She's not very chatty though."

Mrs. Petersik scooped up the little girl and hoisted her onto her hip. The little girl shoved one hand into her mouth and the other into her mom's hair.

"This is Kayla," Mrs. Petersik introduced. She gently pried her hair out of the little girl's chubby fist. "Frank and I call her our miracle baby."

'Miracle.' It seemed like the polite alternative to an 'accident' or 'mistake.'

"Let me just put her down for her nap, and then we can talk."

Mrs. Petersik began to walk down the short hallway that led to bedrooms and a bathroom. I couldn't explain, but I felt compelled to follow her.

Mrs. Petersik talked while she walked. "Do you have any children, Detective …"

"Miller," I reminded her. "And, no. I don't have kids."

Mrs. Petersik clucked her tongue. "You're young. There's still time."

"Now you sound like my mom," I chuckled.

She entered the first door on the right, which turned out to be a nursery. A giant white crib took up most of the room. A wooden rocking chair sat in one corner, and a changing table and clothing bureau rounded out the remainder of the furniture.

I stayed in the doorway while Mrs. Petersik gingerly lifted Kayla into the crib. Her eyes remained locked on the child as she tucked her under a light blanket. "You should listen to your mom; you'll never know love until you've had a child of your own, Detective."

I could barely take care of myself most days without adding a kid to the equation.

We left Kayla in the nursery and Mrs. Petersik quietly closed the door behind us. "She was always smiling. Always happy."

"Kayla?" I questioned. Her verb tense confused me.

"Kennedy," she corrected. "Would you like to see her room?"

I didn't want to admit that I'd already seen it, so I nodded.

Kennedy Petersik's bedroom looked like she could walk back into the room at any time. I'd only given the room a cursory glance the first time around, but now—surrounded by all of her personal belongings—I could appreciate all the details. The open closet, spilling over with clothes. The photographs of friends and family wedged into the corners of a vanity mirror. Bottles of nail polish lined up on the top of her bureau. Random chargers, but no electronics sticking out from every outlet. A tall stack of spiral notebooks on top of a wooden desk.

Mrs. Petersik noticed where my attention lingered. "She loved to write. She kept a diary since the fourth grade. Didn't miss a day, even when she got older."

"Did the police take any of them?" I couldn't recall seeing any journals in the evidence boxes when I'd gone to retrieve the bullet to send to the crime lab, but I hadn't been looking specifically for a diary then.

"No. Kennedy was very protective when it came to her journals. She never let anyone read them—not even me. I wasn't going to let the police just take them."

I pursed my lips in thought. If there was a chance this was suicide and not homicide, those diaries could tell us what we needed to know about Kennedy Petersik's mindset in the days before her death. And if she'd been killed, she might have shared a rivalry or bad feelings with her diary.

"Ma'am, I know it must feel like a violation of your daughter's trust to have a stranger look through her private thoughts, but every little lead counts. Kennedy may have left important clues as to what happened in these notebooks."

Mrs. Petersik was understandably hesitant, but at the same time I couldn't understand her reluctance. If she wanted us to find out what had happened to her daughter, why put up any road blocks?

"I'll read through them and let you know if I find anything," she decided.

I nodded grimly. I could have produced a search warrant that gave me open access to Kennedy's diaries, but I didn't want the Petersiks to withdraw themselves or see me as an adversary. We were on the same side. I would have to trust that Mrs. Petersik would let me know if she found anything.

A shrill sound like screaming pierced the awkward silence that had fallen between us. I worried that something had happened to Kayla, but Mrs. Petersik looked unaffected.

"That'll be the water for tea."

I had visited under the guise of investigating Michael Bloom's death, so I stayed for a cup of tea and asked a series of questions regarding his death for which Mrs. Peterson didn't have any answers. She'd been right about not being able to help me.

Before I left, I thanked Mrs. Petersik for her time and reminded her to let the police know if she found anything in her daughter's journals. I had serious misgivings about leaving the notebooks behind and trusting Kennedy's mom to report anything unusual, but I wasn't technically assigned to the girl's case. We still didn't have anything concrete to connect Michael Bloom's murder with Kennedy's death. If Mrs. Petersik complained to my superiors, I would probably get suspended for nosing around an active investigation that wasn't mine.

I started to walk down the Petersik's paved driveway towards where I'd parked my patrol car on the street, but I stopped when I saw movement from the neighboring home. Someone had been watching me, but had hastily closed the front window curtains.

I changed directions and hopped up the concrete steps to the home where Landon Tauer lived. I didn't see a doorbell, so I knocked briskly on the screen door. A short moment after, a small middle-aged woman, whom I assumed was Landon's mother, answered the door.

"Hi," I greeted. "Is Landon home?"

I didn't introduce myself as police since I suspected it had been she who'd been the peeping tom.

"No. It's Tuesday. He's at the ice rink."

I flashed her what I hoped was my winningest smile, but it probably looked a little manic. "Do you happen to know which one?"

In Minnesota, ice rinks were like Starbucks—one on every corner.

She gave me the name of a local public high school, which must have been Landon's alma mater. It hadn't occurred to me until then that even though they'd lived next door to each other, Landon Tauer and Kennedy Petersik had attended different high schools—hers private and exclusive, and Landon's just around the corner.

I thanked the woman for the information, and, after consulting the directions on my phone, I steered my old Crown Vic to the area high school.

+ + +

The ice rink was a stand-alone structure, not physically attached to the high school. Normally I would have felt obligated to sign in with the high school's front office, but I entered through the hockey arena's separate entrance instead. I inhaled upon entry and a small shiver of remembrance tickled down my spine. Nothing else smelled like a hockey rink. The scent of ice, buttery popcorn, and rubber brought me back to my own high school days. I'd been a pool rat, not a rink rat, but I'd gone to my share of high school hockey games.

The hockey rink was brightly lit. The names of local businesses tattooed the boards, and state championship banners hung from the rafters high above the ice surface. The concession stand was closed, no one was out on the ice, the bleachers were empty, and yet classic rock piped through the P.A. system.

"Hello?" I called out. "Anybody here?"

As if in response, I heard an engine fire up. A small garage-like door lifted in the far corner of the arena and the zamboni machine slowly pulled out onto the ice. I was too far away to make out the figure seated behind the wheel and had to wait until the ice re-surfacer drove closer.

The man's dark hair was cut close to his scalp, but not quite high and tight as if he'd been in the military. Despite the chill of the indoor ice rink, he wore only a t-shirt and jeans. He looked different without the oversized suit he'd worn to the funeral, but I readily recognized the driver as the man for whom I'd been looking.

I was in no hurry, and he'd just begun to re-surface the ice, so I took a seat in the lower risers and watched the surprisingly calming movement of the zamboni machine. It brought back memories of the zamboni man at my hometown rink in St. Cloud. We'd watch him drive around on ice, our noses pressed against the foggy Plexiglas, pining for the opportunity to get behind the wheel. He'd been a giant. A hero.

Landon Tauer drove with care and precision around the edge of the rink, careful not to bump the vehicle against the hockey boards. His features looked grim and serious as he drove around and around, neglecting no part of the ice. I wondered if this young man had thought his life would turn out like this.

I stood up after he raised the re-surfacing blade, and I walked in the direction of the garage door where I knew he and the zamboni would soon disappear behind. I knocked on the clear Plexiglas that separated us. I wasn't sure he would be able to hear me over the classic rock and the zamboni engine, but his head turned toward me.

I removed my badge from my belt and pressed it against the clear glass. "Can we talk?" I spoke over the rumble of the engine.

Landon responded with a thumbs up and a nod of his head. The engine cut out, and he gingerly climbed down from the elevated zamboni seat.

"What's this about?" he asked as he approached me.

"Mind stepping off the ice so we can actually talk?" I proposed.

I didn't like having a conversation with a thick panel of Plexiglas between us; it reminded me of visiting hours at a prison, but without the plastic phone on the wall.

He jerked his thumb in a backwards motion. "Do you mind waiting? I'm kind of on the clock. I've gotta set up the nets before the water freezes over their piers."

There was nothing pressing at the office, and Stanley and Sarah knew to call my cell in case we finally heard back from the crime lab about a potential bullet match. But I didn't know how long it might take him to finish up the rink, and I'd already spent too much of my day tracking him down.

"I'll come out to you," I decided.

"Are you sure? It's icy," he warned, as though I had no knowledge of the properties of ice.

"I'm from Minnesota, too," I returned evenly.

Landon's mouth curled into a small smile. "Fair enough."

He opened the side board door for me, and I carefully stepped out onto the ice. After being freshly resurfaced, the ice was more damp than slick, but I was still cautious as I shuffled along the ice to follow him towards the end boards.

It might have been because we walked on wet ice, but Landon Tauer walked with a noticeable limp. There was something off about his gait. He looked stiff, as if his hips or knees had once been injured.

"So what's this about?" he repeated his original question.

"Kennedy Petersik."

I carefully watched his reaction to hearing her name, but surprisingly, he had none. "Oh yeah? What about her?"

"You were at the memorial service."

I didn't exactly have a list of questions at the ready for him. I'd thought his conflict at the party with Kennedy's ex-boyfriend was of interest, but it also could have been nothing. Either way, he might be able to provide some valuable context for Kennedy's life since her mother had denied me access to her journals.

"I didn't make it to the church service, but I thought I should at least pay my respects afterwards," he noted.

"Were you and Kennedy close?"

"We grew up next to each other," he said, offering up information I already knew.

"But you went to different high schools," I observed. "Were you still close then?"

"No. I was always here," he said, gesturing to our surroundings, "and she'd made a new group of friends at Pius."

"Friends like Chase Trask," I supplied.

"He was a dick. Still is," Landon snorted. "Couldn't play hockey worth shit, either."

Landon appeared to struggle with moving the hockey net to its original location. He'd had to move both out of the way while he'd re-surfaced the ice. I grabbed onto the top crossbar with him, and together we dragged the net back into place.

"Thanks," he approved.

"You and Chase had a disagreement at the funeral," I observed. "What did you fight about?"

Landon passed his hand over his face. "Shit. I was wasted. I have no idea. I bumped into him or something. Stepped on his fancy shoes."

"Are you typically drunk on a Sunday afternoon?" I inquired.

"Are the Vikings playing?" he tried to joke. "Death makes me uncomfortable. I had a little too much whiskey before going over there. But I called and apologized to Mrs. Petersik afterwards. That wasn't my best self."

I nodded, moving on. "Do you know how long Chase and Kennedy dated? Or the reason why they broke up?"

Landon shrugged. "Can't help you there. Like I said, we didn't really talk in high school."

"What about after?"

"After what? After high school?" he asked.

I nodded.

"I was in Canada for a year."

I vaguely recalled what Kennedy's gossipy aunt had told me about Landon's history.

"Can you tell me more about that?" I pressed.

"Not much to tell. I used to be really good." He looked up at the lofted ceiling of the hockey arena. "I'm responsible for a lot of the banners hanging in here. I was offered a full ride to play for Minnesota, but then I got the call from Canada."

"To play Junior hockey."

"Yeah." He paused and stared. He was probably wondering how I knew so much. But instead of asking me about my informant, he continued. "My parents wanted me to play for the Gophers, but Canada was offering money. Money beat out going to college."

"But now you're back here," I observed.

"I got hurt." He lifted one of his pant legs up to his knee. Pale, white scar tissue cross-crossed his kneecap.

I had my own scars, but this wasn't a competition.

"I got checked low," he explained. "Tore up my MCL and my ACL." He pulled the leg of his jeans back down. "No team wanted to keep around an 18-year-old kid who was already damaged. And all those colleges that had wanted to give me a full ride were no longer interested."

He bent down, kneeling on the ice so he could secure the hockey net to the piers in the ice. "You got anything else for me?" he asked.

"Yeah. One more question," I said. "Do you think Kennedy killed herself?"

Landon didn't have a ready response. His face wasn't in my line of vision, but his body visibly stiffened before he returned to his task. "I don't know."

He stood up and brushed at his knees. His jeans were wet from where he'd been kneeling on the damp ice. "Like I said; we didn't talk."

I left the high school hockey rink with more questions than answers. I tried not to read too much into Landon's noncommittal response to my final question, but it was hard not to. Mrs. Petersik had been so sure—so adamant—that her daughter couldn't have killed herself while Landon had given me reason to doubt her certainty.

But I wasn't a parent. I couldn't know the shock and probable denial that had to come with the unexpected death of a child. Maybe there had been warning signs that the Petersiks had been blind to. I needed to know more about the mindset of this young woman. I needed to see beyond the smiling fresh face reflected in a photograph of a high school graduate with her whole life still in front of her.

But before I could do any of that, I needed to be officially assigned to the case.

CHAPTER FIVE

A light rain struck against the closed bedroom windows. The grey sky and partially closed curtains made it difficult to identify the hour. It was early though; Julia's alarm hadn't yet gone off. Julia slept on her side with her back turned toward me. Her pajamas were modest—a thin v-neck t-shirt and sleep shorts—but the bottom hem of her maroon t-shirt had crept up her torso in the night, leaving a gap between her shirt and shorts. I maneuvered closer until I could feel her firm backside press against the tops of my thighs.

I liked to watch her sleep. It sounded creepy, but on nights when I couldn't get my brain to shut off or when a bad dream had me waking up before the sun, I liked to observe the evenness of her breath, the rise and fall of her chest, the slight flutter of her eyelids. It was more cathartic than counting sheep. I envied how unencumbered she looked.

I gently traced my fingertips along her exposed waistline, barely ghosting my touch above the bare ribbon of skin. I walked the pads of my fingers across her hipbone. A small gap existed between the curve of her hipbone and the waistband of her shorts. I continued to skate my fingertips along her waist before just barely dipping below the elastic of her sleep shorts.

Julia shifted in bed, and I heard her quiet groan as my touch began to rouse her from sleep.

"Good morning," she husked. Her lower register was deeper and raspier than usual. "What time is it?"

"Still early," I murmured.

I slid my palm along the lower plane of her stomach until my fingertips reached trimmed, coarse hair. The meticulously maintained landing strip guided my blind fumbling towards the cleft in her pussy lips. I bypassed her clit and lightly rubbed up and down her slit.

"Mmm …" she quietly hummed. She arched her lower back and pressed more solidly against me. "What's the occasion?"

I pressed my nose against the back of her head and breathed in. She smelled sweet. "It's Tuesday."

"And what's so special about Tuesday?"

"Nothing." I nuzzled my nose deeper into her hair. "Do I need an excuse to fuck you in the morning?"

"Absolutely not." She drew out each syllable as if savoring the feeling of the word on her tongue.

Her t-shirt was loose around her neck, giving me unencumbered access to her creamy breasts. Her breasts were warm and soft, the skin smooth and firm. I palmed one breast and then the other; I lingered long enough to pinch her nipples and make them hard. I rolled the spongy flesh between my fingers and lightly scratched my nails across the sensitive area. Her nipples—along with the rest of her body—began to wake up.

I returned my hand to her shorts and forced my way under the top elastic band. From this angle, it was an awkward fit. Her shorts were loose in the front, but in this reclined position, her thighs were clamped together. I nudged my fingers as far as they could go until she rotated her hips and parted her thighs for me.

I trailed my fingertips along the silky shaved skin of her outer pussy lips. Everything about her was soft. I moved my fingers in long, lazy circles, but avoided her clit. Her breathing became more labored the longer I stroked her up and down.

"So good," she approved in a breathy sigh.

I used my index and ring finger to spread her open and slid deeper across the source of her wetness. Her velvety folds wrapped around my middle finger as I dipped inside, just to the first knuckle. She opened her thighs wider, and I slid in deeper until my palm mashed against her clit. I heard the staccato hitch of her breath, followed by a needy whine. I withdrew my finger and spread her juices on her outer lips and clit.

When I sunk back inside, I curled my single finger against the spongy upper wall of her G-spot. I slowly eased my finger in and out with deliberately unhurried movement. Her pussy made a wet clicking sound each time I withdrew my finger as if she didn't want to let go.

I gathered her hair with my free hand and held it like a ponytail. I kissed and nipped at the nape of her neck as I began to quickened my thrusts. I pressed my lips against the back of her neck and sucked her flesh into my mouth. It was a safe place to leave bite marks. As long as she wore her hair down, the bruised skin would be hidden from view.

I curled two fingers around the curve of her pubic bone and slid between her pussy lips. Her sex clamped around my fingers like a vise. I ground the heel of my palm against her clit each time I bottomed out.

"Fuck, Cassidy," she groaned. She reached back and loosely hooked her arm around my neck.

My wrist ached from the awkward angle and my bicep began to burn. But I wasn't going to stop until she was satisfied.

Julia moved her hips and lower back in time with my fingers, matching each of my thrusts with one of her own. "Close. Almost," she gasped.

I rubbed my thumb against her clit while I continued to penetrate her with two fingers.

"Cum for me," I growled into her ear. "Cum all over my fingers." Her earlobe was too tempting, so I sucked it into my mouth.

A partially contained cry escaped her throat. Her body tensed and jerked in short, stilted movements.

When the movements subsided, I gingerly eased my fingers out of her tender sex. Her juices coated my fingers down to their root.

"Good morning," I murmured into her hair.

She hummed appreciatively and pressed her backside more firmly against my front. "Good morning indeed." She intertwined our fingers even though my hand was still sticky with her arousal. "Tuesday might be my new favorite day."

+ + +

"Darling? Have you seen my grey dress? I could have sworn I picked it up from the dry cleaners."

I sat at the dining room table eating my morning toast and drinking black coffee from my favorite mug. Julia rushed around the apartment, doing a million things at once in order to make it to work on time. Her morning ritual was excessively complicated compared to mine. I showered and pulled my hair into a bun, sometimes without even blow-drying my hair. My biggest dilemma was choosing which color button-up blouse to pair with dark slacks.

"Which one?" I called down the hallway.

Her voice carried from the direction of the bedroom. "Sleeveless. Wool. Buttons on the hips."

"Sorry. I have no idea." I paid attention to her wardrobe, but I didn't keep an inventory.

I heard her high heels first before she appeared around the corner. She apparently hadn't found the grey dress in question, as she was still in her bra and slip. She grabbed my coffee cup and helped herself to a quick sip. The thin muscles in her biceps and triceps flexed as she brought the mug to her lips. I wanted to kiss the lipstick off her mouth.

"I can stop by the dry cleaner after work and double-check they don't still have it," I offered.

She set the mug back in front of me. "Thank you, dear. That would be a big help."

Even though I knew she was in a hurry, I grabbed her arm and pulled her down onto my lap. She didn't complain that I was going to make her late, so I wrapped my arms around her waist.

"Am I crushing you?" she worried.

"You're like a feather."

"And you're a liar," she laughed.

Her hands went to the sides of my face, and she drew me in for a soft, lingering kiss. Her tongue slid against mine; she still tasted minty from her toothpaste.

"Thank you for this morning," she murmured. "It was unexpected, but very much appreciated." The low burr in her voice made me want to ditch my responsibilities and bring her back to bed with me.

"I'll be your alarm clock every morning," I earnestly offered.

She shook her head. "You'd get tired of me."

I shook my head harder. "Never."

Her mouth curled at one edge. "We'll see," she hummed.

"Oh!" I lightly tapped my hand against her thigh as I remembered a forgotten question. "Have you thought about your costume yet?"

Her features pinched. "Costume?"

"For Brent's party," I reminded her.

"Halloween isn't for several more weeks," she pointed out.

Ever since we'd been in the academy together, my friend Brent Olson—whom everyone affectionately called Viking because of the resemblance—had hosted a Halloween party at his apartment. Halloween fell on a Friday that year, which meant the bars of the Twin Cities would be wilder than usual. The revelry of the holiday would no doubt spill from the bars and onto the streets. It was a challenge being a cop and trying to have fun while off-duty. I tended to spend my time eyeballing bar patrons who looked younger than 21 and resisting the desire to ask them to produce identification. Taking the party out of the bars and into a private space was the best way to assure everyone could actually have fun.

"You'd better not procrastinate," I warned. "You don't want to be the loser who shows up to the party in an after-thought costume."

"Loser?" She arched an eyebrow. "I don't think I've ever heard you talk like that before."

"That's because this is a big deal! People go all out!" My hands waved for emphasis. "They start planning their costumes months ahead."

Her lips curled into an amused smile. "And what are you going as?"

"It's a surprise," I denied.

"Even from me?"

"*Especially* from you," I emphasized.

"But what if we end up with the same costume?" she teased in a sing-song voice. "I'm sure that would be an embarrassment."

"I can pretty much guarantee you won't pick this," I denied.

Julia's eyebrows raised on her unlined forehead. "Well, now I'm even more intrigued. How about a hint?"

"Nope. Never gonna get it out of me," I refused.

"Never? That sounds like a challenge." She leaned closer so her lips just barely brushed against the outer shell of my ear. "And you know how I feel about that."

Even though we were only talking about silly Halloween costumes, her words and tone produced a shiver of excitement. I loved how we pushed each other, teasing limits and testing willpower.

She remained a breath's length away, and her voice dropped lower. "If I want something from you, Miss Miller, I *will* get it."

My insides clenched and I swallowed hard. "Do your worst."

Julia laughed musically, and her temporary spell over me broke. I released the breath I hadn't realized I'd been holding.

My relationship with Julia was like a never-ending game of chicken. We pushed each other, challenging each other to blink first. I tended to give in more easily than Julia, but after our handful of months of being together, the balance was tipping more favorably towards me.

"I miss you when I'm at work, but we live together," I blurted out. "We see each other all the time, but I still miss you. Is that pathetic?" I worried aloud.

"No, darling," Julia said, a smile in her voice. "That's not pathetic. That's love."

+ + +

As much as I would have loved to play hooky and stay in bed with Julia that morning, I somehow managed to make myself go to work. Sarah and I were on our own again in the office while Stanley dusted off the tops of old evidence boxes, or whatever he did when he was scheduled to be at the Freezer.

I hovered over Sarah's shoulder so we could both look at her computer screen. Her fingers moved over the keyboard as she pulled up the various social media accounts for our persons of interest: Chase Trask, Landon Tauer, and Kennedy Petersik.

"What do you think of my new perfume?" she asked.

Sarah was smart and quick-witted, and one of her favorite pastimes was making me uncomfortable. She was attractive, and she knew it. She also knew that I had a girlfriend.

I didn't divert my attention from Kennedy Petersik's Facebook page. "It's nice," I confirmed before changing the subject. "What do you think about Kennedy Petersik?"

Thankfully Sarah stayed on task. "You mean is this the Facebook feed of a suicidal girl?"

"Mmhm," I confirmed.

"I can't tell; it's private. Everything is locked."

"What does that mean?" I asked. "Can we unlock it?"

Sarah glanced up at me. "Do you not have a Facebook page, Miller?"

"I was in the Marines for nearly a decade," I deflected.

I'd never seen the point of social media. I could count my friends on two hands—I didn't need an app for that. I was also a very private person; if I wanted someone to know what I was up to, I'd pick up the phone and tell them.

"You're like an alien," Sarah murmured. "*Anyway*," she said with more volume, "I can't get access to most of her content because she's got her privacy settings set to the highest level. I can only see her full page if we're online friends."

"Is that unusual?" I asked.

"Not so much for a young woman," Sarah noted. "There's a lot of creeps on the internet."

"All the more reason not to be on there," I continued to defend myself.

Sarah made a noise. "Hmm. Her parents must have memorialized her account."

"Should I know what that means?"

"Not unless you know a lot of dead people." Sarah tapped at the monitor. "*Remembering* is posted next to her name. People can share stories and pictures to her page even if they didn't have access to her content when she was alive. Content Kennedy shared is still visible to her Facebook Friends, but she's not going to show up in people's birthday reminders."

I sighed. "Death in the age of social media is pretty creepy."

Sarah scrolled through the dozens of messages posted to Kennedy's page. She moved too quickly for me to really read any of the sentiments. "The court of public opinion seems to be split," she observed. "About half of these comments are about suicide and the other half wants vengeance for her murder." Sarah spun away from the monitor. "What do *you* think happened?"

"I'm not going to speculate," I refused. "That only leads to bad police work. If I go into it expecting a certain outcome, I might be tempted to ignore a line of questioning or some observation that doesn't fit with my circumscribed view of the case. One of the worst things a cop can do is start with a conclusion."

Sarah nodded thoughtfully. "Makes sense. Luckily, I don't have to decide either way. Regardless of how Kennedy died, I'm the advocate for her family to help them get closure."

"*If* the case ever gets passed on to us," I noted. The reminder was more for myself than Sarah.

"Is it weird that Stanley knew this girl?" Sarah proposed. "Like, isn't it a conflict of interest for us to be looking into her death?"

"We're the only Cold Case division," I noted. "It's not like we can pass it on to some other team. Besides, Stanley doesn't have a badge. He's not going to be making any arrests."

"That's true." My reasoning seemed to settle her doubt.

"Can you tell if Stanley was online friends with Kennedy?" I proposed. "Maybe we can get to her accounts through him."

Sarah snorted at the suggestion. "Does Stanley seem the type to be on Snapchat?"

"Hey, I would never assume anything about a person," I defended.

"Like how you immediately assumed I was straight when we first met?" Sarah countered. Her mouth curved into a smug smile.

"Th-that's different!" I protested. "You're very feminine in appearance, and there aren't a lot of queer women in Minnesota. And you actually *are* straight, so it's not like I was wrong."

"Easy there, Miller," Sarah laughed. "You're gonna give yourself a coronary."

My head started to throb from my co-worker's roasting. I was also frustrated from so many dead ends. We couldn't even get access to Kennedy Petersik's social media accounts. I grabbed my leather jacket from the back of my office chair.

"Where are you running off to?" Sarah pouted. "I hate when you abandon me."

I rolled my eyes at her dramatics. "I'm not abandoning you. I'm going to drop in on the crime lab. Maybe I can convince them to hurry up a little on that ballistics match."

Sarah scrambled to her feet. "Well don't leave me behind."

I pulled on my jacket and turned up the collar. "I really don't think this is a two-person job."

Sarah ignored my insistence and pushed past me. She walked close enough that her shoulder brushed against mine. "But it might be a two *woman* job, Miller," she grinned, showing her teeth. "How else do you expect to get those lab techs to do what you want?"

+ + +

"Well, shit."

The profanity had come from my co-worker nearly the moment we'd walked through the crime lab's office door.

I leaned closer to Sarah so I could speak without us being overheard. "Didn't count on the lab techs being female, eh?"

Sarah stubbornly lifted her chin. "I'll just have to find another use for my feminine wiles."

I couldn't hold back my smirk.

The business side of the crime lab was unremarkable. A half-wall partition separated us from the lab's all-female employees. Three women in long, white lab coats stood behind computer screens at stand-up desks, but beyond their jackets, nothing else suggested that any evidence testing or analyzing took place in that space.

One of the benefits of working in a large city like Minneapolis, compared to being a cop in a small town, was the proximity of the forensics lab. Instead of mailing evidence away or having to call someone long distance, I could drop by their City Hall office to check on the status of evidence yet to be processed.

The Minneapolis Crime Lab Unit provided the police department with a variety of services: computer forensics—which also involved help with subpoenas involving cell phone providers—video forensics, vehicle forensics, and field operations. They analyzed blood stain patterns, footwear, and tire track marks. They also maintained AFIS—the national fingerprint database.

Of all of the ways the crime lab complimented the police work we did, I was most interested in their firearm expertise. I needed a ballistics match. If the bullets found in Kennedy Petersik's car didn't match those from the Michael Bloom case, I didn't have anything beyond coincidence to connect the two deaths.

Sarah loudly cleared her throat, apparently annoyed at the gender of the lab's employees and that no one had acknowledged our presence.

"Christ, it's like trying to get a drink from a female bartender in here," she muttered.

"You've been going to the wrong places," I said under my breath. Sarah would have been the star attraction at any gay bar.

"I've been waiting for your invite, Miller," she returned with a grin.

"Can I help you?" One of the lab coat women rescued me from Sarah's wheedling. She left her stand-up desk and approached the half-wall partition that divided us.

The woman re-adjusted her tortoise shell glasses at the bridge of her nose. Her skin was nearly as pale as the long lab coat she wore. The rectangular jacket obscured her figure, but delicate bones peeked out from the wrist openings. A name was stitched on the right breast pocket of the white coat: Celeste.

"I hope so. I'm Detective Cassidy Miller, and this is my colleague, Sarah Conrad," I introduced. "We sent in two recovered bullets last week to determine if they're from the same firearm. One is from a current possible homicide and the other is from an unresolved case. We wanted to check on their status."

"Did you receive confirmation from our office that we received them?" the woman asked.

"Yeah, but, uh, I was hoping to kind of speed things up," I floundered.

The woman's grey-blue eyes narrowed behind her thick glasses. With her white-blonde hair pulled back in a tight bun, she reminded me of a librarian who was determined to have silence in her library. "We process evidence in the order in which it was received, Detective Miller," she informed me. "It's policy. We'll get to it as soon as we can."

I held up my hands in retreat. "I'm not trying to cut in line or anything," I insisted, "but we can't re-open this old case unless we can confirm the bullets are a match."

The formerly severe look on the woman's face perceptively softened. "You're from Cold Case."

"Yes, ma'am," I confirmed. She wasn't much older than myself, but the formality tended to slip out when I became uncomfortable.

"Is Stanley still there? How is he?" she asked.

The change in her demeanor was dramatic. At first, I'd thought she might rap our knuckles with a ruler, but now she radiated warmth and concern. I was too taken aback to immediately reply.

"Stanley's actually the reason why we're pushing this case so hard," Sarah jumped in. "He was very close with the victim, and we're pooling all our resources to figure out what happened. It's probably not kosher to prioritize a case just because of Stanley, but we're doing all we can to help out our friend."

The woman bobbed her head. "Of course. Let me see what I can do to speed things along. Wait here just a second."

The woman turned her back to us and rummaged through a large storage container.

I dug my elbow into Sarah's side, but not hard enough for her to make a scene. "Laying it on pretty thick with the Stanley thing," I quietly observed.

"I saw an opportunity, so I took it," Sarah returned. "Don't be mad that it worked and I didn't have to show her my tits to speed things up."

I covered my mouth and loudly coughed to mask my discomfort.

"Here it is!" the lab tech proclaimed. She'd unknowingly saved me twice from Sarah's harassment in a short amount of time.

When she returned to the half-wall, I recognized the padded yellow envelope in her hand. The envelope bore my handwriting on the address label and contained the bullet samples retrieved from Kennedy Petersik's car and the Michael Bloom cold case.

"I'm Celeste, by the way," the woman confirmed the name stitched on her lab coat. "Celeste Rivers."

Celeste opened a hidden gate and ushered us to the business side of the crime office.

"I really appreciate this, Celeste," I recognized.

"Stanley will appreciate it, too," Sarah piped up.

I resisted the urge to roll my eyes.

"Technically, I'm not supposed to be doing this," Celeste said, looking over either shoulder as if expecting someone to bust us, "but Stanley and I go way back, so it's the least I can do."

I was curious to dig more into the pretty lab tech and Stanley's shared past, but Celeste asked a new question before I could.

"Did you check the newer bullet against NIBIN?" she asked.

My eyebrows knit together. "Sorry?"

"NIBIN. It stands for National Integrated Ballistic Information Network. It's the national database of digital images of bullets and cartridge cases found at crime scenes."

"Oh. I didn't even know that was a thing," I grimaced.

"That's okay," she appeased. "Homicide should have done that when they first processed the evidence, not your team. We can still do it manually from our lab though. Both samples are in this envelope?"

"Oh, uh, yeah," I managed. My inexperience embarrassed me, but I supposed that learning about these kinds of procedures would come with time. Good soldiers weren't made overnight either.

Celeste led us deeper into the crime lab. The further we got away from the half-wall partition, the more laboratory and less office-like the space became.

"Most of the forensics work happens off-site at an actual laboratory," she informed us, "and we maintain our major databases in this office. But we can also conduct a few basic tests."

Celeste stopped in front of a contraption that looked like two-microscopes connected by one eyepiece. She pulled on a pair of latex gloves and opened the padded envelope that I'd given her. She then carefully positioned the two bullet samples under the microscope's separate bodies.

Her blonde bun prevented her hair from falling into her face as she leaned over the microscope to look through the centralized viewer.

"What is that thing?" I asked.

"This is a comparison microscope," she said. "It lets me see both samples—in this case bullets—at the same time. Want to look?"

"Sure," I agreed.

Celeste relinquished the double microscope to me, and I peered through the double ocular lenses.

"What exactly am I looking for?" I asked.

I had expected to see the bullets at a molecular level, but instead the two samples were simply magnified.

"When a gun is fired, the bullet makes contact with the spiral grooves inside the barrel. Those grooves spin the bullet for better accuracy, but they also produce individual markings on the bullet. It's these unique markings that we evaluate to determine if a bullet was fired from a particular gun."

I righted myself. "So it's like a gun's fingerprint."

"Pretty much," Celeste confirmed.

"Do you think it's a match?" Sarah asked.

Celeste took another look. "I'd say so. The rifling—the thin lines on the sides of the bullet—seem to match up."

"Really?" I'd been hopeful to find a connection that would allow us to investigate the Kennedy Petersik case—if only for Stanley—but I hadn't let myself become too invested since it was such a long shot.

"I'd like to still send images of these samples to NIBIN to confirm, but I'd say you all have a match," Celeste remarked.

"Wow. This sounds like the easiest open and shut case we'll ever see. And it's two cases in one!" Sarah self-congratulated.

I shook my head. "It's not that easy."

"But we've got the weapon. The bullets match. We just find out who the gun is registered to and the two cases will basically solve themselves, right?" Sarah proposed.

Celeste looked to me. "Do you want to tell her or should I?"

Sarah's eyes traveled back and forth between Celeste and myself. "What am I missing? What aren't you telling me?"

I made a pained face. "There isn't an actual database that you can use to look up gun registrations."

"What? Of course there is," Sarah insisted.

"No," Celeste corroborated. "Most people think gun registration numbers are like the VIN on a car. You find a gun, run some numbers, and find out who it's registered to. But there's actually no searchable database for guns. There's no centralized record of who owns which specific guns. There's no hard data on how many people own them, how many are bought and sold, or how many even exist."

Sarah blinked. "You're kidding me. How is that even possible?"

"I'll give you one guess," I said.

Sarah's features grew grim. "The NRA."

"Yep." I let my mouth pop at the end of the confirming word.

"But all those police shows on TV," she protested.

"All made up," Celeste said. "It's been federal law since 1986 that no searchable gun database exist. The NRA doesn't want the government to know who has the guns in case they decide one day to take them away."

"Can't take away someone's gun if you don't know they have it," Sarah said, the gears in her brain churning away.

"Exactly," Celeste confirmed. "The closest thing we've got is Martinsburg, Virginia."

"What's there?" Sarah asked.

"Oh, I know this one!" I chimed in. "It's where the National Tracing Center is located."

Sarah's confusion returned. "But I thought you just said guns couldn't be traced?"

"There's no searchable database," Celeste qualified. "But all of the gun records are stored at the Tracing Center. Imagine an old-school library, but without the card catalog. But those are just the records of out-of-business gun retailers. The majority of gun records stay with the stores where someone bought the gun, like a Wal-Mart or a hunting store."

"This sounds like a needle in a haystack," Sarah complained.

"Pretty much," I confirmed.

"We can ask the Tracing Center to look for the information," Celeste noted, "but they might never find anything."

"So now what?" Sarah huffed. Where she had previously been excited, she now appeared deflated. I could relate to her frustration, but we couldn't let this hurdle stop us altogether.

"Now we let Homicide know we've potentially got a double homicide on our hands."

CHAPTER SIX

"*Corpus Juris Secundim*," I read aloud. I had probably butchered the pronunciation. "Sounds like a Harry Potter spell."

I stood before the impressive bookcase in Julia's law office while she worked at her desk. On the evenings she kept late hours for clients who worked second shift I dropped off dinner knowing that she would never take a break to do so for herself. That night's meal was a red pepper hummus vegetable wrap from a Greek restaurant close to the Fourth Precinct.

"It's Latin for 'Second Body of Law,'" Julia explained. "It's an encyclopedia of state and federal laws."

"Isn't that what Google is for?" I said, only half joking.

Julia awarded me an indulgent smile. "Lawyers use it to look up relevant case law. Precedents that might help the current cases we're working."

I slid a single finger down the well-creased binding on one of the texts. "Did they come in a Lawyer Starter Kit? Complete with red pens and yellow legal pads?"

My joke fell on deaf ears. "No. My father gifted me his collection when I passed the bar exam."

"Oh."

I didn't know what to say. Julia's family in general was a sensitive subject, and her father, William Desjardin, the former mayor of her hometown, was even more so.

Julia removed her reading glasses and set them down on her desk with a sigh. "I know I need to see him."

I held up my hands in retreat. "I didn't say a word."

Her lipsticked mouth twisted. "I know. But it's been weighing heavily on my mind these past few weeks. Each day that passes, my mother's memories become more and more vulnerable to her disease. How long until she forgets me altogether?" She shuttered her eyes with the weighty statement.

I ached for her. Julia was so strong, so proud and capable; it was these qualities and more that I admired about her. But her mother was her kryptonite. It was the only time I'd seen her let her guard down when we'd first met, months ago.

Julia inhaled sharply, collecting and reorganizing her emotions. "As much as I'd prefer to never speak to my father again, he—by court order—is my mother's keeper. If I want to spend time with her, I'm going to have to make up and play nice."

"Are you thinking about going up there soon?"

Embarrass was just over a three-hour drive from the Twin Cities. I myself had done the round trip in one day when I'd needed to escape Embarrass. If Julia was going up to visit her parents, however, I assumed it would be at least one overnight. Maybe more. Selfishly, I didn't want her missing from my bed for even one night.

"It's just a thought right now," she said. "I'll let you know though if they become plans."

I worried my lower lip. "I've got something I want to talk to you about, but it's really sensitive and definitely not any of my business."

Julia cocked her head and looked concerned. "You know you can talk to me about anything, Cassidy."

"Even Jonathan?"

She quirked an eyebrow. I was sure she hadn't been expecting me to ask a question about her brother. He'd killed himself at her family's cabin in Embarrass, not long after returning from a tour of duty.

"What about him?" she inquired.

I cleared my throat, feeling more awkward than any conversation I'd ever had with her—and that was saying a lot because I typically felt awkward.

My questions about Jonathan were part curiosity and part professional. I didn't see much overlap between Julia's brother and Kennedy Petersik beyond unnatural deaths, but maybe there had been warning signs that had predated Jonathan taking his own life that could be used to better identify Kennedy's death as a suicide or homicide.

"You can ask me whatever you need to," she encouraged.

"Are you sure?"

I watched her lips thin as if reconsidering her offer, but she nodded.

"Before he killed himself, did anyone suspect Jonathan had been depressed or suicidal?"

Julia exhaled like a deflating balloon. "I'm going to need some wine."

+++

Julia sat on her white couch with her legs tucked under her body. She'd exchanged the pencil skirt and Oxford button-up blouse for black leggings and an oversized t-shirt. I did my best to ignore how the fine bones of her clavicle peeked out of the top of the too-large shirt. We weren't there for that.

She'd poured herself a large glass of red wine. Both it and the rest of the bottle sat on the coffee table between us. She took an introductory sip from the glass. Her lipstick stayed on her lips and not on the edge of the glass.

"Alright, Detective. What do you want to know?"

"What was Jonathan like?"

It was a softball of a question compared to my initial inquiry back at her office. Even then, however, she sat for a minute with the request.

"Jonathan was the favorite," she began. "He was everyone's favorite—not just with my parents. Everyone in Embarrass only had glowing words for him. Handsome. Charming. Genuine. Athletic. Smart. Accomplished. I think enlisting in the military was the first time he'd done something my parents disapproved of."

"Why?"

She'd mentioned something to the effect when she'd first told me about his death. As much as I wanted to remain silent and let her control the trajectory of the conversation, I was too personally invested to keep my curiosity to myself.

Julia wet her lips before her response. "My parents aren't pacifists; they've never shared a strong opinion about the country's involvement in foreign affairs. I think they were disappointed because—to them," she qualified, "you enlist when you have no other options. It's something poor people or those without direction do. It's not something a Desjardin was supposed to do."

She paused, waiting for my reaction. I swallowed my pride, but at the same time, I couldn't very well argue with her; I'd had no noble reasons for becoming a Marine. My family wasn't poor, but I'd certainly been directionless. I hadn't enlisted for love of country or to defend democracy across the globe. I'd been bored and had stumbled into a local recruiting office.

"You told me he came back from his tour … different."

"Haunted." She said the word with the conviction of someone who'd sat with the idea for a long time. "If you didn't know him well, you might not have noticed anything was off. But he was my brother, and I noticed."

"I was living in Minneapolis when he came back," she continued. "I'd recently passed the bar and was courting offers from a number of criminal law firms. My parents came down from Embarrass and we all went to the airport together. I hardly recognized him when he first walked out. It was more than the new beard or how tan his skin was. He'd become …" it was his eyes. He just looked … haunted." She shook her head. "I don't have another way to describe it."

I knew that look all too well. It was the same stare I saw when I looked around the therapy circle I sometimes attended at the local VA hospital.

PTSD is a modern acronym, but the diagnosis is as old as war. Each generation has had their own name for it, and yet it persists. In the Civil War it was described as 'exhaustion' or 'soldier's heart.' During World War I, the symptoms were called 'shell shock.' They named it 'battle fatigue' in World War II. Some memories from combat fade with time, but there are sounds you can't forget, scents you can't get rid of.

I nodded tightly for her to continue.

"We had dinner in the city," she resumed. "Jonathan didn't talk much—not about himself, at least. He asked a lot of questions about what was new with all of us, and we were more than happy to fill the silence by talking about ourselves." She paused to take another fortifying sip from her glass of wine. I knew this conversation was taxing, but I loved her a little bit more for her openness and honesty.

"After that, he went back to Embarrass with my parents, and I stayed on in Minneapolis." Her mouth drooped at the memory. "My mom wanted me to come back, too. She told me it was selfish to stay in the city since Jonathan was newly home. We fought about it, and I resented Jonathan for it. He'd never said anything about me coming back, but I still resented the insinuation that I should drop everything going on in my life just because he was back."

"So you weren't in Embarrass when he died?" I asked.

Julia's eyes closed. "No." The word came out with difficulty. "I visited when I could, but when you're a new junior associate, you're working around the clock to make an impression with the partners."

"Did he ever talk to you about what it had been like over there?"

"No more than you do."

It wasn't intended as a shot against me, but I knew that Julia wanted me to talk more about my tours in Afghanistan. She knew the big stuff though—which I'd only ever shared before with doctors and therapists who I needed to convince I was mentally stable enough to return to being a cop. All of that disclosure had been coerced.

"Something here would remind him of a story from over there," she said. "The stories came out in bursts. Stories without beginnings or endings. But I never witnessed him being, ah … confused."

"Confused?" I questioned.

Julia's eyes dropped from my face to her hands. She twisted the stem of her wine glass between her fingers. Her voice was quiet. "Confused like you get sometimes."

I sat up a little straighter. "Oh. You didn't witness his PTSD."

Julia eventually looked up. "No." She wet her lips. "I don't know if those same things triggered him. But I also don't think he experienced a traumatic event like you did."

I held up one hand to stop her. "It's okay. You don't need to make excuses for why I am the way I am. Or why I'm more screwed up than other veterans."

Her painted lips twisted into a frown.

"It's really okay," I reiterated. "I didn't want to make this about me."

Julia nodded. "What else do you want to know?"

"Did he leave a suicide note?"

She shook her head. "No."

"Do you know why it was ruled a suicide and not homicide or an accident?"

She drew in an audible breath and hollowed out her cheeks. "The police found gunpowder residue on his hands. Well ... on *everything*. And I suppose it could have been an accident that he'd been staring down the double barrel of a shot gun at the exact moment it went off."

Her shoulders lifted and fell in a gesture of helplessness. Her explanation and tone had been casual. Flippant, almost. But I recognized the defense mechanism. It was the same nonchalance I witnessed in my fellow soldiers in Afghanistan. We treat death with a casualness so we don't go mad.

+ + +

"I've never been down here before," I heard an amused voice. "Guess I wasn't missing out on much."

I looked up from my computer screen to see Detective Jason Ryan standing in the open doorway of the Cold Case Division office.

My lip curled at his attitude. Our office was a shit hole, but only *we* were allowed to say that.

"Can I help you?" Sarah spoke up from her desk. Her clipped tone indicated she'd been similarly unimpressed with Detective Ryan's attitude.

I expected Ryan to stumble over himself—most unsuspecting cops did when they first saw Sarah. But he appeared equally unimpressed with my colleague as she with him.

"I heard you found your matching bullets, ladies. Congratulations."

The way he said the L-word sounded patronizing.

I pushed away from my desk and leaned back in my office chair. "To what do we owe the honor of your company, Detective Ryan? Need some help on another one of your cases?"

His lips twitched, but he didn't take the bait. "I'm going to need everything you've collected regarding the Petersik case."

"What makes you think we're keeping intel from you?" I posed.

"I know you've been poking around, Miller. Talking to the dead girl's parents. Going to the crime lab."

"I told you I thought there could be a connection. Don't get mad that I was right."

"Since you're so chummy with the folks at the crime lab and seem to have all the time in the world," Ryan sniffed, "why don't you go see about Kennedy Petersik's cell phone records? I want to know exactly where she went on the day of her death. If she went to the mall, I want to know. If she went to the movies, I want to know which one. If she took a detour to shit in the woods, I want to know what it looked like."

Sarah stared blankly at Detective Ryan and his posturing. "You could say 'please.'"

Ryan ignored my colleague. "And I need information and contact numbers from the original cold case. I want to talk to everyone involved."

"I can look up Michael Bloom's family to let them know we're re-examining his case, but it may not be welcomed news," Sarah remarked. "Sometimes opening a case back up only re-opens the wound for the family. If they've moved on, they're not going to want us to drag them back."

Ryan's eyes narrowed to a squint. "Who are you again?"

Sarah straightened in her office chair. "Dr. Sarah Conrad. Victim's Advocate. In other words, I don't work for *you*, Detective."

I held up my hands, hoping to keep the peace before egos spun out of control. "Hold up, guys. We've got to work together as a team. We're all here for the same reason—to find out how and why a young woman died."

Neither Sarah nor Ryan blinked or budged from their respective spots, but they had gone silent, at least for the moment.

"*Doctor* Conrad, why don't you come with me to see about procuring cell phone records from the crime lab?" I proposed. "*Please.*"

Sarah continued to glare at Detective Ryan. Her nostrils flared. "Sure."

I waited until we were outside of the building to confront my colleague. Even though we'd left Detective Jason Ryan behind, Sarah continued to look annoyed. Her hands were shoved deep in the pockets of her jacket and the heels of her ankle boots stomped against the pavement of the Fourth Precinct parking lot.

"What was all that doctor business about back there?" I asked.

"I'm not just a pretty face, Miller," she snipped. "I've got a doctorate in social work."

"Yeah, but you've never thrown around your title before," I observed. "I didn't even realize you had one."

"Because *you've* never treated me like a second-class citizen," she said. "But you're like a unicorn. You'd be surprised how many cops around here think they're better than us civilians. And the fact that they even refer to us as 'civilians' is ridiculous." She threw her hands in the air out of frustration. "Just because you have a badge doesn't mean you're some god."

I let Sarah continue to vent without interruption. I wasn't about to defend myself or my fellow police officers. I knew firsthand how the badge tended to attract arrogant individuals who simultaneously suffered from inferiority complexes.

Sarah drew a long breath, and I chanced a smile. "Am I driving or you?"

Sarah rolled her eyes. I wasn't sure what kind of reaction she'd expected from me—something, certainly. But instead of laying into me about my lack of commentary, she started to walk in the direction of the employee parking lot.

"I'll drive," she tossed over her shoulder. "I've had enough of that tin can you call a car."

+ + +

Celeste Rivers was behind her stand-up workstation when Sarah and I arrived at the City Hall crime lab office. Unlike our first visit, she was the only employee present. She wore the long white lab coat again, which seemed to be an unnecessary uniform, and her white blonde hair was pulled back in a tight bun.

When she noticed our entrance, she left her desk and approached the half-wall partition. "Uh oh," she clucked. "I hope you at least brought a bribe this time."

I opened my empty hands. "Next time," I promised.

As if sensing the nature of our visit, she opened the hidden gate on the partitioning and let us into her side of the office.

"More bullets?" she inquired. Her voice was almost teasing.

"What do you know about acquiring a person's cell phone records?" I asked.

"As in using GPS to track a person's whereabouts?" she posed.

"Not in real time, no," Sarah corrected for me. "As in recreating where a person *used* to be."

Celeste bobbed her head as if she'd forgotten. "Cold Case. Right."

"Is that something we can even do? And is it accurate and reliable?" I asked.

I'd seen my share of murder documentaries, but those had all been decades-old criminal investigations. I wondered how the technology had been refined over time.

"Our phones are constantly tracking our movement, but it's not as precise as say—tracking the chip in your dog or mapping out a running route," Celeste began. "Anytime your phone uses data—not just when you're making or receiving phone calls—it's connecting to a cell phone tower. Bigger cities have more people and therefore need more cell towers, which helps us more accurately pinpoint someone's location. But the cell phone tower that provides voice and text messages is different from the cell tower that provides data usage."

"So you're actually pinging on two cell phone towers?" I questioned.

"Correct," Celeste nodded. "And where that coverage overlaps gives us a pretty good indication of where you might have been. But," she cautioned, "it can still be pretty inaccurate. The towers your cell phone accesses for data or voice aren't necessarily the closest in proximity. Several factors influence which towers handle the call or data request, like which one is most cost-effective."

"In other words, it wouldn't be responsible to base a case only on cell phone records," Sarah observed.

"Exactly," Celeste confirmed. "Ideally, you would want to have other evidence to corroborate the cell phone information, like an eyewitness or a credit card record for a business visited."

I nodded my understanding. It was a start at least, and if we could compare the cell phone information to other records or witnesses, even better. "Would you be able to help us contact the service provider to get a head start on this?"

"Please," Sarah added.

I caught Sarah's side-long stare. "Yes," I quickly corrected myself. "*Please.*"

"Manners are important, Miller," Sarah remarked as Celeste left to start on the appropriate paperwork. "They're the only things that separate us from them."

"From who? Animals?" I guessed.

"No. Men."

There was a bounce to Sarah's step as we exited City Hall. I was glad to see her mood had improved since her interaction with Detective Ryan. The man had a talent for ruffling feathers.

"I thought you would have thrown Stanley's name around like last time," I cracked.

"Oh, no," Sarah clucked. "Stanley's our secret weapon. We can't overuse him or he loses his power."

"What do you think is the deal with Stanley and Celeste?" I asked.

Sarah walked to the driver's side of her vehicle. "I have no idea. Let's embarrass him and find out." Her grin couldn't have been bigger.

A chuckle was still in my throat when my phone rang. I fished my cell out of my jacket pocket; my laughter went silent when I saw my mom's name come up on the phone.

Normally I wouldn't have taken a personal call during work hours, but I rarely heard from my family. My parents didn't text, and I didn't use social media, so unless we called each other, I had no idea what was going on in their world.

I answered the call, anticipating the worse.

"What's wrong?" I demanded in lieu of a greeting.

Was someone sick? Had my dad experienced a heart attack? Had there been a car accident?

"Why hello to you, too, sweetie."

+ + +

"Cassidy? Is something burning?"

I stood in the hallway, frantically waving a kitchen towel in front of the smoke detector. Luckily I'd caught it in time—not in time to salvage dinner—but in time so the smoke detector didn't detonate the entire building. My culinary shame would be confined to the apartment I shared with Julia and not the entire apartment complex gathered on the front sidewalk.

I'd been trying to make a pizza with a cauliflower crust to show Julia I cared equally about her heart and her waistline. But the burnt smell billowing from the oven let me know we'd be ordering real pizza that night.

Julia's high heels clacked towards the kitchen. "Darling, what's going on? I smell something burning."

I abandoned the kitchen towel and the smoke detector. "I ruined dinner," I sighed. "I ruin everything."

I grabbed the pizza stone from the stovetop and hollered in surprise when I realized it was still hot. "Goddamn it!"

The pizza stone fell from my hand, the failed cauliflower crust with it. Both clattered to the kitchen floor and shattered on impact.

Julia grabbed my stinging hand and thrust it into the sink. She turned the kitchen faucet on full blast so cold water bathed my hand.

"Are you okay?" she worried. She stood close to my hip and we jointly watched the cold water cascade over my pink flesh.

"I'm a disaster," I said numbly. "I can't do anything right."

Julia frowned. "That seems like a bit of an overreaction to burning pizza."

"I just wanted to do something nice for you." I turned off the kitchen faucet and inspected my hand. My palm and fingers were bright pink, but I'd survive.

"You do nice things for me all the time, dear."

I bent down to pick up the broken pieces of cauliflower crust and pizza stone, but Julia stopped me. She ushered me to the dining room table and made me sit down. Instead of sitting down in her own chair, she sat down lightly on my lap.

"You're a complete mess, Detective." She pushed the hair out of my eyes. "What's got you so agitated?"

I swiped at her hand, the one that had brushed the hair away from my forehead. "My parents want to visit." I made a sour face. "More like my *mom* wants to meet for dinner, and my dad has no say in it."

Julia's features turned serious. "That's as good of a reason to be frazzled as I've ever heard."

I could feel her body shift and move as though she was about to stand up. My hands moved to her waist, and I held her firm against me. "You're not supposed to say that," I protested. "You're supposed to be my rock."

"And I will be." She dipped her head so her lips brushed against mine. "When are they coming?"

"Tomorrow," I grumbled. "They're only in town for one day and then they're going back to St. Cloud. Will you come with me?"

Julia pursed her lips in thought. "Cassidy—are you Out to your parents?"

I dropped my eyes. "Not exactly, no."

"Not exactly?" she repeated.

"I didn't date in high school, and then I was in the military for eight years. You're my first relationship that counted."

"Do they know I exist?"

"Uh ..."

"Cassidy." Her censuring tone had me hanging my head.

"I'm not close with them, you know that!" I squeaked.

Julia exhaled. "Would it be easier if I didn't go to this dinner?"

"Easier, sure," I admitted. "But that doesn't mean I don't want you there."

"You're asking me to come to dinner with you and your parents ... but you're also asking me to pretend like we're not in a relationship?"

I cringed. It sounded awful. "Yes."

"So, I'm what—your *roommate?*" Her voice wavered between anger and disbelief.

"Would that be so terrible?" I proposed.

"Cassidy, I'm a grown ass woman. And so are you—sometimes. Are you really so concerned about what your parents think about whom you're dating?"

"Weren't you the one who wanted to be discreet in Embarrass?" I deflected.

"That was different. We didn't have a label for what we were doing. We weren't *living together.*"

I couldn't defend myself.

Julia sighed and ran her hand over her face. "Fine. I'll do it."

I blinked once. "Are you sure?"

She nodded, but the displeased look remained on her features. "I of all people should be able to appreciate that when it comes to family, things can be complicated."

I exhaled. "Thank you."

"So, *roommate*, when and where is dinner? Do you want me to make a reservation somewhere?"

"They're not fancy," I warned. "I mean, they made *me*, so that should tell you something."

She smiled at my self-deprecation. "So no *Etoile Blanche*, I gather." She named the fancy French restaurant where we'd once shared a meal with my Marine buddy, Pensacola, and his wife, Claire.

"Definitely not. They wouldn't know what to do if there's more than one fork at their place setting," I noted.

"What will be easiest for them?" she asked. "I imagine they won't want to drive and have to park downtown. It can be a little overwhelming for even the most seasoned city driver."

"Have you ever been to the Mall of America?" The words felt ridiculous the moment I said them.

Julia pinched the bridge of her nose. "Christ, I must really love you."

CHAPTER SEVEN

"Miller, party of four. Your adventure is about to begin."

The Mall of America was a short drive outside of the Minneapolis city center, close to the Twin Cities airport. It first opened in 1992, and now boasted over 500 stores, an amusement park, an aquarium, two miniature golf courses, and a variety of eating choices. I'd implored my parents to meet at an actual restaurant—something more substantial than the mall's Food Court. The image of Julia, in her pants suits and red-bottomed heels, sitting at a sticky table in a loud, crowded mall food court might have actually been worth the awkwardness, but I couldn't do that to her. She was already setting her pride to the side to help me through a meal with my parents.

We'd met up with my mom and dad in front of the restaurant entrance. I'd simply introduced Julia by her name—no qualifiers about who she was to me: a friend, a work colleague, a roommate, *the love of my life*. They hadn't asked for more information, and, like a coward, I was satisfied to let them think what they may.

My parents, Julia, and I followed the smiling hostess from the front of the restaurant to our table for four. We passed groupings of animatronic monkeys and elephants and larger-than-life insects until we reached our table near the robotic tigers. I felt Julia's hand in the small of my back. It lingered for a moment before she pulled her hand away.

I regretted my decision to keep our relationship closeted. But my parents had a hard enough time dealing with a daughter who had PTSD. They already didn't know how to approach my condition.

Would I only be piling on if I added *gay* to that growing list of things that made them uncomfortable?

My parents claimed the booth seating against the wall while Julia and I sat in the individual chairs on the other side. Julia picked up her laminated menu and inspected the restaurant's offerings. If the deep-fried appetizers and the two-for-one combos insulted her sensibilities, she at least had the kindness to school her features and hide her displeasure.

"This is something, isn't it?" my mom openly marveled as she took in our animated surroundings. "I've never been to one of these before, but they have them at all the theme parks and in big cities, so I thought why not?"

"It's a charming choice, Mrs. Miller," Julia approved.

Julia's words sat well with my mom; her pleasure unabashedly radiated across her features. I knew how she felt. A compliment from Julia was all I needed to smile, too.

My dad sucked on his teeth while he looked over the menu. "Kinda pricey," he tersely observed. "Don't know how I feel about spending $15 on a burger."

"Don't worry about the price, Dad," I jumped in. "You guys traveled all this way; dinner's on me."

His frown lines deepened. "Don't know how I feel about my daughter picking up the check either. Parents are supposed to—."

"I know, I know," I interrupted. "Parents take care of their kids." I'd heard the mantra a million times. "But I've missed, like, your past ten birthdays," I exaggerated. "Let me do this."

My dad's eyes flicked from my face over to Julia's before returning to his menu. He was a proud guy who didn't take handouts. Accepting my offer in front of Julia—a stranger to him—must have been eating away at him. But he didn't put up further protest so I considered the matter settled.

I nearly shot to my feet at an animatronic clap of thunder and flash of lightning, which was followed by the sounds of rain falling in a lush forest. My body tensed and jerked, but I somehow remained in my plastic molded seat. It probably had something to do with Julia's hand, which she'd innocently rested on my knee, hidden from my parents beneath the cover of the table.

My thigh muscles twitched erratically, but the subtle weight of her hand kept me anchored—tethered—to reality instead of being mentally transported to an Afghan desert.

My parents were too busy exploring their menus to notice my altered behavior. But even if they'd noticed, I knew they wouldn't ask how I was managing my PTSD.

Julia's shoulder pressed imperceptively into mine even though we had plenty of room on our side of the table. It was a nonverbal question, asking if I was going to be all right. I bobbed my head, more for my own benefit than hers. I could do this. I could handle outbursts of fake jungle sounds without losing my shit.

A waitress dropped by to take our food and drink orders. I wanted to request appetizers for the table, but I knew my parents thought pre-entrée food was too showy. I wondered what they thought about the woman sitting to my right. I was thankful she had somewhat dressed down for the occasion. She still looked like a million bucks in a cowl neck cashmere sweater, dark skinny jeans, and ankle boots, but at least it wasn't her typical uniform of pencil skirt, Oxford blouse, and high-priced heels.

A server who wasn't our waitress delivered our food to the table in a suspiciously short amount of time. Cheeseburgers and fries for everyone at the table. I'd been stunned when Julia hadn't ordered something with more vegetables.

We dug into our respective meals. Table conversation was stilted until my mom opened up with a question: "Cassidy, are you coming home for Thanksgiving?"

I wasn't expecting the request, but luckily my mouth was full of cheeseburger so I had some time to chew before having to respond.

I hated when my mom referred to St. Cloud as my home. I hadn't lived fulltime in the city for a decade, and since then, my return visits had been sporadic and infrequent and typically ended with me leaving in dramatic fashion after fighting with my dad. I didn't want this dinner to end in the same way, so I didn't bother to critique my mom's word choice.

"I haven't thought that far ahead," I told her. It wasn't a lie; I hadn't given much thought to the holiday since it was more than a month away, but I also had no intention of spending more time in St. Cloud.

"So, I guess that means you're not planning on coming home for Christmas either?" my mom pressed.

I couldn't help my exhausted sigh. "No, it doesn't mean that, Mom. I'm kinda playing it by ear."

"I get it. You don't want to spend your birthday with your stuffy, old parents. I just thought it might be nice to have the family together for once."

I rubbed at my face. I could sense my mom starting to gain momentum. I was in for a massive guilt trip. "Mom, we're together right now."

"Wait a minute." Julia interrupted the trajectory of the conversation and turned in her chair to look at me. "Are you a Christmas baby? How did I not know that?"

"Christmas Eve," I clarified. "But growing up I still basically had to share my birthday with Jesus."

"Oh, it wasn't all that bad," my mom clucked. "You got a birthday cake every year. And think about all those children who don't get *anything* for their birthdays."

I stuck out my lower lip. "I still got the shaft."

My mom dropped her voice to a low hiss. "Language, Cassidy."

"'Shaft' isn't a bad word, Mom," I complained.

"Maybe not. But it's vulgar. Julia—" she unexpectedly turned to my girlfriend. "What do you think about my daughter's language?"

Julia looked as surprised as me to have been directly addressed, but the shock on her features didn't last long. "I would have to agree with you, Mrs. Miller," she responded. "I'm forever reminding Cassidy to refine her word choice. Just because she was in the military doesn't mean she needs to talk like a sailor."

I bit back an acrid response: *You weren't complaining about my mouth last night.*

There was no mistaking the smug, triumphant look on my mom's face. She was clearly pleased that Julia had sided with her. She reached across the table and patted the top of Julia's hand. "Oh, you can call me Nancy."

Dinner passed pleasantly enough, largely because we stuck to safe, neutral topics. How nice the weather had been lately. If the Vikings were going to win the North division this year. My mom shared the latest St. Cloud gossip, but nothing particularly scandalous. My dad, as predicted, ate his meal and kept mostly to himself, only offering up a grunt or a growl when prompted by my mom to participate in the conversation.

Before long, our empty plates had been cleared away and dessert menus had been refused. The only thing left to do was settle the check so my parents could head back to St. Cloud. My mom and dad excused themselves to the restroom; St. Cloud was only an hour and a half away from the mall, but my dad hated having to stop for bathroom breaks. I could vividly remember as a child having to hold my bladder on long road trips because he refused to deviate from his driving plan. Only scheduled stops were allowed.

While my parents were in the bathroom, I took advantage of their absence. I leaned close to my girlfriend and kissed her mouth. It was quick and chaste, but only because I knew my mom and dad would be back to the table soon.

Julia leaned her shoulder against mine. Just the residual heat from her body made my insides hum.

"How are you doing?" she asked. "I got worried for a second when I heard that fake thunder."

"I was worried, too," I admitted. "But no flashbacks. Go me."

"Maybe you're getting better?" she proposed.

I shook my head. "Let's not get carried away."

Julia leaned closer and tucked a stray blonde lock behind my ear. The hair hadn't been bothering me, but I grinned knowing that it was an excuse for her to touch me.

"Your parents seemed to enjoy the restaurant," she observed. "Your mother especially."

I hummed in agreement. "Thank you for being so nice to them. I know they're kind of country."

Julia arched an eyebrow. "Did you expect me to be rude?"

"No. Of course not," I denied. "But you've been downright bubbly tonight. And, you ordered a cheeseburger and ate the whole thing!"

"It's all part of the plan, my dear."

"Which is?" I was curious, but hesitant to ask.

She batted her long eyelashes and pressed even tighter against my shoulder. "To charm your parents so much that they practically *beg* me to date their hapless daughter."

I didn't have time for a response before my mom returned to the table.

"The animal sounds are even in the bathroom," she chuckled. "I almost had a heart attack when I flushed the toilet and heard a lion roar."

I didn't bother to jump away from Julia or put more space between us. But I was curious as to what my mom might have seen. She may have missed the chaste kiss, but she would have at least observed the intimacy of our close proximity. I inspected my mom's face, but saw no sign or signal of recognition. She either had an excellent poker face or was still too enchanted by the animatronic monkeys to notice anything else.

My dad returned from the bathroom shortly after my mom. "Time to hit the road, Nancy. We're losing daylight."

I spied our server and waved her down. "Can I get the check when you have a second?"

"Oh, he already took care of it." She pointed in the direction of my father.

"Dad!" My voice pitched in complaint. "You weren't supposed to do that!"

He only shrugged.

The heels of Julia's ankle boots clicked crisply against the concrete floor of the parking garage as we walked back to her car. Her black Mercedes chirped when she unlocked the doors from a distance.

My loud exhale echoed in the cavernous parking lot.

"Having second thoughts about finishing my French fries, dear?" Julia playfully teased.

"They didn't even ask."

"Who?" she questioned.

"My parents. They didn't ask who you were."

"Are you surprised?"

"I guess not," I shrugged. "They're too passive aggressive, disguised as politeness to ask about the stranger at the table."

"That's a good thing though, isn't it? At least you didn't have to lie," she pointed out.

"But they didn't give me the chance!" I practically whined.

"Were you having a change of heart?" she asked. "Did you *want* to tell them?"

I reached for Julia's hand and intertwined our fingers. We'd been play-acting as 'roommates' for far too long.

"I'm sorry I'm not Out and Proud," I apologized.

"I don't expect you to wear a rainbow, dear," she pacified.

I stopped walking. With our fingers entwined, Julia had no choice but to stop as well. "I don't want you to think I'm embarrassed or ashamed to be with you. Because *look* at you. Who wouldn't want to show that off?" I gestured with my free hand. "You're the sexiest woman on the planet. Plus, you're a brilliant lawyer."

Julia silenced my effusive praise with her mouth. Her full lips pressed against mine, and I couldn't hold back a guttural moan when she trapped my lower lip between her top and bottom rows of teeth.

She twisted her fingers around the lapel of my leather jacket and drew me closer. "I don't think you're ashamed of me. And I never want you to feel like I'm embarrassed to be with you either. I know I'm not always comfortable showing affection in public, but I've always been a private person. I'm not about to put on a show for anyone."

I wiggled my eyebrows. "I wouldn't mind a private show."

She lightly swatted at me and laughed, showing off her perfect teeth. I knew I'd interrupted a serious moment, but I couldn't help myself.

Julia curled her fingers around my blonde tendrils. She leaned in close so her lips brushed against the outer shell of my ear. "Well now that I know when your birthday is …"

+ + +

I lay on my stomach in bed, flipping through one of the many police catalogs I'd somehow gotten on the mailing list for. I skimmed over bulletproof vests, tactical sunglasses, combat boots, and more—all of the accoutrement that used to get me excited, like a kid at Christmas. These days, shopping for that kind of gear only made me wistful, now that I spent the majority of my time behind a desk.

Beside me, her head propped up by the headboard and a pile of decorative pillows, Julia flipped through file folders and yellow legal pads. She didn't bring work home often, but if her case load started to pile up she had to sneak in a few hours of work before bed. I didn't mind though; I typically watched some sports event on TV in the background. As long as we were together, l was satisfied.

I rolled onto my side and watched her, unnoticed, while she worked. A skinny headband held her thick, glossy hair out of her face. Her black-framed reading glasses had fallen halfway down her nose, but she didn't bother to rearrange them. She picked up a thick book from the floor, maybe one of her case law encyclopedias. She licked the tips of her fingers before carefully turning its pages.

"I love you," I announced.

Julia hummed in acknowledgment, but she didn't look in my direction.

I ran my hand across her smooth stomach. Her silk nightgown was nearly transparent. "I adore you."

Julia smiled down at me. "And I, you," she returned.

"I *worship* you," I growled.

Julia's smile was replaced with a raised eyebrow. "Worship. Really?"

"Yes." I jumped to my knees on top of the mattress, suddenly more sure of myself. "Marry me."

Julia slowly lowered her legal pad. "Cassidy," she said in a disapproving tone.

It was the most brilliant thing I'd ever thought of: "Marry me, Julia." I was emphatic.

Her lips pursed. "I'm not the marrying kind."

"Bullshit," I exclaimed. "You weren't the dating kind either when we first met."

Julia's caramel gaze steadied. She took off her reading glasses and carefully folded them on her lap. "You're serious about this?"

"As a heart attack."

"I don't see a ring," she pointed out.

"You can pick out whatever you want." I would give her the moon if I could.

She paused and tucked her lower lip between her top and bottom rows of teeth. "Let me think on it."

"What's there to think on?" I chafed. "It's either yes or no."

"*Cassidy*," she said more sternly. "Let me think on it."

I swallowed hard. "Okay."

The rush of adrenaline I'd experienced from the proposal left my body, leaving me feeling like a deflated balloon. I crawled under the top covers and rolled onto my side, giving Julia my back.

"How much longer do you need the light on?" I asked.

Julia ignored my question. "Are you pouting, darling?"

"No," I huffed. I pulled the cotton sheets tight under my chin. "I'm tired, and I'm going to sleep."

"Not much longer," she promised. "Don't you have some writing to do yet?" She gently referred to the dream journal that my therapist, Dr. Susan Warren, had me write in before I went to sleep.

"I'm skipping it tonight," I grunted.

I expected to receive a lecture about consistency with my therapy, but she wisely left it alone: "Okay."

The mattress shifted as Julia leaned over me. She pressed her lips against the back of my head. "Sweet dreams, dear."

I shut my eyes and lay silent, certain I wouldn't get any sleep at all.

CHAPTER EIGHT

"Give it up, you little fucker."

I smacked my palm against the clear glass that separated me from the bag of Skittles I'd just paid for. The red rectangular bag swung in the balance, not quite sold, not quite mine.

Just like Julia.

To say I was having a hard time concentrating at work would be an understatement. I'd lost count of how many times I'd picked up my phone that day, intent on texting Julia that I'd changed my mind about wanting to marry her or that I hadn't really meant it. But each time I returned my phone to the top drawer of my desk.

"Come on," I mumbled. I smacked the clear partition again. The bag of candy wobbled, but stubbornly continued to hang on.

"I'm still waiting on those files, Miller."

Detective Jason Ryan appeared at my elbow. He'd forgone the suit jacket that day or had left it at his desk. His badge continued to hang from a chain around his neck like a desperate plea for attention.

"What for?" I challenged.

"Because Homicide is taking over Bloom and Petersik cases."

"Like hell you are," I denied. "You wouldn't even know there was a connection between the two cases without us."

Ryan pressed a hand to his heart. "And we're eternally thankful to you all," he said with mock sincerity. "But this is now an active investigation, so I'm gonna need all of your files."

"You're right. They're *our* files. So why don't you give *us* everything you've got on Kennedy Petersik, and we'll take it from there?"

"Because it's an active investigation," he reiterated.

"I'm a detective, too, you know."

His lips ticked up. "Yeah. But you're ..."

"I'm what?" I cut him off. "I graduated top of my class in the police academy. I'm a decorated war hero. I'm a goddamn national treasure," I spat.

I never threw around my accolades—in fact, I tended to hide them—but Jason Ryan's attitude was wearing on my nerves. Women were supposed to be timid. They were supposed to let men feel superior. But I'd never been any good at being a woman. I was a Marine.

Ryan's eyes widened comically. "Jesus, Miller. Is it that time of the month?"

A loud, booming voice interrupted our interaction: "Detective Ryan, get in here!"

I didn't have time for a smug look before I heard that same voice calling me as well: "Miller—you, too!"

The disembodied voice belonged to my previous supervisor, Inspector Garnett. He was old school and liked to resolve conflict internally rather than getting the higher ups or Internal Affairs involved. When my FTO had refused to clear me from my probation, following my voluntary leave of absence from the Minneapolis Police Department, it had been Inspector Garnett who'd recommended me for Cold Case. He was probably the one person within the entire city police department whom I respected the most.

Sitting in the Inspector's office felt a little like getting called to the principal's office, although I had no experience with that. I'd kept my head down and my nose clean in school. Detective Ryan looked more injured than I felt. I guessed he was used to being teacher's pet.

Inspector Garnett gave us both a hard look. "I've got this girl's parents breathing down my neck, busting my balls to find their daughter's killer. And apparently some senator's kid might be involved, too," he told us. "I can't afford to throw more resources at this, but I can bring in another department."

Ryan raised his hand to be recognized. "But—."

"No. Not another word from you, Ryan," Inspector Garnett shut him down. "You're collaborating with Cold Case on this one. They've got resources that could prove valuable to the Petersik case. And I think it would be good for you to work on this with someone."

Ryan tried again: "But Inspector—."

"This is not up for negotiation. I've made up my mind. Now go play nice and do your jobs."

I didn't want to look like the bird who'd eaten the canary, so I schooled my features. But I'd be lying if I said I didn't take at least a little bit of pleasure from the outcome of our meeting.

I followed Ryan's sulking form out of Inspector Garnett's office. He dragged his feet over to the vending machine that had confiscated my money earlier and struck the side of the machine with the flat of his hand. The whole machine shuddered and the Skittles bag that had been denying me fell from its metal coil. Ryan retrieved the candy bag from the bottom dispenser and handed it to me.

I was slightly taken aback, but I managed to find my words: "Look. I don't like this anymore than you. But if the end result is us clearing two unnatural deaths, I'd say that's a pretty good day."

"Two: you think it could be a serial killer?"

I could practically see the gears churning in Ryan's head. If he was overly ambitious like I suspected and was using Homicide to catapult his police career, I could only imagine how much he was salivating at the thought of a potential serial killer.

"Easy there, tiger. Let's not put the cart before the horse. We don't even know if the Petersik girl's death was a homicide."

"Her parents say there's no way it could be suicide," he dismissed.

"Sure, that's what they say. But how many parents actually know what's really going on in their kid's life?"

Ryan shrugged. "Just relaying to you what they've been telling me, Partner."

I held up my hand. "I'm gonna squash your buddy cop dreams right now, Ryan. We're not partners. We work in totally different departments."

"Yeah, but 'partner' sounds so much better than 'teammate' or 'colleague,' don't you think?"

"Just call me Miller," I grunted.

+ + +

My serrated knife skid across my plate as a stalk of steamed asparagus dodged out of the way. The utensil shrieked against the ceramic plate below.

"Sorry," I winced.

From across the dining room table, Julia offered a placating smile.

Polite conversation about our respective work days had dominated that night's dinner. Neither of us had broached the topic of my wedding proposal from the previous night. Julia was playing avoidance, and I was too terrified of her rejection to bring it up again.

Julia set down her knife and fork. It hadn't escaped my notice that she'd barely eaten anything. She'd barely nibbled on her baked chicken and several stalks of asparagus remained whole on her plate. "I have to go to Duluth tomorrow."

I dug into my own skinless chicken breast. "You don't have to run away to avoid me," I said, only half joking.

"The timing is a coincidence, nothing more," she assured me. "I have to try a child custody case."

"Don't they have lawyers in Duluth?" I questioned. I hadn't realized her public defender duties might take her out of town.

"It's a favor for a friend. Charlotte had hoped the custody dispute wouldn't actually go to trial, but it looks as though there's no getting around it."

"You've never mentioned this friend before," I noted.

"She's more like a former student of mine. I was the teaching assistant for one of her classes when I was in law school and she was an undergrad."

"Oh. Is she …" I hesitated, "one of your college flings?"

Julia laughed. "Don't be ridiculous. She was far too young for me." She laughed again.

Her words did nothing to satisfying me and her bubbled laughter made me even more self-conscious. "What's so funny?"

"I just realized that you and Charlotte are about the same age."

I dropped my knife. "That's it. You're not going."

Julia arched an eyebrow. "I'm afraid you don't get a vote in this, dear."

I poked at the chicken on my plate, no longer very hungry. "How long will you be gone?"

"It's hard to say." She folded her long, elegant hands on the table. "I'll know more once I get there."

"I don't want you to go," I refused.

She shook her head. "It's only a short while. And just think of all the fun you'll have when I'm out of town. All the dirty dishes you can leave in the sink, the socks you can leave on the floor."

I grumbled unintelligently and resumed eating my dinner. The food on my plate had lost all its flavor.

I plucked the decorative pillows from my side of the bed and threw each one on the floor. Julia sat on her side of the mattress, applying lotion to her hands and quietly watching my temper tantrum.

"Why do you want to get married?"

Her question made me feel a little wild. "Because I love you."

"And that's what people who are in love do?" she calmly posed.

"Well, sure." I rubbed at the back of my neck.

She pressed her lips together. "I've made my decision. I've decided to say no."

I chewed on the inside of my cheek. I bit down hard to distract me from the tingling in my tear ducts.

"We've only been dating a handful of months," she carefully reasoned. "We've barely been living together."

I turned away from her steady gaze.

"Cassidy, please," she called to me. "Don't be upset."

I cleared my throat to dislodge the remorse that had settled there. "It was premature, I get it."

I couldn't bring myself to look at her. I pulled back the covers and slid into bed. I thumped at my pillows and flopped my head deep into their feathered comfort.

I heard the rustle of Julia climbing into bed and adjusting the sheets. She wiggled closer to me and pressed her ice block toes against the back of my calves. I knew she was doing it so I would say something, but my stubborn pride had me ignoring her.

"Would you be able to drive me to the airport in the morning?"

Her question had me rolling over. My forehead crinkled. "I thought you were going to Duluth?"

"I am. But the sooner I get there, the better. I'll already be playing quite a bit of catch-up when I arrive. The flight is less than an hour compared to at least a two and a half hour drive. And who knows what morning traffic will be like." Her lips pursed. "If it's too much of a hassle, I can order a car."

"No, no. I'll drive you."

"Thank you, dear," she softly smiled. "I don't know what I'd do without you."

Probably take a cab, I bitterly thought to myself.

She cuddled closer and nuzzled the tip of her nose against the expanse of my neck. "How can I ever repay you?" Her mouth was hot and wet against my skin.

I felt her fingers begin to creep under the bottom hem of my t-shirt. She scratched her nails across my abdomen before starting the journey up to my bra-less breasts.

I closed my fingers around her wrist to keep her hand from traveling. "Maybe when you get back from Duluth," I mumbled.

Julia pulled away. Her eyes narrowed shrewdly. "Are you punishing me?"

"No," I said darkly. "I'm just not in the mood."

"I love you."

"I know you do," I couldn't help snapping. I took a deep, calming breath. "I just—I need a little time, okay? My ego's a little wounded, I guess."

She nodded curtly, mouth drawn in a tight line. "Good night, dear."

I rolled onto my side and sighed. "Night."

+ + +

Julia wasn't the type to hit the snooze button. The alarm on her phone chimed and she immediately rose out of bed. Her feet were silent on the carpeted floor and she only turned on the bathroom light after she'd closed the door.

I heard the shower turn on. I remained in bed and reached over to her side of the mattress. Her pillow was still warm. It was still dark outside; I had no idea what time it was. I could hear the light patter of rain against the bedroom windowpanes.

The shower turned off. I stared at the ceiling. What if I'd ruined everything? Why had I been so stupidly impatient to propose marriage to her after only a few months of dating? I'd barely gotten her to agree to *date* me; why would I ever think she'd want to get married?

I heard the sounds of the bathroom faucet turning on and off as Julia brushed her teeth behind the closed bathroom door. Her hairdryer turned on a few moments later. She hadn't even left, but I missed her already.

My mind raced to the ridiculous. What if she'd made up the excuse about needing to go to Duluth? The timing was impossibly coincidental. What were the chances that she'd have to go out of town immediately after I'd proposed? And who was this Charlotte person that Julia had to go save? I didn't have a last name, so running her name in the system wasn't even an option.

The bathroom door opened and Julia stepped out. My eyes had adjusted to the dim bedroom lighting, but I could only make out her silhouette.

"Cassidy," she whispered.

"Yeah?" My voice sounded too loud. Hollow and foreign.

"Do you still want to give me a ride?"

"That suggests I want you to go."

The edge of the mattress dipped as Julia sat down. Her fingers went to my hair, twirling tendrils that had worked their way out of my bun. I closed my eyes and suppressed the urge to lean into her touch. I was literally wrapped around her fingers.

"I can call a cab," she offered.

"No, no. I'm up. I'll drive you." I sat up in bed and threw the covers off of me.

Julia remained seated on the bed. I could feel her introspective stare. "Are we okay?"

Her complicated question pressed against my chest. "Yeah. Sure. Of course." The words moved with resistance like a thick, sticky syrup.

She nodded, my halted assurances apparently enough to satisfy her.

I pulled on jeans and a sweatshirt while Julia finished getting ready. She'd packed a medium-sized suitcase. It wasn't the largest bag she owned, but it also wasn't her smallest. I imagined it packed with meticulously folded blouses and pencil skirts. Red bottomed high heels and pearl necklaces.

Julia dropped her key ring into my hand, and I knew it was time to go.

"Feel free to use my car while I'm gone."

I nodded, hands at 10 and 2. I knew I wouldn't use it. As soon as I finished chauffeuring her to the airport, I'd park it in her spot at the apartment complex and leave it there until she needed me to pick her up from the airport again.

"When's your return flight?" I asked.

"I bought a one-way ticket."

I glanced once in her direction. Her eyes were on the dark road ahead of us; she'd tucked her lower lip beneath her top row of teeth.

"Are you *sure* you're not running away?" I tried to joke.

"I don't know how long the trial will take."

It was a logical, reasonable answer, but it did nothing to ease my nerves.

The drive to the airport took no time at all. The sun was still sleeping along with most of the Twin Cities' commuters. I pulled Julia's Mercedes up to the drop-off curb in front of her airline. She turned towards me, but I unfastened my seatbelt and hopped out of the car before she could complete her hasty goodbye.

I grabbed her wheeled suitcase out of the trunk and set it on the curb. The persistent rain had dropped the air temperature. My leather jacket cut through the chill, but Julia was practically shivering in her thin trench coat.

I roughly rubbed the outside of her arms. "You should get inside."

She ignored my advice. "Are you *sure* we're okay, Cassidy?"

The look of concern on her beautiful face made me ache.

"Because I won't get on this flight if we're not."

"Don't say that," I barked out a laugh. "You'll have me lying to keep you here."

Julia's mouth twitched with the hint of a smile, but she still wasn't convinced. "I'm sorry I couldn't say yes."

I wrapped my arms around her figure and pulled her to me. I felt her rigid posture slip as she leaned against me. "I get it," I said, my voice hoarse. "I don't like it, but I get it. Now go," I ordered. "The sooner you're on that plane, the sooner you'll win your trial and can come back to me."

Instead of pulling away, Julia buried her face into my shoulder. "Just a little longer."

I would have been content to stand in the cold and hold her all day, but the sound of a shrill whistle tried to interrupt our embrace.

"Black Mercedes!" A traffic cop in a yellow safety vest yelled at us. "Get moving!"

I locked eyes with the cop and waved to let him know I'd heard him. Julia, however, refused to let me go.

I pressed my face against the side of her head. The scent of her spicy shampoo hit my nostrils. "You're gonna get me arrested," I chuckled.

Her arms tightened around my waist. "I'll visit you in prison."

The airport cop blew his whistle again. I heard Julia's low growl. "I will have that man's head on a plate."

"Easy, Counselor. Save some of that for the court room."

Fingers curled around the collar of my leather jacket. She tugged me to her height. Our lips met, and I heard the police officer's whistle go silent.

"I hope he choked on that damn thing," Julia murmured against my open mouth.

I slipped my fingers through her silken hair and deepened the kiss. When she hummed against my lips, I wanted to toss her into the back of her Mercedes, but I knew I was only delaying the inevitable.

I broke away from her mouth with an unreasonable amount of willpower. "You've got a flight to catch," I rasped.

"Why don't you come with me?" she proposed. "You're due a vacation."

I let my head fall back and I breathed out. "A vacation in glamorous Duluth, Minnesota. Sure."

"Who cares about the destination?" Her voice lowered to a rough burr. "We wouldn't leave the hotel room anyway."

If I'd still been sleepy from the early hour, her promise had my body at full attention. "Oh God, that's not fair," I groaned.

Julia batted her dark lashes in faux innocence. "Thank you for the ride, Detective. I'll have to think of some way to repay your kindness."

You could let me marry you.

I forced a grin to my face. Julia's mood had turned playful, and I wasn't about to sour it again with my selfishness.

"I'm sure you'll think of something." I jammed my hands into the pockets of my jacket and started to walk backwards toward her car. "Text me when you land?"

Julia nodded. She looked as though she had more to say, but there was an airport police officer marching in our direction, and I really didn't want to go to jail.

I drove back to Julia's apartment in silence. I didn't turn on the car radio; only the rhythmic sound of the windshield wipers broke the quiet inside the car. It was quiet in the interior of the car, but not inside of my head.

Everything about Julia's demeanor as I'd dropped her off suggested that she was sensitive and sorry for having damaged my feelings. But her leaving was more powerful than any reassuring words or sweet gestures. Selfishly I'd wanted her to cancel her trip altogether to baby my bruised ego. But Julia had been a lawyer long before we'd met. She had a reputation to consider and apparently a mysterious friend to help in Duluth. I wanted to shove down feelings of inadequacy, but in my current position it was hard to feel anything but abandoned.

I came home to an equally quiet apartment. I didn't have to be to the office for a few more hours, so I shed the clothes I'd been wearing and purposefully left them in a sloppy pile on the bedroom floor. I considered calling in sick, but I knew what would have followed—me wallowing in self-pity, drinking too much beer, and ordering takeout. Going to the office would at least distract me during daylight hours. I could self-destruct later.

I rolled over to Julia's side of the bed; her pillow smelled like her. I was probably imagining it, but the sheets were still warm.

CHAPTER NINE

"Hey, Miller. Truth or Dare?"

I stopped typing the weekly report that my immediate supervisor, Captain Forrester, required of me. He didn't physically keep tabs on our goings-ons in Cold Case—he was too busy dusting the taxidermy in his office down the hallway—so the review served as his way of staying in the loop without having to do any actual work.

I shook my head at Sarah, who sat at her computer work space on the other side of the room. "You really have nothing better to do?" I charged.

"I can multitask, can't you?" she seemed to challenge.

The click-clack of high heels against the linoleum basement floor pulled my attention to the open doorway of the Cold Case office. A Pavlovian response kicked in at the distinctive sound. Since I'd just dropped her off at the airport, I didn't really expect it to be Julia, but I also didn't expect to see Celeste Rivers away from her crime unit laboratory.

Her white-blonde hair was down from her usual bun and fell in loose curls against her shoulders. She'd left the white lab coat at work in favor of a white angora sweater that accentuated the soft swell of her breasts underneath. The overhead lighting in the basement tended to be unflattering, but she appeared to be wearing more makeup than before.

She approached my desk and handed me a stack of computer paper.

"What's this?" I asked.

"Kennedy Petersik's cell phone records. I went as far back as two days before her death."

"Wow," I blinked. "You didn't need to bring them all the way down here."

"It's no problem," she dismissed. "I thought you might be in a hurry to see them. Is, uh, is Stanley in?" she asked, suddenly looking unsure of herself and her surroundings.

I scanned over the material on the thick printout. "No, he's babysitting the Freezer today."

"He's what?" she questioned.

"Oh. Sorry," I apologized. "That's insider speak. He's out at the evidence warehouse today."

She made a humming noise. I wanted to ask her more questions about her relationship with my hairy, awkward colleague, but I also didn't want to embarrass her, knowing how likely it was that Sarah would pounce on her discomfort.

"I also tracked down the names associated with each phone number," she remarked.

"Damn. You're thorough," I approved.

"Are you cheating on me, Miller?" Sarah accused from her computer screen.

"Go back to your Minesweeper game, Conrad," I shot back.

I flipped through the stack of paper. My eyes scanned greedily over the list of names and numbers, looking for patterns or familiar names. I paused when I saw an unexpected name on the list of outgoing calls.

"Richard Trask," I read aloud. "Isn't that the State Senator?"

"Yeah, I noticed that as well," Celeste noted. "I wonder what she had to talk to him about."

"She used to date his son," I said absently. "The call was made the day before her body was found. Can we tell where she was when she made these calls?"

Celeste pointed to a column of numbers on the printout. "Each of these represents a different quadrant related to a specific cell tower. I included a map on the last page that identifies which quadrants are associated with different city landmarks as well as her parents' house."

"Hey, Sarah. I'm replacing you with Celeste," I called over to my colleague.

Sarah made a noise and stuck out her tongue.

"Where was Kennedy when she called the Senator's house?" I questioned.

Celeste reclaimed the cell phone printouts and flipped to the map at the back. "The quadrant associated with her parents' house."

I chewed on my lower lip. "You're back from college for fall break. You call up your ex-boyfriend to see if he's back, too?" I thought aloud. "But you don't have his cell because he's your ex, so you call his parents' number?"

"That's one idea," Celeste remarked.

"You have any better ones?" I challenged.

To her credit, Celeste didn't back down. "You're kind of prickly when you're working a case," she shrewdly observed.

"I've been called worse," I deflected. "How long was the phone call?"

The printout rustled again while Celeste consulted the numbers. "Just under four minutes."

"So the ex-boyfriend was at home—unless you chat up your ex's parents for that long?"

"Doubtful," Celeste opined.

"They talk for little bit, and then what—they meet up? When does her quadrant location move?"

Celeste consulted the copy of the cell phone records. "Not long after the phone call ended," she confirmed. "She doesn't ping again for a while though."

"About halfway between the Senator's house and her parents'?" I questioned.

"I don't know; I'd have to look up where he lives."

"Do it. And then can you text me the address? I've got a house call to make. Sarah," I said, bringing my colleague back into the conversation, "have you been able to track down Michael Bloom's family?"

I was hesitant to bring up the topic since Sarah had lashed out at Detective Ryan earlier about it.

My co-worker frowned. "I was able to track down their DMV information. They moved out of state. They're in Arizona now. It looks like they left Minnesota not long after their Michael's death. Both are a little older—retirement age. With Michael gone, maybe they didn't see a reason to stay in the state."

Normally I would have found it suspicious for someone to flee the state so soon after an unsolved murder, but I didn't have children. I couldn't judge how anyone grieved.

"I suppose the weather is better in Arizona," I noted.

"And they wouldn't be constantly reminded of their lost son every time they walked by his bedroom door," Sarah reasoned.

Her sage words reminded me of how much longer Sarah had been doing this job than me.

"Do we call them?" she wondered. "Let them know the case has been re-opened?"

"Right now our focus has been on Kennedy," I said. "I think the likelihood of discovering what happened to her is greater than us being able to re-establish an old case. And hopefully, if we can find out how she died, it will shed some light on how Michael Bloom died. You said it yourself—let's not re-open old wounds unless we have something substantive to tell them."

Sarah nodded. "You're pretty empathetic for a cop, Miller."

I was going to say something about her being pretty smart for a civilian, but knowing how she'd responded to that word before with Detective Ryan, I kept the quip to myself.

"Thanks. I'll take what I can get."

+ + +

I knew I should have alerted Jason Ryan that we'd gotten Kennedy Petersik's phone records and that I was going to question the State Senator—or at least the Senator's son—but I felt like I was racing against the clock. It was another long shot. Chase Trask had been present at Kennedy's memorial service, but he may have already returned to college on the East Coast. The more I delayed, the greater my chances were of missing out on questioning the young man before he left town.

A text from Celeste with the Senator's home address came through by the time I returned to the parking lot and my Crown Vic. She'd also included the name of the Senator's wife—Rhiannon—in case the Senator was at work in the capitol building. Celeste Rivers really was thorough.

After a half hour's drive out to the affluent suburbs, I stood in front of a cookie-cutter McMansion whose address matched the address from Celeste's text. I pressed the doorbell and smoothed back any flyaways that had worked their way free from my bun. I didn't have to wait long before the door opened.

The woman standing on the other side of the doorway was petite. Her short, dark hair was permed tightly against her scalp. Her mouth was pursed and thin, her dark eyes narrowed in question. I spied a pearl necklace above the collar of her cream-colored cable-knit sweater that she'd paired with dark dress pants. She didn't look much older than my own mother.

"Rhiannon Trask?" I guessed.

"Yes, that's me," she confirmed. "I'm sorry. Did you not see the 'No Soliciting' sign?"

"I'm not selling anything, ma'am," I assured her. "I'm Detective Cassidy Miller, Minneapolis Police."

"Oh, how silly of me!" she exclaimed with a laugh. Her hand came off the door handle and rested on her neck to fidget with the iridescent pearls of her necklace. "I'm sorry—the way you're dressed—I thought you were the Mormons again."

I tried to not feel offended. My clothing had always been the least interesting thing about me, and I liked it that way.

"Mrs. Trask, is Chase home?"

The brief mirth disappeared from her features. "Chase?" she echoed. "What is this about?"

"I'm investigating the deaths of Kennedy Petersik along with Michael Bloom," I told her. "I have a few questions for your son."

"Bloom," she breathed. "I haven't heard that name in a while. You think there's some connection between the Bloom boy and Kennedy's death?"

"I can't go into more detail, ma'am," I begged off. "But I'd like to ask Chase some questions about Kennedy, specifically. I know he was at her memorial service, and I'm hoping he's still in town."

Mrs. Trask shook her head. "If you'd like to speak with my son, our family lawyer needs to be present, and he's currently out of the country on vacation, so you as can see, it's just not going to be possible."

"Ma'am, with all due respect, I'm not accusing your son of anything. I only have a few questions for him. In fact," I added, "he might be a big help to this case since he was one of the last people to speak to Kennedy Petersik before her death."

Mrs. Trask visibly flinched. "And how do you know that?"

"Cell phone records, ma'am. Kennedy called your residence the day before her death. Someone at this address spoke to her for about four minutes. I'd like to be able to confirm that that person was your son and find out what he and Kennedy spoke about. It may give us insight into her mindset at the time."

"I'm very sorry, Detective. I wish we could be of more help; Kennedy was a sweet girl. But my son is not available for questioning."

I opened my mouth in continued protest, but I didn't have the opportunity to double down on my request; the front door had already been shut in my face.

+ + +

My police boots squeaked on the linoleum floor of the Fourth Precinct basement as I came to an abrupt stop. Jason Ryan was sitting at my desk. He leaned back in my chair and rested his designer dress shoes on my desktop. I scanned the room for Sarah or Celeste or even Captain Forrester, but Ryan and I were the only ones in the office.

"Did you show up unannounced at the residence of Senator Richard Trask?" Ryan demanded.

I was surprised he'd found out so quickly, but there was no point in denying it. "Yeah," I grunted. "The crime lab retrieved Kennedy Petersik's cell phone records. She called the Senator's house the day before she died."

"Didn't get very far with the Trasks, did ya?" he mused, a smug smile on his idiotic face.

I clenched my jaw. "No."

"Did they teach you that technique in the Marines, Miller? Storm the beaches, guns blazing, at the first whiff of new evidence?"

His question didn't require a response, so I didn't give him one.

"The Senator's office called the Inspector to chew him out," he told me. "Apparently, his wife didn't appreciate being interrogated about our case, even if it came from a goddamn national treasure like yourself."

"I guess I should stick to questioning grieving families at funerals instead," I retorted.

"Whatever," Ryan scoffed. He removed his shoes from my desktop. "Just remember that we're working on this case together. The next time you get new intel, I expect to be included."

"Yeah, sure. You will," I sighed. I didn't have the energy for a fight.

Ryan popped to his feet. "Are you gonna start the paperwork or should I?"

"For what?"

"To assemble a grand jury." Ryan grinned and rubbed his hands together. "If the Senator's son still refuses to cooperate, a judge can hold him in contempt of court. He'll go to jail until he agrees to talk to us."

My eyebrows arched in surprise. "Geez, man. Isn't that a little much? This kid is a minor player; he talked to our victim for four minutes."

"It's textbook overkill," Ryan admitted, "but the Trasks don't have to know that. They'll be down here with their high-priced lawyer before you have time to kiss my ass for being so brilliant."

Another long shot.

"If you say so," I shrugged.

"Stick with me, Miller," he winked. "I know all the tricks of the trade."

+ + +

"How's Duluth?"

"Charming.

"That's Julia-speak for 'primitive,'" I spoke knowingly.

Her laughter filled my ears. She'd only been gone a few hours, but I already missed her. I didn't know how I was going to handle more than a few days of being apart. But her laughter told me we were going to be okay.

I plugged my cell phone into the wall and propped myself up on the decorative pillows on her side of the bed. Work had been mentally exhausting and I had big plans to spend my first night on my own eating pizza and watching zombie films—two things I rarely had the opportunity to do when Julia was home.

"There's only so many hotels to choose from, especially on such short notice, but I'm making do."

"You're not staying with Charlotte?" I hoped I didn't sound as jealous as I felt.

"No. It would be a bit of a tight fit in that apartment between herself, her daughter, and her girlfriend."

"Girlfriend? As in *girlfriend* girlfriend?" I squeaked. "How am I just hearing about this?"

"I didn't know myself," Julia promised. "It's a bit of a new development apparently. But as it turns out, Charlotte's girlfriend is the reason I'm up here."

My jealous outrage paused long enough for me to consider Julia's words. "What do you mean?"

"Charlotte and her ex-boyfriend have been separated for some time," Julia explained. "He had never shown any interest in their daughter's life before, and then suddenly there's a petition to take her away from Charlotte."

I blinked as the words rattled around in my head. "He wants custody of his daughter because Charlotte is dating a woman?"

Julia sighed. "So it would seem."

"And a judge is actually allowing this to happen? They're actually considering her sexuality as grounds to take her daughter away?" My voice pitched higher and my body tensed the more I spoke. I couldn't muster the appropriate rage because the idea was so ludicrous.

"Not if I can stop it," she observed.

I tried to settle back onto the bed despite my irritation. "So what happens next?"

"Out of court negotiations failed, which is why I'm here. I'm going to have to pull an all-nighter tonight to get caught up on the background of the case because tomorrow we're already in court," she said. "Tomorrow will largely be character witnesses and questions about which parent is best suited to serve as the primary caregiver."

"Have you ever tried a child custody case before?"

I knew she'd represented herself when she'd tried to sue for custody of her mother, but this was probably different.

"No," she admitted. "And it's been some time since my family law coursework in law school. I won't be versed in loop holes or know the minute details of random court decisions, but at its core the law is all the same. I'll convince the judge that I'm right and the other side is wrong."

She sounded confident, but I still worried. "Don't let this guy take Charlotte's kid, okay?"

"I'm going to do my very best not to let that happen," she promised.

+ + +

Chase Trask sat on the other side of the interrogation table, sandwiched between his mother and a man who introduced himself as the Trask's personal lawyer. I couldn't imagine having counsel on retainer, but I also wasn't from an ambitious political family. Chase, understandably, appeared far less comfortable in a police interrogation room than when he'd been holding court amongst high school friends in the Petersik's living room. He wore the same blue suit and tie from Kennedy's memorial. The outfit was getting unexpected use on his extended return home.

I was loath to admit it, but Ryan's bluff had worked. As soon as we faxed the beginnings of the grand jury paperwork to the Trask's family lawyer, we'd immediately received a phone call indicating that Chase Trask was willing to answer our questions—in the presence of his mother and their lawyer, who apparently wasn't out of the country, after all.

I pulled out my copy of Kennedy Petersik's cell phone records that Celeste Rivers had procured and set it in the center of the table. The Trask family's home phone number was highlighted in bright yellow in the center of the top page.

"The day before Kennedy died," I began, "someone in your house spoke to her. Was that person you, Chase?"

The boy didn't immediately respond. I noticed how he looked first to his mom. Only when she nodded did he address us.

"We talked, yeah," he finally confirmed. "I was surprised to hear from her. I hadn't heard from her in a while."

"Not since the breakup?" I posed.

He shifted uncomfortably in his chair. "Yeah."

"What did you talk about?" I asked.

"Nothing, really. Smalltalk. How school was going. Our parents. She asked if I would meet up with her."

"But he didn't go," Mrs. Trask spoke up.

I tried to ignore Mrs. Trask's outburst because it was her first, and I hoped, her last. "No?" I questioned.

"We never met up. I agreed on the phone, but I didn't actually go." Chase glanced at the woman sitting beside him. "My, uh, my mom didn't want me to go."

"And look at how right I was," Mrs. Trask defended. "I won't be uncouth and say I told you so, but I told you it was a bad idea to reconnect with Kennedy after all this time."

"You always do what your mom says?" Ryan poked.

It was an obvious jab at Chase Trask's masculinity, but instead of being annoyed by Detective Ryan's unorthodox question, I appreciated it. A rattled witness might inadvertently spill information they'd intended to keep to themselves.

"I didn't go," Chase reiterated, ignoring Ryan's question. "We talked on the phone a little. That's all that happened."

"How did she sound on the phone?" Ryan asked. "Happy? Sad?"

Chase shrugged beneath his suit jacket. "I dunno. Normal, I guess."

I bit back a groan. We were getting nothing from the Trask boy. I started to worry that perhaps this was a serious dead end and that we'd played grand jury chicken with a State Senator's family for no reason.

"You hadn't spoken since the breakup, but did you ever talk about her with anyone else?" I tried. "Did you ask mutual friends how she was doing or what she was up to? Did you check up on her online?"

Chase wiggled a little more. "We were friends online, but we never, like, talked. I'd make a comment on a photo or something, but she never responded."

"She must have been pretty mad that you broke up with her," I innocently remarked.

His eyes suddenly focused on me. The blue orbs had taken on an intensity that hadn't been there before. "I didn't break up with her. She broke up with me."

His admittance didn't match the information I'd received from Kennedy's aunt, but I should have known not to put much stock into the gossip of overly involved extended family.

"Did she say why?" I asked.

"Is all this high school drama really necessary?" Mrs. Trask jumped in.

"Why did Kennedy break up with you, Chase?" I tried again.

"She said it was for the best," Chase told us. "She said we were from different worlds and that it would never work between us."

"Romeo and Juliet over here," Ryan snickered.

Chase struck his palm against the table. He hadn't hit it that hard, but the metallic clang echoed in the bare room. "I loved her!" he shouted. "And I know she loved me back. My parents thought she was a gold-digger and was only dating me because of who my father is, but it wasn't like that. She was special. What we had was special. And then she ended it, with no warning!"

Chase's face had become flushed and his breathing was labored. Ryan and I remained unflinching and unimpressed on the other side of the table. Chase Trask was cracking.

"Why did you stay for the funeral, Chase?" I was curious to know. "Your fall break from college must be over by now."

I thought about Detective Ryan and his intrusive police work at the memorial service. I'd found him to be obtrusive and rude at the time, but he'd been right about one thing: perpetrators often attended the funerals of their victims.

Chase swallowed. He looked again to his mom, but she gave him no cues, verbal or nonverbal, on how to respond. She appeared annoyed that he'd revealed so much to us.

"I think that's enough, Detectives," the Trask family lawyer spoke for the first time since introductions. "The Trasks have been more than cooperative, and I think everyone can agree that Chase had nothing to do with Kennedy Petersik's death. If you have further questions for my client, I advise you to call my office first and not show up at Senator and Mrs. Trask's front door."

He stood up and tossed an embossed business card onto the table like throwing scraps of food to a wild animal.

Ryan and I remained in our seats while Mrs. Trask, Chase, and the lawyer collected their belongings and filed out the door.

"We'll be in touch!" Ryan cheerfully called after the retreating threesome.

No one in the group acknowledged his statement.

Ryan tapped at the top of the metal table like he was playing the drums. "What do you think of the man-child? Jilted ex-boyfriend still sore about a bad breakup?"

I stared at the interrogation room door through which Chase and his entourage had exited. "He didn't pull the trigger," I decided. "But that doesn't mean he's innocent."

CHAPTER TEN

"How are you surviving?" I asked. "Need me to send you a care package?"

"There's an in-room coffee maker," Julia noted wryly. "I think I'll survive."

Julia had now been gone for three days. Three days of coming home to an empty apartment. Three lonely dinners in front of the TV. Three nights of sleeping by myself. Three mornings of waking next to an empty space where my girlfriend should have been.

"How much longer will you be, do you think?" I needed to know.

"Each case is different. But the law guardian seems like a reasonable woman, so hopefully this goes fairly quickly in our favor."

"That would be Charlotte's daughter's lawyer, right?"

I knew a little about custody proceedings from course work at the police academy.

"That's right," Julia confirmed. "It's a random appointment, so we have no control over who will represent the child's interests. She could have been assigned a homophobic twit who believes a child can't possibly be raised by two loving adults, regardless of sexual orientation. It appears we've been lucky in that regard, at least."

"What about the judge? Have you gotten a good read on what they think about the situation?"

"Unfortunately, no," she sighed. "And it's been a point of frustration for me," she admitted. "Normally I'm able to coax *some* kind of emotion from them. But our guy has been stone-faced for the entire proceedings, so it's been a challenge to determine which way he might decide."

A thought popped into my mind. "Does Charlotte know you date women, and that's why she contacted you?"

"No," she stated evenly. "She asked for my services because I'm a good lawyer."

"I'm sorry. I'm like a dog with a bone," I self-chastised.

"Have I ever given you reason to suspect me as unfaithful?" she challenged.

"Only with your cousin."

When Julia and I had first begun our unlabeled arrangement in Embarrass, I'd observed her on the arm of a dark haired, dark eyed, dazzling man. I'd stupidly assumed the worst, when it was only her cousin Reggie. Good genes and all that. Unintentionally, however, it had become a kind of turning point for our relationship.

"Oh, that's right," she mused. "I'd almost forgotten about that."

And let's try to forget this little jealous tantrum, too," I implored.

"You're in luck—I find it endearing rather than without decorum."

One would think that my confidence regarding our relationship would only grow the longer we'd been together, but I was discovering the opposite to be true. If anything, the deeper I fell in love, the more paranoid I became of screwing up and losing her. She had my heart and could do with it what she pleased. We had left the cat-and-mouse games behind in Embarrass and yet my paranoia threatened daily to ruin everything we'd built over the past few months.

"Come home soon, okay?" I sighed into the phone.

"I'm doing my best, darling," she assured me. "But in the meantime, how are you enjoying the bachelorette life?"

"You mean am I having fast food for every meal?" I chuckled.

"I hope you'll have the good sense to get rid of your debauchery before I get home."

"Beer bottles will be recycled, fast food wrappers will be in the dumpster, hookers will be buried in the backyard," I solemnly vowed.

She hummed in amusement, and I felt its vibrations all over.

"What are you wearing?" I needed to know.

"Miss Miller, we are *not* having phone sex."

"I totally didn't mean it like that," I promised. "I just wish I could see you."

The internet in her Duluth hotel room was limited, making video chat unreliable. Julia also hated having her photograph taken, so selfies were out of the question.

"I called you as soon as court recessed for the day, so I'm still in a shirt and skirt."

The admittance that I'd been the first thing on her post-court agenda warmed me more than any explicit language.

"I need more details than that," I implored. "I need more than 'shirt and skirt.'"

"Do you have some clothing fetish I wasn't aware of?" she posed. "*Please?*"

"My shirt—my blouse—is blue."

"What color blue?"

"I don't have a box of crayons at my disposal."

"*Julia*," I whined.

"Fine," she sighed. "It's *dark* blue. Almost black."

"Unbuttoned to the third button?" I guessed.

"Yes?"

"I thought so," I congratulated myself. "What else? Go on."

"The skirt is grey. It's a vintage wool Burberry pencil skirt. High waisted, hits just below the knee. Very court appropriate."

"Nylons?"

"Black. Sheer."

"High heels?"

"They're on the floor now, but yes. Black patent leather. Red bottoms."

A contented sigh escaped my lips. "Red bottoms."

"Are you certain you're going to be okay, dear?" Amusement, not concern, colored her question.

"I just miss you is all," I wasn't too proud to admit.

"Your turn."

"For what?"

"What are *you* wearing, Miss Miller?" Her voice seemed to drop a full octave.

I looked down at the clothes I'd changed into after work. "Uh, a t-shirt and shorts."

She clucked her tongue. "You're going to have to be more specific than that, dear. How else are we going to do this if I can't mentally paint a picture?"

My insides clenched.

"It's a free t-shirt I got for running a 5K on Nicollet Island. It's grey with some neon screen printing on the front."

"And the shorts?" she pressed.

"They're actually boxers. Navy blue with little pizza slices all over."

The stark contrast between our clothing choices had me feeling ridiculous.

"Underwear?"

I coughed a little. "No."

"Bra?" she questioned.

"Nope."

"What would you say if I told you I was unbuttoning my shirt?" she posed. "Down to the fourth button. Down to the fifth button. Until it was completely undone?"

I sat up a little straighter against the headboard. "Yes, please."

"And I suppose the skirt will have to go, too. So it doesn't get unnecessarily wrinkled," she added with mock innocence.

"Right," I husked. "We wouldn't want that to happen."

My tongue felt thick in my mouth.

"Darling?"

"Yes?" I could barely breathe.

"You never asked about my bra or underwear."

"How rude of me." I laid my free hand, the one not clutching a phone, between my thighs, but over my shorts.

"Do you want to know?" she asked.

"Please," came my strangled response.

"Black. Lace. They leave very little to the imagination."

"Oh, I'm imagining alright," I blurted.

Her laughter was musical.

"Will you—." I stopped and cleared my throat. "Will you touch yourself for me?"

"You're going to have to be a little more specific than that, Miss Miller," she purred.

"Skim your fingers across your collarbone."

"Well that's unexpected," she admitted.

"Baby, I'd put BBQ sauce on that thing and gnaw on you," I said in earnest.

Her chuckle was low and throaty.

"Touch a little lower now," I instructed. "Just at the swell of your breast, above the cups of your bra. Feel how warm and soft you are."

I heard a quiet intake of air on her end. "Have you done this before?" There was an edge to her question.

"No," I answered truthfully. "I only know what I'd do to you if I was there."

"What else would you want to do, Miss Miller?" My honesty seemed to satisfy her.

"I'd dip my fingers into the cups of your bra," I said. "I'd pull those cups down so I could see every inch of your tits."

"And what else?" she breathed.

"I'd scratch my fingernails across your nipples and make them hard."

"Already hard."

Fuck. I shut my eyes. "Are you pinching your nipples, baby?"

"Mmhm," she replied. "I wish they were your fingers though. Pinching and pulling, just on the other side of pain."

I bit down on my lower lip. "Is that pretty little pussy feeling neglected?"

"Yes," she hissed.

"You'll have to be quiet. I can't imagine the walls of your hotel are very thick."

I heard her whimper.

"Touch yourself, Julia," I said thickly. "Slide beneath those delicate lacy panties and touch yourself."

Another sigh.

"Are you wet?" I asked, although I already knew the answer. "Rub your clit. I know you want to."

"Cassidy," she breathed.

"How many fingers do you want?" I asked.

"How many do you want to give me?" she returned.

"Jesus," I moaned.

"Are you fucking yourself yet, darling?"

"No," I admitted.

"Are you waiting for my permission?" she mused.

My free hand immediately went into my boxers.

"Fuck yourself, Cassidy," her voice encouraged. "I want you to cum with me."

My fingers slipped through my liquid arousal. I was wet and ready for her. It had been several days of neglect because of my stubborn denial of sex when she'd refused my marriage proposal.

I plunged one finger and then two into my waiting sex. I imagined Julia doing the same. I pictured her on a hotel bed, full breasts hanging over the cups of her bra, black lace underwear down around her knees, her hand between her legs. Her glossy black hair falling in front of her eyes. The thin muscles in her biceps and triceps flexing as she pushed and pulled her fingers in and out of her tightening sex.

"Fuck," I cursed.

"Are you close?" she panted into my ear.

"Uh huh. You?" I gulped in great breaths of air.

"Same."

With only the sound of her voice, she'd awoken the familiar coiling in my abdomen and the tightness in my throat. With anyone else, my eagerness would have embarrassed me. I was too wet, too flushed, too ready. But with Julia, that's how it had always been, and she had never made me feel self-consciousness about it.

This wasn't going to take very long.

"Julia? Still there?"

I worried with the poor cell reception that we might have gotten disconnected.

"Mmhm," came her lazy reply.

"Did you get off without me?" I accused.

"I'm sorry, dear. It just … happened."

"You okay?" I couldn't help but laugh.

"I don't smoke," she breathed, "but I think I need a cigarette."

CHAPTER ELEVEN

I didn't know what to do with myself with Julia gone. It wasn't that we did post-workday activities all the time; I just didn't know how to be single anymore. Even though I'd spent the vast majority of my life on my own, I didn't know how to function without her.

Cooking for one brought me no joy despite getting to eat whatever I wanted. I took hotter and longer showers than usual. Watching television was depressing despite not having to argue with her about how loud the TV was or if we should watch an educational documentary versus the latest superhero film. There was no one to scold me for empty beer cans in the trash instead of the recycling bin, no one to curl her lip at toothpaste residue in the sink or my dirty socks in literally every room.

I had absolute freedom, and I hated every second of it.

I looked forward to evenings when Julia would call me to tell me about her day. We fell into a routine of me updating her on the Petersik case and she relaying what had transpired in the courtroom that day. I wasn't even tempted to bug her for more phone sex knowing the seriousness of her trip.

Well, maybe a little bit.

The worst was the not knowing. There was no real timetable for when she might return even though she assured me that child custody cases had a relatively quick turnaround. I missed her every moment without even the solace of a return date.

When I arrived at work that day, it was a bit of a zoo. People whom I didn't recognize had gathered in our basement office. That kind of activity was more usual upstairs, but not in our office. I shoved down a protective impulse as I observed strangers sorting through our evidence boxes and file folders.

I spotted Stanley at one of the work tables, talking about something with one of the newcomers. He spoke animatedly, motioning with both of his hands. I waved from the doorway until he saw me. He said something to the woman standing beside him and left her to come speak to me.

My Cold Case partner looked pleased, but overwhelmed. "I had to ask for some extra help; we've been fielding phone calls all morning. I didn't even know our phones were actually connected to the wall."

"What's going on?" I asked.

Sarah left her computer and joined our conference by the door. "We found our needle in the haystack."

"You heard back from the National Tracing Center?" I guessed.

"They found who the gun's registered to!" Sarah practically cheered.

I couldn't believe our luck, yet I remained cautious. The handgun might have been originally registered to someone completely unconnected to our two deaths. It could have been transferred without proper paperwork to someone else or even stolen by whomever had pulled the trigger.

"Do we know the name?" I asked.

"Kind of," Stanley confirmed. "It's registered to Steven Tauer."

"Tauer," I echoed. "As in related to Landon Tauer?"

Stanley nodded. "It's his dad."

"Does Jason Ryan know?" I demanded.

Stanley looked down at his shoes, almost guiltily. "I ... well ... yeah."

I quickly ascended the basement steps and strode with purpose to the Homicide division. I entered the open office space just in time to see Detective Ryan standing from his assigned desk and pulling on his suit jacket.

His eyes locked with mine. "Miller. Good. I was just about to call you. Did you hear the news?"

I nodded. "Steven Tauer, eh?"

"I'm going to get the warrant right now if you want to tag along."

"Search warrant?" I questioned.

"Hell, no," Ryan scoffed. "I'm going for the arrest."

"Wait-wait-wait." I held him up. "Stop and think. What reason would Steven Tauer have to kill Kennedy Petersik and the Bloom kid?"

"I don't need motive," he refused. "I've got matching bullets and a gun registration." He looked too eager to get his arrest.

"Are you coming or not?" he pressed.

We took Ryan's car to make the arrest. I was thankful for his silence in the vehicle. I wouldn't have been able to handle his gloating or cockiness. He didn't turn on the siren or lights, but he drove quickly and efficiently to the neighborhood where Kennedy Petersik had grown up.

The car was barely parked before Ryan had removed his seatbelt. His long strides up the driveway to the Tauer residence were evidence of his eagerness to make an arrest. I followed closely, but cautiously, behind.

Ryan opened the screen door and knocked loudly on the inner door. "Police!" he yelled.

I mentally shook myself awake; we were there to arrest a suspected murderer. We weren't there to talk or ask questions. I realized I'd never made an arrest in plainclothes before. I wasn't even wearing my bulletproof vest. I self-consciously unfastened the top clasp of my gun holster.

A tall man who took up much of the doorframe answered the door. His hair was beginning to thin, and his jeans were too big for his meager frame. He wore a faded University of Minnesota sweatshirt and no shoes or socks.

"Steven Tauer?" I asked. I couldn't see much resemblance between the man and his son. This man looked too old, too worn out by life.

"Yes?" he responded.

Ryan flashed his badge, too quickly I thought, before producing the silver handcuffs attached to his hip. "Steven Tauer, you're under arrest for the murder of Kennedy Petersik."

He spun the man around and began to read him his rights. He flicked open the handcuffs with a flip of his wrists. The movement was so fluid, I wondered if he practiced at home in front of a mirror.

Steven Tauer didn't put up a fight.

As the metal handcuffs closed around Steven Tauer's wrists, I felt a similar clenching in my stomach. Arresting someone was supposed to feel good. It was supposed to represent the culmination of rigorous researching and evidence finding and interviewing. This just felt like dumb luck. Nothing had pointed to this man before. He hadn't been on our radar.

A voice called out from inside the house. "Steve? Who is it?"

"The police," he replied. "They think I killed Kennedy."

I was in awe of the clarity and calmness in his voice. His wife, however, didn't react in the same way.

I flinched when I felt the pinch of fingernails digging into my forearm. "What are you doing?" she shrieked in my ear.

"Mrs. Tauer, I need you to step back." I tried to match the same neutral tone of her husband.

If anything, her grip tightened. "This isn't right! We didn't do anything!"

I split my attention between the active arrest and the woman clinging to my arm. "Mrs. Tauer," I spoke more forcefully, "you need to let go."

Only her husband's words seemed to register with her. "Mary, don't get in trouble, too."

Mrs. Tauer immediately dropped my arm. She watched, helpless, as Ryan and I led her husband down the driveway to where the police car was parked. Ryan opened the back door of the squad car and guided a cooperative Steven Tauer into the backseat.

Mrs. Tauer continued to cry in disbelief from the front stoop of her home. Her former words of grief and denial had become incoherent sounds. The noise had brought several curious neighbors out of their homes, including the Petersiks next door.

I felt everyone's eyes on me. I felt the phantom pain of Mrs. Tauer's nails biting my skin. I felt ashamed to be there.

"Everybody back to your homes, please," I barked out.

I scanned the perimeter and watched folks reluctantly walk back to their houses. I knew they wouldn't go far, however; they'd probably only remove themselves to the closest street-facing window or to their police scanner to listen in, like some strange form of voyeurism.

In spite of my words, Mr. and Mrs. Petersik remained on their front porch, their arms wrapped around each other. Their eyes looked hopeful, but afraid. I couldn't bring myself to tell them why we were arresting their neighbor. I didn't know the nature of their relationship. Were they friends? Did they barbeque together on hot summer evenings? Had they babysat each other's children?

I made purposeful eye contact with the couple before climbing into the front passenger seat of the police car. "We'll be in touch," I promised.

+ + +

Newly arrested suspects aren't immediately thrown into a jail cell to await a trial. They first have to be processed by the arresting police department. Personal belongings are confiscated and inventoried. Since I wasn't technically a member of the Homicide team, I waited on the peripheral while Steven Tauer had his mugshot taken and his fingerprints collected, among other procedural requirements.

His arrest didn't sit well with me. It felt far too premature. We should have questioned the man, gotten a search warrant for his home, and then gone from there. But Jason Ryan was like a toddler with a new toy that he couldn't wait to show off.

I stood, chewing on my lips, while Ryan received congratulations from the other Homicide detectives and beat cops; he looked ready to pop the champagne. The giant whiteboard at the center of the room still displayed the number 35, representing Kennedy Petersik's death, however. There was still much to do before that number could be cleared.

"You guys think you might want to slow your roll?" I spoke up. "All we have is a gun registration."

"We've got a helluva lot more than that. The extra print we pulled from the cartridge is a match," Ryan grinned, showing his teeth.

"Yeah, because Steven Tauer put bullets in his gun," I said, stating the obvious. I shook my head. "Nothing puts him in that vehicle though."

"He didn't do it!" a loud, desperate voice proclaimed.

All action and conversation stopped in the Fourth Precinct lobby. I turned and frowned when I realized I knew to whom the voice belonged. Landon Tauer stood on the other side of the intake desk at the police station. He wore a Twins baseball cap and a plain blue t-shirt. He looked as though he might have attempted to hurdle over the reception desk had it been any shorter.

"My mom called me at work," he said. "She told me you arrested my dad."

Ryan took a few swaggered steps toward Landon. He tugged at his belt. "And who are you?"

I realized suddenly that Ryan had never actually met Landon Tauer before. He'd been too busy interviewing family members at Kennedy's funeral to notice the boy. I'd been the one who'd done the leg work to follow up with him despite not being assigned to the case yet.

"This is Landon Tauer," I explained. "Steven Tauer's son. He and Kennedy grew up together."

Landon's desperate eyes fell to me. "Where's my dad?" he demanded.

"Awaiting his court hearing," Ryan said. "Unless you're his lawyer, you'll have to wait until then to see him."

"But my dad doesn't know anything about this!" Landon insisted. "You've got to let him go."

"The gun found in Kennedy Petersik's car belonged to him," Ryan revealed.

"I know," Landon breathed. "I'm the one who gave Kennedy the gun."

"What for?" Ryan demanded.

I jumped in before Landon could supply an answer. "Let's not do this out here, guys. There's gotta be an available interview room somewhere."

I looked warily at the several sets of prying eyes regarding us, uniformed cops and plainclothes detectives. This was not the place for any kind of conversation.

The interrogation room was grey and sterile. A metal table was fused to the ground. On either side of the table were two wooden chairs. A mirror monopolized one of the walls, but it was a façade. No police officers stood on the other side to listen and observe our interview.

"You're gonna release my dad, right?" Landon fidgeted in his chair. The legs of the chair were slightly uneven and he rocked back and forth on the linoleum floor. "Cause his heart's not so good."

"That all depends on what you have to tell us," Ryan said. He pressed the record button on a small video camera that sat atop a tripod.

"Are you sure you don't want a lawyer present?" I interjected.

"Can't afford one," Landon mumbled, dropping his eyes to the table. "Besides, I've got nothing to hide."

I thought about Chase Trask and his overly-protective mom. I thought about the high-priced lawyer in his high-priced suit that people like Landon Tauer would never be able to afford. I wanted to tell him about public defenders, about people like my girlfriend, whose job it was to protect him from incriminating himself in a situation like this, but Jason Ryan was too eager to start the interview.

"Let's try this again," Ryan started. "How did your dad's gun end up in Kennedy Petersik's car?"

"Kennedy called me up when she was in town on her fall break," Landon said. "She asked if she could borrow my dad's gun. She said she needed it for protection."

"A gun. Not pepper spray?" I wondered aloud. It felt like an overreaction unless there was something we were missing, like a stalker situation. I really needed to see her journals.

"She didn't really explain," Landon admitted. "She only said she needed it."

"You know this doesn't look good for you, right?" Ryan noted.

Ryan was trying to intimidate Landon into some kind of confession, but I had more questions. I hadn't been allowed to interview Steven Tauer, but as far as I was concerned, Landon Taurer was my witness.

"How did she know your dad had a gun?" I asked.

Landon's eyes shifted in his skull. "I, uh, I brought it to a party once."

Ryan jumped on the question before I could. He was practically salivating. "As in the graduation party where Michael Bloom was shot and killed?"

"Uhm, yeah," Landon mumbled. "That's the one."

I heard Ryan's excited hiss, but I tried to ignore it. My heart pounded in my head. "Landon—I want you to be very sure and very careful about what you say next," I prefaced. "Are you admitting to shooting Michael Bloom?"

Landon's eyes widened. "Hell, no. I didn't do that! I didn't even know the kid!"

"The bullets retrieved from Kennedy Petersik and Michael Bloom's bodies are a match," Ryan practically gloated. "We know they came from the same firearm. The one registered to your dad."

Landon quietly swore under his breath. He took off his baseball cap and ran both of his hands over his buzzed brown hair.

"I never should have brought that gun," he muttered with regret.

"Why *did* you bring a gun to a party?" I questioned.

It wasn't as though the Twin Cities suburbs were dangerous. And a bullet from a handgun like the one found in Kennedy Petersik's car would have felt like a bee-sting to a 500 lb. bear.

"I was a dumb kid," he said. "I didn't know how to impress girls."

Ryan scoffed. "And you thought bringing a gun to a party would do the job?"

It was clear he didn't believe Landon's explanation. I wondered what else he might not believe.

"Like I said," Landon shrugged. "I was dumb."

We were tip-toeing around the important details—namely who had killed Michael Bloom. "What happened that night at the party, Landon?"

He stared at the grey metal table, chewing on his lower lip. I could only imagine how his heart and his thoughts must have been racing. Finally, he looked up and spoke:

"I decided to crash Pius's graduation party. Everybody knows they have a rager at the end of the school year, but it's by invite only. I'd just signed my contract with Junior-A hockey, and I was feeling pretty cocky. I never made it inside the house though because I saw Kennedy sitting outside by herself."

As he recounted his memories from that night, he picked at an aggravated cuticle on one of his fingers.

"I could tell she was depressed, upset about something, and I wanted to cheer her up. I mentioned I had the gun and offered to let her shoot it at some beer cans." His gaze dropped to his hands and his voice came out like a rough whisper. "I thought we were alone. I don't know what that kid was doing in that field. Taking a piss maybe because the bathroom lines were too long."

I swallowed hard. "So Kennedy shot Michael Bloom?"

Landon lifted his head. His eyes seemed wobbly and unsteady. "It was an accident. We were just messing around. The last thing either of us wanted was for someone to get hurt, let alone die."

"I've looked over witness depositions from that night." Ryan leaned forward in his chair. "No one at the party reported hearing gunshots. How do you account for that if you two were popping off rounds at beer cans like you say?"

"It was a party. The music was loud," Landon shrugged. "You couldn't hear yourself think inside. That's part of the reason Kennedy came outside in the first place."

"And the other part?" I asked.

"She and Chase were fighting," Landon said.

I shared a quick look with Detective Ryan. Maybe we had another reason to drag the Trask boy and his mother back to the police station.

"What did they fight about?" Ryan asked.

"I don't know. She wouldn't say." Landon shook his head. "I wasn't trying to find out; I just wanted to cheer her up."

I exhaled, trying to process all of this new information. "If it was an accident, why not tell the police what had happened?"

Landon's features grew sharp. "Oh yeah—tell the police and ruin my life? Ruin my parents' lives, too. R-ruin K-Kennedy's life," he stuttered. "I was getting out of this town and so was she. I couldn't mess that up for us."

"So you ran away," Ryan accused.

"I was protecting Kennedy." Landon's temper continued to flare. "And yeah, I was saving my own ass, too. I took the gun with me, and told Kennedy to call 911 from a landline inside the house."

"So it couldn't be traced back to her phone," I observed. "Pretty smart thinking for something that happened so fast."

Landon flashed me a wild look. "We didn't leave him there to die. We got help, but we didn't want to get in trouble, too."

"What did you do with the gun afterwards?" Ryan asked.

"I put it back in the lockbox by my dad's bedside table. No one knew I'd been at the party—I wasn't supposed to be there. The gun was better hidden in my dad's bedside table than me tossing it into a lake."

I had another question that I didn't want to ask, but my job required it of me: "Landon, where were you the day Kennedy died?"

"At the hockey rink."

"Can anyone vouch for that?" Ryan questioned.

"I'm there every Tuesday."

"But did anyone *see* you on that specific Tuesday?" Ryan emphasized.

"Oh. Uh, n-no, I don't think so," he verbally stumbled. "I'm usually the only one there during the day."

"Do you have to sign in and out at the high school office?" I probed.

Landon shook his head. "No. Since they know me, they let me come and go as I please." He blinked a few times. "Shit. Does this mean I don't have an alibi?"

I shut the soundproof door to the interrogation room with Landon Tauer still inside. Detective Ryan and I conferenced in the hallway just outside.

I leaned against a wall and crossed my arms. "We've got to release Steven Tauer." I kept my voice low to make sure none of the swarming cops overheard us. "There's no reason to keep holding him."

Ryan nodded in agreement. I knew how much he wanted to erase that number 35 from the board, but I was glad he wasn't so fanatical about it as to charge an innocent man.

"Kennedy Petersik killed Michael Bloom," he said wistfully. "Do you buy it?"

"I don't know yet," I admitted. "We'll need to go over the Cold Case files again with this new information. Look for extra bullet casings collected from the scene. Beer cans with bullet holes, maybe. Something to corroborate Landon's story."

"What do we do with him?" Ryan tugged his thumb in the direction of the interrogation room.

"Is it a crime to be a dumb, love-struck kid?" I posed.

Ryan arched an eyebrow. "You think he was in love with her?"

I shrugged. It wasn't my job to head-shrink the kid, but it seemed like he'd gone through a lot to protect a girl he didn't at least care for.

"We've got him for tampering with evidence, at least," Ryan noted.

I pursed my lips in thought. "That's peanuts. The D.A.'s office is going to want something bigger. I say let him walk for now. Tell him to stay close—not to leave the area. Maybe the Inspector will give us a badge to tail him. I want to know what he does once he leaves this place."

Ryan's mouth curved in a peculiar way. He didn't say anything about my idea, but he stood with an idiotic grin on his idiotic face.

"What?" I demanded.

"I never thought I'd say this, Miller, but I think you might actually be a cop."

CHAPTER TWELVE

My heavy leather boots crunched through dead flowers and overgrown grass. The wind swirled around me, kicking up loose, fallen leaves like a miniature tornado. I popped the collar of my leather jacket to shield myself from the worst of it. Detective Ryan, Stanley, and I had taken an impromptu field trip out to the property where the Pius High School graduation party had occurred. The house had been removed as a rental property following Michael Bloom's death. Inappropriate as it was, I wondered what kind of zero-star reviews the property owners had received in the aftermath.

I kicked at the damp ground, not really sure what we might find, three years later, that the original police investigation had overlooked. Ryan had rented a metal detector and busied himself at the edge of the property to search for brass bullet casings. An abundance of them in a central position might suggest that Landon had been telling us the truth—that Michael Bloom's death had been an accident, the victim of a stray shooting range bullet.

The physical evidence related to Michael Bloom's death was scant. With so many reluctant witnesses, police at the time hadn't known what objects to collect from the scene. There were no shell casings to suggest an impromptu target practice and no beer cans with bullet holes. Michael Bloom's clothing had been separated into several evidence bags. The original DNA testing hadn't produced any interesting results, but that could have been predicted since forensics had already determined that Bloom had been shot at a distance.

I thought it was notable that Landon had known that detail. It was unlikely that news coverage of the death had been specific about the kind of gunshot wound the boy had suffered. Ryan ordered a second round of DNA tests on Michael Bloom's clothing now that we had both Landon and Kennedy's profiles to compare against, but I didn't believe the crime lab would find anything.

A number of other details from that night that only the persons involved would have known about were starting to pile up. The biggest detail was that the 911 call had come from the landline connected to the rental property. Every single high schooler at that graduation party would have had a cell phone on them. Why, then, had the call been made from a landline? And how else would Landon have known that detail if he hadn't been the one to instruct Kennedy to make the emergency call?

Stanley held up one of the oversized photographs that the original forensics team had taken of the crime scene. He spun on his heels, trying to decipher where on the property Michael Bloom had been shot. The task was made more difficult because the Bloom boy hadn't died on the property. He'd still been alive when the first responders had arrived, and he'd died overnight at the hospital.

"What do you think?" he asked me. "Does that tree look like it's three years older than the one in the picture?"

I took a cursory look, but shook my head after a moment. "I have no idea."

The property surrounding the home was largely flat and monolithic, with no distinguishing features beyond the floating pier and docked pontoon on the lake.

Stanley continued to trod through the tall grass, periodically comparing a new photograph to his surroundings. The landscape hadn't completely changed in three years, but the lawn had become overgrown and unkempt.

"Hey!" I waved down Ryan, who continued to scan the perimeter of the property with the rented metal detector. "Find anything?"

"Not yet!" he called back.

Beside me, Stanley pulled a large ball of yarn from the pocket of his trench coat with some difficulty.

"What are you doing, Stanley?" I wondered what else he kept in those jacket pockets.

"If we can figure out the epicenter—the place where Michael was standing when he got shot—we can use this yarn to draw a radius around the center to figure out the likelihood that he was killed by a stray bullet."

I hadn't known how Stanley might react to Landon Tauer's claim that Kennedy Petersik had killed Michael Bloom, even if it had been an accident. I knew he felt a responsibility to the girl as her former mentor at Pius High School, but first and foremost his duty was to the Cold Case division. In his position, I might not have been so gung-ho about proving Landon's story to be true.

Another brisk wind rustled through the long grass. Tiny ripples skated across the surface of the nearby lake. A thick cloud cover had hidden the sun for the majority of the day, making our task even more difficult. I wished I'd worn a thick sweater or had thought to bring a hat and gloves. Julia would have made sure I'd been properly bundled up. I was so lost without her.

I didn't have a specific assigned job, so I rambled along the property and stared at the ground, looking for anything that seemed out of place. Every other step had me sinking into the soft turf. The level of the lake must have been on the rise because the land was uneven and soggy.

"I think I've got something!" Ryan's voice carried from across the yard. "Disregard," he said almost immediately. "It's just a coffee can!"

I stopped my fruitless search by a dilapidated fence. Doubt about our errand began to creep into my bones the longer we worked without discovery. I kicked at the fence posts to dislodge some of the mud that had collected on the bottom of my work boots. The wood creaked in response, but I heard another sound: something metal and crinkling.

I bent down and wedged my fingers into an empty fence hole where one of the posts had fallen off or had rotted away. My fingers closed around a cylinder-shaped object. I thought it might be another coffee can—an impromptu ash can or bait bucket—until the soft metal bent in under the pressure of my grip.

The ground made a sucking sound as I wrenched the object out of the mud. I wiped away at the wet dirt that coated the half of the canister that had been partially submerged. The grey clouds seemed to part at that moment. The sun was warm against my back. I twisted the dirty beer can in my hand. Sunshine pierced through a bullet-sized hole.

+ + +

I hold my hand up like a visor and squint into the sun. I hear a motor, an engine of some kind, but I can't be sure if it's friend or foe, real or imagined. A commercial airplane, too high to ever see us, streaks through the periwinkle blue sky, leaving a white, puffy trail behind it.

"Chemtrails," Pensacola grits out. Speaking in full sentences has become increasingly difficult for him. "My mama always told me that's what those were."

"You mean the water condensation?" I question.

I've heard all about this conspiracy theory before, but I egg on my friend, hoping that talking will distract him from the severity of his injuries.

He uses his arms—the only part of him that escaped the dirty bomb—to prop himself up. I reach to help, but he waves me off. My back in on fire though, so I don't know how much help I'd actually be.

"Government's trying to kill us: EPA, NOAA, FAA," he lists off. "They're trying to control our minds." He taps a dusty finger against his blood-caked temple. The dried blood crumbles off his dark skin.

"What'd she say when you told her you were going to be a Marine?" I ask.

His cracked lips purse. "Said I was gonna die." An even drier tongue tries to wet his lips, but it's useless. There is no water. There hasn't been for some time. "Guess she was right about something."

I want to tell him we're going to be alright. I want to say we're going to survive—that help is on the way. But I can't force the lies to my lips. I need to conserve my energy to prove Pensacola's mom wrong.

I flinch and duck down a little lower when I hear the bombs. I can tell from the sound that the explosions are far away, but that doesn't make them less alarming. Sometimes I'm thankful for the noise, however. It's the only reminder that Pense and I aren't the only ones left in the world.

The bombs and the chemtrails.

I jerked awake at the sound of the next explosion. This one was closer. I shot up in bed; my breath came in short bursts and my heart felt like it might explode inside my chest. The bedroom filled with light, followed by a loud crack and a rumbling. Thunder. Lightning. It was storming outside.

I looked with bleary eyes to Julia's bedside table. The alarm clock read the time in large, neon green numbers: 3:12 a.m.

I flopped back onto the pillows and exhaled. Without Julia taking up her side of the bed, I'd started to sleep in the middle. It made me feel like the bed wasn't so empty, and I wasn't so alone.

I let the furniture of Julia's St. Paul, Minnesota apartment flood back in and replace the sand, blood, and crumbling structure of the safe house in Afghanistan. I liked to sleep with the windows open, but I jumped out of bed and hastily shut the glass when I realized that a hard rain had started to penetrate the window screen.

Another flash of lightning. Another rumble of thunder that seemed to shake the entire apartment complex. I'd written in my dream journal before bed, but apparently it hadn't been enough to stave off the nightmares. It had been some time since I'd had one of those dreams—memories of my time in a different world, another life. Of the struggle not to die and to bring back Terrance Pensacola alive.

I looked around the darkened room for something that might help me—something that might ground me. Julia had been my anchor, but I would have to weather this literal storm without her. I grabbed one of her unlaundered t-shirts from the clothes hamper and pressed the cotton material to my nose. Fabric softener tried to mask the spicy scent of her skin. I inhaled, like a lunatic, like an asthmatic dependent on their inhaler. I threw the oversized t-shirt over the clothes I already wore and crawled back into bed. I grabbed one of the pillows from Julia's side of the bed and hugged it against my chest. I shut my eyes tight and hoped for dreamless sleep.

I didn't wake up again until I heard the buzz of my cell phone as it bounced across the bedside table. Julia's alarm clock sat sentinel and silent. 9:27 a.m. *Shit.* I'd overslept. Knowing me, I'd probably set the alarm for PM, and not AM. Julia was typically in charge of setting the morning alarm since she was more responsible than me.

I grabbed my phone and answered the call without looking at the caller's number. "Hello?" I grunted.

"You planning on coming in today, National Treasure?" Jason Ryan sounded pissed off.

I was exhausted from uneven sleep, but I still managed a saucy retort: "Miss me that much?"

"Meet me at the Petersik residence," Ryan snapped. "Mrs. Petersik's been calling all morning demanding to know why we let Steven and Landon Tauer walk. The Inspector has politely requested that we see them in person."

"He chewed your ass out, huh?" I couldn't help my private grin. "Not teacher's pet anymore?"

"Just hurry up and get here, Miller," he growled.

+ + +

Detective Ryan and I sat around the kitchen table with Mr. and Mrs. Petersik. I had not been offered coffee or tea upon our arrival this time. Mrs. Petersik was livid.

"How could you just let them walk out of there?" she demanded.

Ryan spoke for the both of us. "We didn't have a reason to hold either Steven or Landon, Mrs. Petersik."

"And now they're both gallivanting over there like nothing ever happened." She gestured wildly in the direction of her neighbors' house. "And I can't even bury my baby because you still refuse to release her body. How am I supposed to get any sleep knowing my Kennedy is in some storage locker? How is a mother supposed to survive?"

"Mrs. Petersik, as soon as we leave here I'm going to speak with my supervisor," Ryan gently tried. "You're right—we've inconvenienced your family for long enough. There's no reason for us to continue to hold onto Kennedy. You should be able to grieve and get closure, not continue for this to drag out."

I was mildly impressed with how tender Ryan was being with Kennedy's parents. It was probably all for show, but he exuded genuine care. In any case, it seemed to have calmed down Mrs. Petersik momentarily.

"Landon said that Kennedy killed that boy? The one at the graduation party?" Mr. Petersik slowly shook his head, like the words he was saying were in a foreign language.

"Kennedy would never hurt a fly," Mrs. Petersik insisted. "This is all Landon. Kennedy was probably going to tell on him about the

Bloom boy, so he killed her with the same gun that he killed Michael Bloom with."

I exhaled deeply through my nose. "There's no evidence to suggest that, Mrs. Petersik."

"Landon told us that Kennedy asked him for a gun—for protection, she said," Ryan noted. "Do you know anything about that? Did Kennedy mention anything to you about being scared or threatened by someone? Someone in a class with her? Someone she might have dated, maybe?"

"No. She was having such a great time at college," her dad said. "That's all we ever heard—how great St. Olaf was."

"But she wasn't having *too* much fun, if you know what I mean," Kennedy's mom interjected. "She was on academic scholarship, so she was very serious about her studies. As long as she kept a B average, all of her schooling was being taken care of."

"That's very impressive," Ryan allowed.

A watery smile appeared on Mrs. Petersik's face. It was obvious how proud she had been of her daughter.

"Did she mention anything about the graduation party in her journals?" I tried.

I hadn't forgotten that Mrs. Petersik had denied me access to Kennedy's diaries. At the time, the case hadn't been mine to press for a search warrant, but now our reasons to not investigate every page of those journals had run out.

The smile fell from her face, and Mrs. Petersik threw me a steely look. "No. There's nothing there. This is the first time I've heard about it."

"Someone died at a party she was at and she didn't think to write about it?" I had major doubts.

"I'm sure she had her reasons," Mrs. Petersik said stiffly. "It was so traumatizing for those kids. Why write about it?"

"Mrs. Petersik, I know you're concerned about your daughter's privacy, but a second set of eyes couldn't hurt," I tried gently. "Maybe we would notice something that you overlooked."

"We're her parents," Mrs. Petersik huffed. "She didn't keep anything from us."

I had an ace up my sleeve that I'd been sitting on. It was a sensitive topic, and I hadn't been sure when or if to ever show my hand, but this seemed to be the moment. "Were either of you aware that Kennedy was into cutting?"

"Cutting?" Mr. Petersik frowned. "What's that?"

"Self-harm," I cautiously explained. "It's a coping strategy for some people who suffer from depression. They cut themselves, usually very small and unnoticeable. The physical pain can serve as a distraction from other kinds of mental trauma. It's not necessarily a suicide attempt, but sometimes the razor blade goes too deep."

"H-how would you ever know that?" Mrs. Petersik stuttered.

I chose my next words with deliberate care. "Because I inspected Kennedy's body at the morgue, ma'am. The insides of her arms were covered with old scars."

"That's ridiculous. This is some kind of trick," Mrs. Petersik claimed. "I never saw any marks on Kennedy. You're not reading my little girl's diary, Detective," she snapped. "So forget they even exist."

CHAPTER THIRTEEN

Mrs. Petersik had been vehement about not letting us see her daughter's private journals, but she hadn't said anything about us not checking out Kennedy's former campus home. Between Kennedy's death, interviews with police, and arranging the details of the memorial service, the Petersiks hadn't had the opportunity to pick up Kennedy's belongings from her college.

Detective Ryan and I planned to make the hour trip down I-35 to Northfield, Minnesota, home of St. Olaf College, and Kennedy Petersik's home away from home for the past three years. It was a long shot among long shots, but maybe she'd kept a journal in her dorm room that would give us more insight into her mindset in the months and weeks leading up to her death. Or maybe someone she knew on campus would know more about why Kennedy believed she needed a gun for protection.

I stopped off at a coffee shop to procure caffeine and snacks to fuel our road trip. I had just set the piping hot coffee containers into the cup holders of my squad car when my cell phone began to ring. A rare photograph of Julia flashed onto my cell screen. It had been sunny the day of the photograph, and sunshine reflected off her glossy, raven hair. Her broad smile made her high cheekbones more elevated than usual. For someone as beautiful as she, Julia really hated having her picture taken.

"Hey, pretty mama," I answered the call with a smile. "What's going on?"

"We won."

Julia's tone was so nonchalant and cool that it took me a moment to figure out to what she was referring.

"You won? The custody trial? Charlotte gets to keep her little girl?"

"Mmhm," she confirmed. "The judge made his ruling this morning, so it was only a short day in court today."

I thought she sounded unnaturally distracted for having such good news.

"Have you booked your return flight yet? When do I pick you up from the airport?" A greedy, eager emotion rushed over me. I wondered if she'd be able to get a flight later that day and be home in time for dinner.

"I'm on my way to Embarrass," she said.

It took a moment longer for my brain to make sense of her announcement. "You're what?"

"I rented a car, and I'm driving to visit my parents. It was totally an impromptu decision," she explained. "I'm this far north already; I might as well drive the extra hour and a half to see them."

My mouth went dry. "Oh."

"That's it? That's all you have to say?"

"Seatbelt on, headlights on?" I said, unsure.

I didn't want to tell her about the dream I'd had in her absence. I didn't want her to feel guilty or like she'd abandoned me. I also didn't want to admit that my sleep and sanity had become so dependent on her.

"You're not upset that I'm going to Embarrass without telling you?" she questioned.

"You're telling me now." I hated how my stomach churned with uncomfortable knots.

"Ask me your question, Cassidy."

"I don't have a question," I denied.

Julia was silent on the other end of the phone call, satisfied to wait for my eventual honesty.

"Fine," I sighed. "Are you *sure* you're not avoiding me?"

My brain flashed back to my stupid, premature marriage proposal. The thought had felt so right, so natural at the time; now my eagerness brought only embarrassment.

"I'm not avoiding you," she promised. "I've been avoiding my father, and I'm going to remedy that."

"When do you think you'll be back?" I asked.

"I'm not sure. A couple of days, at most. I'd like to spend some time with my mother. And I should probably drop in on my grandparents' house to make sure it's still intact."

"Your mansion?"

I could hear her chuckle. "If that's what you want to call it, sure."

I couldn't help my long, loud sigh. I'd been elated to hear that she'd won her case, but I'd also equated that with her coming home, not her staying away longer.

"I won't be long, darling," she promised. "I miss you terribly."

My throat constricted from emotion. "I miss you, too."

+++

St. Olaf College probably received a lot of attention from fans of *The Golden Girls*, it being the fictional hometown of Betty White's character. But in reality, it was a small, private liberal arts college located an hour south of Minneapolis.

I always had a strange feeling when I walked on college campuses. I'd gone directly from high school into the Marines. It was easy to slip into thoughts of What Ifs when I observed seemingly carefree co-eds lounging on blankets on the campus quad, studying from thick textbooks under the canopy of mature maple trees. Maybe I would have still ended up in law enforcement if I'd gone to college, but it was pretty unlikely.

A posted campus map led us to the dormitory where Kennedy Petersik had last resided. St. Olaf was a residential campus, so every student lived in the dorms. Bulletin boards in the front lobby provided a schedule of campus activities and short biographical profiles of the building's resident assistants. With most students in late morning classes, the residence hall was eerily quiet.

I spied an older, balding man in a dark work shirt and Carhartt pants mopping the linoleum floor. Careful to stay on the narrow carpet runner so as to not ruin his work, Detective Ryan and I approached the man.

"Excuse me, sir?" I called to him.

The man looked up from his work and peered at us from behind thick lensed glasses.

I touched the badge that hung at my hip. "Cassidy Miller, Minneapolis Police," I introduced myself. "This is Detective Ryan. We're investigating the death of a St. Olaf student."

"You mean Kennedy."

The man's response surprised me.

"St. Olaf is a small campus," he explained. "Pretty much everyone knows each other."

"We're hoping to see her room. Her parents said they haven't been by to pick things up yet?"

The man nodded thoughtfully. "I've got the keys, but not the authority. You'll have to talk to the Hall Director. I'm just the janitor."

"And where might we find this person?" Ryan asked.

The man pointed down a narrow hallway that dead-ended with a solid door. "Her apartment is right there."

"Thank you." I hesitated before leaving. "Did you know Kennedy?" I wondered aloud.

We had made the trip to inspect Kennedy Petersik's room, but I thought it would also be helpful to interview the people who knew her best on campus. I'd gotten statements from her parents and from Landon Tauer about what Kennedy had been like, but I was living proof that young people tended to be different away from the place and people where they'd grown up.

The man shook his head. "Not really, no. I'm part of the scenery. Like a chair or a trash can. Most of the kids here barely acknowledge me. Kennedy, though, I remember she always made eye contact and smiled when she'd see me. She never spoke to me, but it was a whole lot more recognition than I typically get."

His admission brought a sad smile to the corner of my mouth.

"Thank you for your candor, sir." I made sure to make purposeful eye contact.

The Hall Director—Faith Newman—had her name posted on the outside of her apartment door. Ryan took lead and knocked on the solid wooden door. "Police," he barked.

"Really?" I slowly drawled. "We're not here to arrest anyone."

Ryan dropped his hands to his sides. "Sorry," he clipped, having the decency to at least look a little embarrassed. "Habit."

He didn't knock again, but we didn't have to wait long before the door opened.

Faith Newman's hair was a surprising shock of pink that she wore cropped close to her scalp. Tattoos were visible where her wrists peeked out from beneath a cable-knit sweater. She wore skinny jeans and Converse sneakers. The look was very punk rock meets J-Crew.

She welcomed us into her apartment after Ryan and I introduced ourselves and our purpose for being there. I scanned my eyes around the room we stepped into. The apartment was one large room that served as living room, dining space, and kitchen. I noticed a single hallway in the back that presumable led to a bathroom, bedroom, or both.

"What exactly is a Hall Director?" I didn't know much about college campus residence life, so she explained for me.

"It's pretty much what it sounds like," she said. "I supervise the students who live in the building."

"Are you a student, too?" I asked.

Her laugh was more like a squeak. "Not anymore, thank God. I graduated two years ago. I'm taking some time off before I go to graduate school. Doing this until my mental batteries get recharged."

Ryan pulled a small notebook from the inner pocket of his suit jacket. He flipped it open to a blank page and clicked a ballpoint pen awake. I wrinkled my nose at his robotic and stereotypical mannerisms, but I knew we needed to get back to business.

"Ms. Newman, what can you tell us about Kennedy Petersik?" he asked.

Faith sighed. "Not much, unfortunately. She kept to herself. Didn't have a roommate. Didn't participate in hall activities. I've got just over 100 residents, so if you're not active in the community or you're not high-maintenance, sometimes you slip through the cracks."

"Do you know if she had many friends on campus? People she was close to?" I probed.

Faith slowly shook her head. "Sorry. Like I said, she kept to herself."

Ryan clicked the top of his pen again and returned his notepad to his pocket. "Do you mind showing us her room?"

"Of course," Faith agreed. "I only wish I could be more help."

Ryan and I followed Faith Newman up three flights of stairs. The stairwell smelled like burnt popcorn and body odor. At the top of the stairs was a long hallway. Each door we passed was decorated with posters and little construction paper nameplates.

Faith came to a stop in front of one of the doors. A construction paper caterpillar was taped to the door. The name 'Kennedy' was scrawled across its segmented body in careful, feminine handwriting.

Ryan touched the decoration. "Cute."

It was only then I noticed the makeshift altar on the ground in front of the door. Vases of drooping flowers, deflated helium balloons, and unlit candles cluttered the doorway.

Faith sighed. "I don't know what to do with this or how long to keep it here. We don't even allow candles on campus. But I don't want to seem heartless by throwing all this stuff away. And it doesn't seem worth it to send to her parents. Are they really going to want dead flowers and shriveled up balloons?"

I didn't have an answer for her, so we stepped over the tribute to Kennedy and entered the dorm room. I took a deep breath. Similar to her childhood room, the space looked ready for her return, as if she might walk into the room at any moment.

I looked around the small room, at the family photographs on the walls and the bookshelves of books I'd never read. The single twin bed was unmade. A wooden desk of cheap construction, probably provided by the university, was covered with textbooks and spiral notebooks. My throat constricted when I saw the notebooks, but I didn't immediately grab for them. I didn't want to appear too eager in front of the Hall Director.

Ryan picked up a well-loved teddy bear from the bed. "What do you think—bag it all up or just take pictures?"

"It's not a crime scene," I noted. "Let's take a lot of photos, and if there's something of interest we can bag it up."

Ryan nodded his agreement and removed his digital camera from its carrying case. He started to take photos, starting first with the desk.

"You don't have to stick around," I told Faith Newman. I'd nearly forgotten she was hanging out in the hallway. "We'll probably be a while, processing the room, and I don't want to take up anymore of your valuable time."

Faith looked unsure, a mix of not wanting to leave a resident's room unsupervised with strangers, but also wanting to be more helpful.

"We'll stop by your apartment when we've finished up in here," I promised.

Her anxiety was fleeting and she nodded, relieved, before disappearing down the hallway.

As soon as Faith Newman was out of sight, I stormed over to the dorm room desk. I thought I'd struck the mother lode when I saw the tall stack of spiral bound notebooks. I grabbed the top notebook from the tidy stack. I flipped it open, but frowned at the contents. Lecture notes on the reasons behind the American Revolution. A second notebook was filled with math problems. The third included environmental science lectures.

I hadn't realized I'd made a noise in my frustration.

"What's up?" Ryan asked. "Find anything interesting?"

I shook my head and returned the notebooks to their original location. "Nope. Just school stuff. You?"

Ryan was bent over in Kennedy's closet. I couldn't see his face. "How many shoes do you girls really need? I'm like knee-deep in boots."

"You're asking the wrong girl," I remarked. "I own exactly three pairs of shoes. Black, brown, and running."

The desk drawers were of no interest. Old magazines, books, and school supplies. I scratched my head as I scanned the room. Kennedy Petersik's childhood room had been cluttered with journals. Why couldn't I find a single one in her college dorm?

"Am I allowed to go in her underwear drawer?" Ryan posed.

"I don't know. Are you gonna be creepy about it?" I returned.

Ryan gingerly pulled open the top drawer of Kennedy's dresser. He looked as though he expected something to jump out at him. The tension on his face lifted when the drawer was completely open. "Laptop. Jackpot."

He pulled the thin silver device out of the top drawer and set it on top of the bureau. Ryan opened the laptop's lid, but nothing happened. The matte screen remained dark. He pressed the power button, but the computer remained off.

"The battery must be dead," he observed. "Do you see a charger anywhere?"

A few minutes of searching through unexplored drawers produced nothing, so I packed the laptop into a plastic evidence bag. I was confident that Celeste Rivers would be able to power it up.

Ryan sat down on the twin sized bed. He picked up the well-loved teddy bear again. "If Kennedy Petersik planned on killing herself over fall break, why did she leave all of her stuff here?"

"We don't know that," I contested. "We don't have an inventory; she might have brought the important things home."

"Don't you think her laptop's important?" Ryan posed.

"Then maybe it wasn't premeditated," I reasoned. "Maybe something happened at home to upset her. Chase Trask stood her up."

He rubbed at his chin. "Yeah, but being jilted by an ex isn't worth dying over."

"What about this story about needing protection?" I posed. "I think that's worth following up on."

"Or Landon Tauer made up that story to distract us."

"Do you really think he killed her?" I asked.

"It's not my job to think," Ryan deflected. "I follow leads; I interview witnesses."

I shook my head. "You don't have a gut feeling on suicide or murder?"

"Guts don't put criminals in prison. Clues and confessions do."

"Landon hasn't confessed to anything," I reminded him. "Except for being a dumb kid in high school."

"It's early. Give him some more time to sit with his guilt, and he may start to think about his circumstances differently."

We finished up with the photography and evidence collection, but really had only a dead laptop to show for our efforts. It felt like a wasted trip, but I was hopeful the laptop would contain something useful. We stopped back at Faith Newman's apartment to let her know we'd completed our work.

"I took the liberty of printing up Kennedy's course schedule from this semester," she said. She handed me a piece of computer paper. "Technically I'm not supposed to give out student information, but I figured this was a special circumstance. Maybe some of her professors or classmates can give you more information."

"Thank you, Ms. Newman. This is very helpful."

It was clear the woman felt badly about not being able to answer our questions about one of her residents.

I took a cursory look at the classes listed: U.S. History, Applied Statistics, Environmental Science, Creative Nonfiction.

It seemed quite the range. The creative nonfiction course caught my eye. Maybe her English professor had kept some of her assignments.

"Do you know what her major was?" I asked.

"It should be listed at the top of that page," Faith notes.

"Undeclared?" I read aloud.

"That means she didn't have a major yet," Faith said. "It's not too unusual. When students are just starting out we encourage them to try a variety of things to see what they like best. They only have to declare at the end of their sophomore year."

"But wasn't Kennedy a junior?" I asked.

Faith Newman's eyebrows punched together. "No. My building is only freshmen and sophomores."

She eased the piece of paper with Kennedy's class schedule out of my hands. "Yep. Sophomore," she confirmed. She tapped at the top of the page where her GPA and graduation year was recorded.

The discrepancy had me confused, but I kept those questions to myself.

Detective Ryan and I thanked Faith Newman once again for her help before heading back to his patrol car. It had started to lightly rain since we'd arrived on campus. Grey clouds blotted out the sun.

I had Kennedy's laptop in a duffle bag and her class schedule in my front pants pocket. "How was Kennedy only a sophomore?" I wondered aloud. "She graduated from high school three years ago."

"Maybe she took a gap year," Ryan proposed. His car keys jingled in his hand. "Isn't that all the rage these days? Kids taking a year off before going to college?"

"Yeah, but only if you're wealthy and can afford to not work."

"Maybe she took a year off to work and save up money," he suggested.

"Maybe," I concurred. "But didn't her parents say she was on academic scholarship? What was the money for?"

"Pizza and beer? Hey, I don't know," Ryan shrugged. "I just work here."

CHAPTER FOURTEEN

I was resigned to the fact that Julia was never coming back, and I would have to start foraging for food. The fridge had long become empty, I'd exhausted the pantry, and only a few frozen bags of vegetables remained in the freezer. I stopped at the grocery store on my way home after work that day. I was proud of myself for not filling my grocery cart with frozen pizzas and bagel bites. Instead, my grocery bags overflowed with fresh vegetables and fruit. I would have to remember to take a picture of my grand haul later to send Julia. She would never believe my healthy choices otherwise.

With my arms encumbered by heavy grocery bags, I struggled to unlock and open the apartment door. I could have lightened my load by taking multiple trips, but I was as stubborn as I was economical.

I dropped my key ring on the floor in the apartment foyer. The various keys bounced and clanged noisily against the marble tile. I retrieved the keys from the floor and paused; I might have been imagining it, but an extra pair of high heels were in the foyer that I hadn't accounted for before.

A new noise alerted me from the rear of the apartment. Instead of feeling threatened, however, I was only curious.

"Hello?" I called out.

"Back here," came a voice that sounded uncannily like my girlfriend's.

Still lugging the canvas grocery bags, I traipsed towards the back bedroom. I dropped the bags of food in the doorway.

Julia stood near the bed, which I'd somehow had the foresight to make that day. Her suitcase was open on the mattress. Tidy piles of still-folded laundry covered the duvet.

"You're back," I said with unconcealed surprise. I'd been expecting a phone call later that evening to tell me she'd arrived safely in Embarrass. I wasn't expecting to actually see her. "Did you decide against seeing your parents?"

"No. I saw them."

"And?"

Julia sighed and momentarily paused her obsessive unpacking. "And, it was a very civil, cordial visit."

I sat down on the corner of the bed. "I can't tell if that's good or not."

"It's both. My father and I didn't fight, but we also didn't hug it out."

"Is that why you're back?" I guessed.

"I considered staying on," she remarked, "but I guess I didn't really see the point. It will take more than a long weekend for me to forgive my father. Besides, I couldn't be away from the office for that long."

"Or me?" I offered up hopefully.

Her lips twisted in a painted smirk. "I thought that went without saying."

I stared down at the puffy duvet cover. "Yeah, but a girl likes to hear it every now and again."

I looked up in time to see the tip of Julia's tongue appear between parted lips. It darted to lick the center of her top lip. "Come here," she husked.

I had no reason or desire to refuse her command.

Her delicate fingers curled beneath the collar of my jacket. Her caramel gaze traveled up and down my body once before settling on my face. "I realized something while I was gone," she said.

"What's that?" I asked. I willed myself to keep my cool, but her perfume—something spicy and warm—had me melting in my boots.

"This was the longest we've been apart since our first date."

I considered her words. Even when we hadn't lived together we'd seen each other most days—every other day at least. We definitely had never gone without seeing each other for more than four days. It surprised me that the thought hadn't come to me, too.

"I didn't like it," she told me. Her fingers subtly tightened in my lapel. "I slept terribly."

I cocked an eyebrow. "So you're upset your sleep schedule was disrupted?" I teased.

Her dark eyes narrowed. "Take the compliment, Cassidy. I missed you."

My grin widened. "I missed you, too."

The fingers under my collar loosened and Julia released her vice-like hold. "Well now that that's been decided, I need to finish unpacking."

"Can't that wait until later?" I asked with a pout. "I can think of much funner things we could be doing."

"More fun," she corrected.

"I'll give you the *most* fun."

"I promise I will give you my undivided attention, as soon as I finish up here. And it appears you have some groceries to put away, too," she observed. "I won't be able to properly relax knowing I haven't put these things away."

"I know another way to properly relax you," I sing-songed.

She flashed me a look of warning.

I held up my hands and laughed. "Okay, okay. I'll stop."

Julia continued to dutifully remove clothes from her suitcase and divided them into separate stacks on the bed.

"What are you doing?"

"Making piles. Dry-clean only and machine washable."

My lips twisted wistfully. "I think my dress whites from the Marines are the only dry-clean only clothes I'll ever own."

"There's nothing wrong with that," she defended me. "But it's expected of my profession."

"Even as a public defender?" I wondered.

"Even more so. It gives my clients confidence in my abilities. They don't want their representation to look like they got their degree from a Cracker Jack Box." She paused and smiled. "Are you even old enough to know what that is?"

"Why do you think I'm so young?" I pouted.

"Have you seen what your lip is doing right now, dear?" she teased.

I immediately tucked my lower lip back into place.

"We should do something tonight to celebrate your victory," I suggested.

Julia shook her head. "That's really not necessary," she resisted.

"You won your case. A family gets to stay together because of you!" I exclaimed. "That's not something to casually shrug off."

"I've had a long day, Cassidy," she sighed.

"I know you have," I conceded. "Which is exactly why you should let me take you out."

"I can tell I'm not going to win this one," she remarked.

"Not today, Counselor." I hopped up from the bed with renewed enthusiasm. "Unpacking will just have to wait."

Julia still wasn't all in, so we stayed close to the apartment and walked to a Mexican restaurant only a block away. A line hadn't formed outside of the neighborhood restaurant, but it was standing room only inside. The hostess was able to find us a table after only a few minute's wait, but we were squeezed onto a two-top close to the bar and the kitchen. The surrounding area was a chaotic combination of waitstaff retrieving orders from the kitchen and bar patrons taking advantage of half-price margaritas.

I wanted to, but I couldn't relax. Getting Julia out of the apartment had taken some convincing, so I felt on edge about bringing her someplace that was overly crowded and uncharacteristically loud. A mariachi band, led by a garishly dressed trumpet player, traveled from table to table, entertaining the crowds with traditional songs. It took at least ten minutes for someone on the waitstaff to bring us water and complimentary chips and salsa. The longer we waited without service, the more aggravated I became.

I typically didn't take notice of details like how quickly we were seated or when orders were taken, but Julia's reluctance to come out had me overly conscious about minor annoyances.

"Do you want to get something to go?" I asked.

Julia peered at me over her menu. "Why?"

"It's just, uh, a little overwhelming, don't you think?"

Julia's caramel eyes studied me with concern. "Is it too much for you? Do you need to go?"

My legs bounced beneath the bar top table, hidden from her view. I'd been so worried about the environment annoying Julia that I'd completely forgotten about myself.

"No, no. I'm fine," I insisted.

Julia set down her menu. "Then what's the problem, dear?"

I marveled at her tunnel vision. Every detail about our surroundings had frayed my nerves, but Julia appeared unfazed and unaffected.

"Nothing, nothing," I dismissed.

"Why don't you tell me what's going on with your murder/suicide case," Julia suggested.

I wanted to know more about her day—the details of how she'd won her child custody case or why she'd left Embarrass so abruptly—but I was thankful for the distraction.

"Ryan and I went down to St. Olaf's today to check out Kennedy's dorm room. We found a laptop, but no charger. We processed it as evidence, and next it'll go to the crime lab for analysis. The Petersiks still aren't allowing us access to Kennedy's journals, so I'm hopeful there's something useful on the laptop."

"Are you two getting along better?" she asked.

"Ryan and me?"

She nodded.

"We are," I confirmed. "Some of his tactics still annoy the hell out of me, but at least we're finally working together as a team and not trying to steal the case from each other or hold back newly discovered evidence."

I caught Julia's attention start to drift. Her eyes were no longer focused on me. Her attention had strayed to an adjacent table where a couple—a man and a woman—sat, attempting to cajole a little girl to take one more bite of her taco. I didn't take offense to it though. I knew she'd been driving for most of the day and had had a mental battle with herself over her decision to not stay on longer in Embarrass.

"Amelia's about her age," she remarked.

"Charlotte's daughter?"

"Mmhm," she confirmed. "Such a funny little thing." A small smile played at her lips. "Obsessed with insects. Wild hair, too. A completely untamable puff of blonde fluff."

"Sounds cute," I remarked.

I wasn't really into kids, but I also wasn't against them. Indifferent would be the word. As long as they didn't scream through dinner at a restaurant where I was or an airplane I was on, we were cool.

Our food orders arrived, and I watched Julia poke at her plate of enchiladas. She'd barely eaten anything since we'd sat down. Even the complimentary chips and salsa on the table had been neglected.

"Is your dinner okay?" I worried aloud. "Is it spicy enough? Too spicy? I can ask them to take it back."

Julia looked up sharply from her meal. "Stop trying to make everything perfect, Cassidy."

I opened my mouth. "I'm not," I started to protest. "I'm—."

"You're feeling self-conscious about the timing of our time apart," she interjected. "I didn't run away to Duluth to get away from you. I didn't extend my stay to avoid coming home to you. If anything, I cut short my trip to Embarrass because I'd been away from you for too long."

I choked on the lump in my throat. "Oh. Really?" I squeaked.

"You have two options," she calmly continued. "You can continue to insist we celebrate my winning in court with guacamole and chimichungas or you can take me home and ravage me until I'm begging you to stop." She leaned back in her chair. "It's your choice, dear."

My hand went in the air. "Check please."

+ + +

A giddy, youthful feeling radiated from my chest to the point of explosion. I practically pulled Julia down the street in the direction of the apartment. Her stilettoed feet struggled to keep up with my ambitious pace. We rushed past the doorman and onto the elevator. I silently cursed our luck that we didn't live on the ground floor.

My eagerness spilled out while Julia rummaged through her purse for the front door key. I was like a sprinter out of the blocks the moment I heard the locking mechanism spring free. I couldn't wait any longer. I scooped Julia off her feet and out of her heels. I tossed her over my shoulder in a fireman's lift and traveled down the hallway as fast as my legs could carry me.

I indelicately dumped Julia onto the center of the bed, amongst her organized clothes I had insisted could wait until later.

"My piles!" she protested.

With one long swoop of my arm, I eliminated the distraction. Her carefully separated laundry piles toppled to the floor in an unceremonious heap.

I licked my lips, knowing I would be tasting her on them later. "Lose the pants," I husked.

Julia hadn't bothered to change out of her court outfit from earlier in the day, or more accurately, I hadn't given her the opportunity to change before dinner. I needed her linen pants and blouse on the floor with the rest of her clothes. Julia, thankfully, was of the same mindset. This was no striptease performance. This was efficient desperation.

She lifted her backside off of the bed and her fingers released the top button of her pants. I watched with growing anticipation as she pulled the zipper down. She peeled the front panels apart to reveal satin beige underwear, nearly the color of her skin. It gave the impression of not wearing underwear at all, but I was going to be all too happy to help her remove her underwear in time.

She wiggled the dark pants past her hips. Her hipbones canted towards the ceiling. They jutted out just slightly from the smooth panel of her abdomen. The pants traveled lower still, past her thighs, her knees, her calves, her ankles. Finally, she removed them entirely.

A peculiar smile formed on my lips. "Dry-clean only?"

Her features darkened and she threw the pants to the floor, tidy piles be damned. She was always so careful, always so precise. I loved these moments when she decided to color outside the lines.

Without having to be asked, she started on the buttons of her pressed Oxford shirt. Each button gave way to the next until the front of her shirt was completely open.

I watched the erratic rise and fall of her breasts beneath her beige lace bra. Her normally impeccable hair was slightly tussled.

"Will you hurry up and fuck me, Miss Miller?"

The time for such formalities were long gone, but I couldn't deny how my insides clenched when she called me by a title. I was certain she knew that about me, too, which explained her continual usage.

"I hadn't realized we were on a timetable," I quipped. "Do you have someplace to be?"

"Yes. Between your legs," she said flippantly. "But only if you're efficient on your end."

I swallowed hard. "Yes, ma'am."

I quickly yanked my clothes off and joined her in bed.

I neglected her bra and breasts for the moment, knowing there would be time for them later. I kissed and licked down the center of her abdomen. As much as I wanted to tease her until I had her pleading for release, I knew we both needed this. Time apart had been a challenge, and we'd been on unsteady footing when she'd left. The phone sex had been a welcomed reconnection, but nothing compared to the real thing. We needed a reboot moment. I needed to wipe the slate clean.

I curled my fingers under the waistband of her underwear. She lifted her backside off of the mattress to help me shed the satin and lace barrier.

I lay on my stomach and positioned myself between her parted thighs. I didn't immediately dive in; I pressed soft kisses to either side of her inner thighs. Her skin was impossibly soft, putting our luxury high thread count sheets to shame. Egyptian cotton had nothing on her.

I flattened my tongue and licked the length of her slit, up to her slightly protruding clit. Her ready arousal had me groaning at her taste. Julia's head tilted back, and her painted lips parted in silent praise.

I captured her clit in my mouth, and the jerking of her hips practically bucked me off the bed. I held tight to her upper thighs as I sucked on the bundle of nerves, determined to see this ride through. I flicked the sensitive nub back and forth with the tip of my tongue.

I heard her groan when I sank my tongue into her depths. I plunged as deep as I could reach while my nose bumped and slid against her pulsing clit. Julia's thighs pressed hotly against my ears.

Needy fingers gripped my hair. "Up here," she gasped. "I need to be kissing you."

I was happy to oblige.

My lips and tongue were coated with her juices, but she didn't seem to mind. Her hands rounded to my backside and squeezed. Her tongue battled with mine, neither of us wanting to give in, neither of us wanting to be topped.

Her hand went between my legs, and I moaned into her open mouth. She trapped my clit between two fingers and repeatedly pinched and released the fleshy nub. She stroked the bundle of nerves up and down. It was rough and inelegant, and it was going to make me cum.

"Fuck me, Cassidy." She bit down on the top of my shoulder and my eyes rolled back. "Fuck me with your fingers."

I slid one finger and then two into her waiting pussy.

"Oh, God, yes." Her voice cracked on the praise.

She released my clit and I felt her fingers fill me. She didn't give me time to adjust before she began to dip in and out. I concentrated first on the feeling of her fingers roughly moving between my thighs before I remembered her own needs. I curled my fingers and slid into her to the second knuckle.

"Harder, Cassidy," she commanded me.

I pulled my fingers out and plunged back in. My knuckles slammed against her pelvic bone.

"Harder," she breathed.

Her fingers slipped out of me, but I no longer cared about my own orgasm. I was determined to get her off.

Her hands curled around my shoulders; her short nails bit into my skin. I could mentally picture the half-moon divots she was creating. Her breath hitched in my ear each time I bottomed out.

I sat up on my knees and held her down with my free hand. I pressed my palm firm against her breast plate, pinning her to the mattress. My hand was a blur between her thighs.

Julia's eyes were screwed shut. Her mouth was open, yet she made no sound.

"Look at me, baby."

Her eyes immediately flipped open and her dark stare locked with mine. She silently challenged me with an intense gaze. *Can you do it?* she seemed to taunt. *Can you make me cum with only your fingers?*

The rhythmic sound of skin slapping against skin echoed in the bedroom. My knuckles felt raw from continually striking against her pelvic bone. We would both be feeling this tomorrow.

"Harder. Harder, Cassidy." Her encouragement bordered on desperate. "Fuck me hard."

Her hips and backside bounced off the mattress to keep pace with my relentless fingers. "Don't you fucking stop," she warned me.

I could feel the sweat starting to build a thin layer on my skin. The dampness dribbled down the small of my back. The sweat from my brow started to sting my eyes.

"I'm close," she sharply gasped.

I grunted and refocused my efforts. I rammed into her while wildly pawing at her tightened nipples with my free hand. I remembered her words from phone sex: pinching and pulling, just on the other side of pain.

"Fuck," she suddenly bit out. "I'm cumming! Baby, I'm cumming!" she cried.

Even with her verbal assurances, I continued to fuck her. I thrust between her splayed thighs over and over again until her fingers curled around my wrist, forcing me to stop.

I flopped onto my back with an exhausted grunt. My right bicep and forearm were screaming; I might have even pulled something.

"Damn, baby. I gotta stop skipping arm-day at the gym if you like it like that."

I turned my head to appraise her when I didn't get an immediate response. Her hands were covering her face.

"Babe?" I questioned.

She still didn't respond. Her hands continued to hide her face. I heard the sharp intake of air and observed how her body shuddered.

"Babe, hey," I hushed. "Baby, are you okay?" I sat up and cupped my palm over her shoulder. "What's wrong? Did I hurt you?"

When she finally dropped her hands, I could see her tear stained cheeks. "No. No. I'm fine. I'm fine," she insisted. She made a noise as if to shake away the emotions. "I'm *more than* fine."

"Are you sure?" I desperately needed extra confirmation.

"Uh huh," she verified, wiping at her eyes. "It just hit me, you know?"

"So they're good tears?" My lips formed a crooked grin.

She gave me a watery smile in return. "Very good tears."

CHAPTER FIFTEEN

You guys still coming tonight?

My phone chirped with a new text message from my friend, Brent.

You bet, I responded. *Just waiting for Julia to get home from work.*

Hurry up! came his typed reply. *This beer isn't going to drink itself!*

I followed up Brent's text with one of my own: *Have you left work yet? Where are you?*

I stared at my phone, but received no response from Julia.

Since returning from Duluth, Julia's workdays had been getting longer and her time with me was getting shorter. We both had stressful careers, and it was easy to let those jobs completely take over our time. It was one of the reasons I was really looking forward to Brent's Halloween party, not just for the opportunity to see my friends, many of whom I hadn't seen in a while, but to also spend some quality time with Julia.

My knee bounced anxiously as I watched the hands of Julia's grandfather clock continue to move.

I heard a key in the front lock, followed by the apartment door opening. Julia's heels clicked on the marble tile in the entryway.

"I'm home," she called out. "I just got your text. I met late with a client and then traffic was murder. And I had to go to *two* stores before I could find any candy," she complained. "Who sells out of candy on Halloween night?"

Julia appeared in the archway of the living room where I continued to sit on the couch. Her work bag hung from one shoulder, and her hands were filled with plastic convenience store bags.

"Did you forget about tonight?" I asked.

Julia paused in the hallway. She blinked and shook her head. "Am I forgetting a month-a-versary or something?"

To be honest, I had no idea when we considered the start of our relationship. The first time we'd met? The first time we'd had sex? Our first official date? The pacing and chronological order of our relationship 'firsts' had been anything but orthodox.

"No, Brent's party, remember?"

"Oh. That," she said, her tone flat. "I'm not going."

I hopped up from the couch and followed her down the hallway towards the back of the apartment. "What? But it's tradition!" I protested.

Julia frowned at my reaction. "I hadn't realized it was as serious as that. I was really looking forward to relaxing and handing out candy here. I never got trick-or-treaters in Embarrass," she seemed to pout. "I lived too far out of town."

"Plus, their parents were probably scared of you," I quipped.

She curled her lip, but offered no words in self-defense, most likely because I was right.

My colleague on the Embarrass police force, David Addams, had once referred to Julia as a pitbull, and Grace Kelly Donovan had dubbed her the Ice Queen. Julia's sharp edges had softened some since moving away from her hometown to the Twin Cities, but she still exuded a confidence and class that could come across as haughty or unapproachable.

"We live in an apartment complex, babe; you're not gonna get trick-or-treaters here. Please come with me?" I wasn't too proud to beg.

"I've had a full day of work, Cassidy," Julia sighed with annoyance. "I have so much catching up to do because of Duluth. I don't have the energy to pull double-duty tonight."

"I had a full day of work, too," I pouted. I knew I was whining, but I'd really been looking forward to going to the party with her.

"Yes, but you've got youth on your side," she claimed. "Go. Have fun. Hang out with your similarly young friends."

A frown tugged at both corners of my mouth. "You're not that much older."

In truth, I had no idea how many years separated us. I knew she was older than me, but I didn't know by how much. Every time I brought up the topic of our ages, she deflected or ignored my question.

"Please apologize to Brent for me."

My entire body sagged in disappointment. "You're really not coming?"

"You could stay home with me?" she proposed. "We could order Chinese and handout candy together. Maybe watch a scary movie later?"

A twinge of regret settled in my gut. She was proposing the perfect night in, but I'd been looking forward to this party ever since I'd decided on a costume.

"I already RSVP'd," I begged off. "It would be rude not to make an appearance when Brent is expecting us."

She arched a quizzical eyebrow. "When did you become the etiquette queen?"

"I guess some of your good habits are rubbing off on me," I huffed.

Childishly, I left the room before she could respond. I grabbed my police academy duffle bag from the bottom of the closet in the guest bedroom and shoved my costume inside. I made a big show of storming into the bathroom and loudly shut myself inside, even though I had no idea if Julia was even watching.

The blonde woman in the mirror glared back at me. "Stupid," I mumbled to myself.

I didn't really know what I was doing with my hair, but I tossed it over one shoulder and contained it in a loose braid.

I exited the bathroom and strode purposefully toward the front door. "Don't wait up," I called from the foyer. "I'll probably be out late."

Julia chose to ignore my bratty tone. There was no way she couldn't have heard it. Her steps were more careful than mine as she walked toward the front door with a glass of red wine in one hand. "What happened to your costume?" she asked.

I hugged my duffle bag closer to my chest. "I'm going to change at the party. I don't want my Lyft driver to laugh."

"Is your costume funny?"

"I guess you'll never know." I knew I was being unfair, but I was too disappointed at that moment to be civil or polite.

Julia immediately frowned at my words. "This is really that important to you?" Her tone softened from its usual refined edge.

"No," I lied. "It's just a stupid party."

I felt ridiculously emotional. But I also felt betrayed and disappointed. I didn't want her to know how affected her dismissal had made me, however. Because I felt like a child who hadn't got their way, I did my best to choke down the truth.

I kissed her cheek hastily, my lips barely making contact with her skin. "Don't wait up," I repeated. "I know you've had a long day."

I know you've had a long day.

My retreating words to Julia replayed themselves over and over again in a loop as I sat in the backseat of my ride share. I'd meant my words to sting and to make her feel guilty. I didn't know how they'd affected her, but by the time my Lyft driver dropped me off at Brent's apartment, I didn't feel like partying anymore.

I pressed a button in the front lobby to be buzzed into the apartment building and walked up the two flights of stairs to Brent's apartment. Even if I had never been to my friend's apartment before, I still would have found the location of the party. The rhythmic pulse of deep bass filtered through the front door and into the apartment hallway.

I discovered the front door unlocked and the narrow foyer empty. I still had to put on my costume, so I made a detour to the powder room. I opened my duffle bag and sighed at the icy blue sequined gown inside. I'd been so pleased with my costume—not for the novelty of the idea—but with how unexpected it would be on me. I'd wanted to see Julia's amused reaction, and after the party was over, I'd looked forward to her making good use of the blue gown's thigh-high slit.

I carefully removed my civilian clothes and slipped on the long dress, but all of the joy had been sucked out of the evening. I'd wanted to unwind on the holiday with my friends, but I'd wanted Julia to be a part of that as well.

I left the bathroom and wobbled towards the kitchen in thrift-store high heels I had no intention of ever wearing again. I turned the corner and found my closest police officer friends gathered around the granite kitchen island of Brent's bachelor pad. I made a cursory scan of the open floor plan. The apartment was crowded. I saw a few familiar faces, cops I recognized from the academy or from the Fourth Precinct, but there were even more people I didn't know. I'd always wondered how Brent had come to know so many people, but I'd never thought to ask.

My cheeks flushed red when I heard my friend's wolf whistle and laughter at my appearance.

"Amazing costume, Cassidy!" Brent approved.

He was, predictably, dressed like a Nordic Viking. He recycled his costume every year. His broad chest was barely covered with a leather vest. A plastic hat with a giant horn positioned on either side threatened to spill off his head whenever he moved.

"Here. Hold this," he instructed. He pressed a replica powder horn into my hands. "I'll get you a beer, Your Highness."

I peered down at the mystery liquid sloshing around inside of the horn. I didn't dare take an experimental sip, however. I liked myself too much for that.

I smiled and waved my free hand at the other party attendees whom I knew: my friends Angie, Rich, Adan, and his girlfriend Isabella formed a tight half-circle around me.

"Interesting costume choice," Rich smirked at me.

I crossed my arms across my chest in a defensive position. With the exception of the aggressive thigh-high slit, the aqua-blue dress wasn't revealing, but I still felt uncomfortable. I never wore dresses or skirts if I could help it.

"Hey, at least I put in some effort," I retorted. "What are you supposed to be?"

Rich didn't appear to be wearing a costume at all. There was nothing special about his blue jeans, and the t-shirt he wore had the word 'Life' screen-printed across his chest. I was almost afraid to ask.

"Isn't it obvious?" He pointed to the center of his chest. "I'm the *Life* of the Party."

Rich's pun produced a groan from me and my other friends. He looked too pleased with himself, however, to be concerned by our reactions.

"Where's Julia tonight?" he asked. "Trouble in paradise?"

I smiled tightly. "No. The thought of hanging out with you assholes …" I couldn't finish the cavalier lie. I stopped myself. "She had a long day at work. She apologizes for her absence."

"That's too bad," he clucked. "She makes hanging out with you almost bearable."

I didn't suppress my eye roll.

"How's Grace Kelly?" I asked.

"You would know if you called once in a while."

My mouth fell open. "Wow. I haven't gotten a guilt trip like that since I last saw my mom, Rich."

"Shut it, Rookie," he scowled. "Maybe I just miss my friend."

On a normal day, I would have taunted him without mercy for being so honest and vulnerable. Maybe I was premenstrual, but I hugged him instead.

I could feel Rich's arms and shoulders stiffen. "Easy there. I've got a girlfriend. You do, too."

I pulled back and swatted at his chest. "Shut it, you goon."

Brent eventually returned with a bottle of recognizable beer, thankfully, and not some mystery mead he'd whipped up special for the party. I exchanged his Viking horn for an IPA.

"How's Cold Case treating you?" he asked.

I took a grateful preliminary sip. "I'm starting to get the hang of it, I think."

"That's great," he approved. "Working on anything interesting?"

A strong arm flung around my shoulder. "Party foul! No talking about work!" My friend Angie pulled me close. Her breath smelled like alcohol.

Angie had teased her hair out to a small, puffy halo around her head. She wore a long leather jacket, bell bottom pants, a midriff, and big golden hoop earrings.

"Pam Grier as Foxy Brown?" I guessed.

"You know it, girl."

Angie pulled a snub nose .38 special out of her leather trench coat and posed. I assumed the gun was fake, but with cops—who knows.

Over the next hour or so I made small-talk with strangers whose names I promptly forgot the moment they introduced themselves. I got my picture taken numerous times since I was the only Disney royalty at the party. My friends danced and drank and laughed at juvenile pranks, but I felt like an outsider.

As much as I wanted to be in the moment, my thoughts continually strayed to the woman I'd left behind. I periodically checked my phone for messages from her, but either Brent's apartment building blocked all incoming messages or Julia hadn't bothered to text me. Even though she'd been the one to bail on our plans, I couldn't help feeling guilty about how I'd stormed out of the apartment.

I had just gotten to the bottom of my second longneck beer bottle and had a decision to make. I could grab another beer and be on the road to getting good and drunk, or I could call up a ride share car and head home early. Rich and Angie were engaged in a heated conversation if her wild gesticulations were any indication. Brent was chatting up a pretty woman dressed as Little Red Riding Hood, and Adan and Isabella looked cozy together on a couch in the living room.

I grabbed my duffle bag which contained the clothes I'd worn to the party and quietly exited Brent's apartment without saying any goodbyes. My friends would only make me feel guilty for bailing on the party so early.

I didn't quite know what I'd find when I returned to the apartment. I entered quietly in case Julia had decided to go to bed early. The front of the apartment was silent and dark. I didn't need the lights on to maneuver around, so I didn't bother turning on any overhead lights.

I didn't call out to find out where she was. My heels clicked on hardwood floors until I made it to the master bedroom. My shoes sunk into the carpeting as I hovered in the doorway.

Julia's normally meticulously arranged wardrobe was strewn haphazardly across the bed and had collected in piles on the floor. Empty hangers littered the ground like land mines. Julia herself was half-dressed in only a bra and black dress pants.

I announced my presence with a question: "What happened in here?"

Julia's attention snapped from the closet to the doorway. Her dark eyes looked wild and unfocused. Her ribcage heaved as if she'd been exercising. I saw her take in my unorthodox outfit before she launched into her explanation.

"I never got a costume. I had no intention of ever going to that party with you, so I never bothered to even come up with a costume idea. I was selfish and stupid, and I thought you'd just do what I wanted and would skip your party to stay home with me."

I held up my hands. "Hey-hey … calm down. It's okay. It was just one dumb party."

"That's not the point," Julia resisted. "I'm manipulative, Cassidy. I only think of myself and not how my actions impact others. I act as though I expect you to bend and give in to all of my petulant demands."

I teetered in my glittery high heels. "We all have our flaws. Do you see me complaining? I do what I want. Like tonight—I still went to Brent's party."

"Then why are you home so early?" she posed.

She had me there. I dropped my eyes to the floor. "It wasn't any fun without you."

"See?!" Julia exclaimed as if I'd proven her exact point. "I ruined tonight with my selfishness."

"But I don't want to force you to do stuff you don't want to do," I said, shaking my head. "I wasn't going to drag you to Brent's party tonight like some cave man."

"You shouldn't have to drag me anywhere. I need to learn how to compromise better."

"We're still new to this." I couldn't help defending her from herself. "We'll figure it out."

Julia hung her head. "Do you still want me to go to that party with you?"

I waved away the suggestion. "It's not a big deal; it was kind of dying down by the time I left. I guess we're all getting old."

"Are you hungry? Did you eat?" she asked. "I could still order Chinese?"

My mood brightened at the prospect of food. "I wouldn't say no to that. Do I get to pick the scary movie, too?"

Julia initially curled her lip, but, remembering herself, her mouth quirked into a smile. "Nothing gore porn, okay? My stomach can't handle it."

I thrust my fist in the air in victory.

"Now when are we going to address this outfit of yours?" Julia remarked. Amusement colored her tone. "Where on earth did you get that thing?"

I looked down at the blue sequined dress wrapped around my body. "I ordered it online."

"I've never seen you in a dress before," she remarked, still smiling. "Although I'm not exactly sure this counts."

I smoothed my hands down the sequined material. "Do you like it?"

"Not at all." Julia gave me a predatory leer. "You should probably take it off."

"Nuh uh," I clucked. I took a self-preserving step backwards as Julia began to stalk toward me. "You're not going to distract me from a scary movie and takeout food with sex."

"Are you sure about that?" Julia slipped one bra strap off of her gently sloping shoulder and then the other so that only the back clasp held her bra together. I involuntarily squeezed my thighs together.

"Are you sure there's *nothing* I can do to convince you?" she questioned.

"You don't play fair," I scowled. She was manipulating me again, but amazingly I didn't mind.

Julia stepped closer, one step at a time. Her dark gaze held me frozen in place. Her hand went first to my waist as she slowly walked in a circle around me. I felt a blush grow on my cheeks, a combination of embarrassment and excitement. The costume was ridiculous and so unlike me.

With my hair tied back in a loose braid that draped over one shoulder, the back of my neck was exposed. She pressed her warm lips against the base of my neck. Her fingers toyed with the thin, gauze material that covered my upper back before I felt her take purchase of the dress's zipper.

"Let it go, darling," she rasped. "Let it go."

The fastening let loose, exposing my shoulder blades. As she released more and more of my skin from the dress, she trailed her mouth and tongue down the top of my spine. She took her time with the zipper, causing my anticipation to heighten. My whole body seized with a shiver at the feel of her talented tongue marking a path down the center of my back. I'd discovered that my scar tissue was incredibly sensitive, and Julia took full advantage of that discovery. It was she who had helped me embrace all of my scars, or at least not feel so damned self-conscious about them.

She pulled away suddenly, her mouth no longer on me. I heard her frustrated noise.

"What's wrong?" I asked.

"You're stuck."

"Stuck?" I echoed.

"Your zipper," she said. "It won't go any farther."

She tugged again at the zipper that traveled down the length of my back. The scooped neckline of the dress tightened around my breasts when she pulled, but the zipper wouldn't budge.

"I'm sorry, dear," she clipped. "It would appear that you're trapped in this outfit for the rest of time."

I tried to reach the top of the zipper myself, but the mechanism had gotten jammed in the center of my back, just out of my reach. No matter how I contorted my shoulders or twisted my arms, my fingers could only uselessly brush against the metal fasten. A claustrophobic feeling began to rise in my chest.

"Julia!" I complained. "*Do* something!"

She pressed her palm flat against the exposed skin in the center of my back. The simple touch of her skin on mine instantly calmed me. I heard her chuckle. "Wait here, Princess. I'll save you."

She disappeared momentarily from the bedroom towards the front of the apartment. I heard the sounds of drawers or cabinet doors being opened and closed. When she returned, she held a silver pair of scissors.

My eyes widened at the sight. "What are you going to do with those?"

She experimentally snipped the scissors in the air. They even *sounded* sharp. "Rescue you, of course."

She returned to the stubborn zipper at the center of my back. "I hope you weren't planning a repeat performance," she remarked.

I didn't have time to ask what she meant before I felt the almost icy touch of metal scissors against my skin. I immediately jerked away, but she held firm to my shoulder.

"Hold very still," she warned. Her mouth was close enough to my ear to ruffle the hair that had escaped from my loose braid.

The scissors slipped under the fabric of my dress. The cool metal felt like an icicle. The sharp blade began to slice just above my exposed skin.

"Wait!"

I felt the scissors pause. "Don't you trust me?" she asked.

"I trust you, I do," I promised. "But if you have to cut off the dress ..." I bit down on my lower lip. "Could you ..."

Julia and I were experimental when it came to sex. We pushed each other's limits and tried new things that might make the other person uncomfortable. What I wanted to ask of her, however, brought a blush to my cheeks.

The scissors were removed and Julia spun me around to face her. I felt her knuckle under my chin, and she raised my head so my gaze met hers. She kept her hand there so I couldn't look away. My request was stuck, just like that damn zipper.

Her warm caramel irises searched my face. I hadn't intended to make her worry, but she looked concerned. "What is it, darling?"

"The scissors," I gulped. "Instead of cutting down my back, would you ...could you ...you know, uh ...cut *up*?"

She dropped her hand from my chin.

I immediately panicked. "That's a weird question. Never mind. Forget I said anything. What you were doing was fine."

Her nostrils flared and she spoke very calmly, very quietly. "Get on the bed, Your Highness."

CHAPTER SIXTEEN

I lay on my back in the center of our bed. The scissors sat on the bedside table. Julia had taken off her pants and remained only in her matching bra and underwear. I could still feel the hot flush on my cheeks from what I'd asked her to do. Julia's face, however, didn't reflect the same embarrassment. She looked completely at ease, almost business-like.

She approached me from the bottom of the bed. She climbed onto the mattress and crawled towards me. The delicate lace of her demi-bra offered me a generous peek of her breasts. The bra struggled to keep the supple flesh from spilling over. I could hardly wait to get my hands and mouth on her, but first I needed to get out of this damn dress.

Julia didn't immediately reach for the scissors. Her hands went first to my ankles. She lifted my right leg and rested my heel on her shoulder. The movement strained my hamstring and pulled at the seams of the dress, but I was in no position to complain. Her dark gaze locked on mine. She turned her head slightly, but maintained her stare. She pressed a soft kiss to the inside of my ankle.

I watched intently as she retrieved the scissors from the end table. My breath caught in my throat. The blades somehow looked even longer and sharper than before. I expected her to focus on the thigh-high slit, but Julia rarely did the expected.

She pressed tip of the closed blades lightly against my inner calf. She slowly dragged the pointed end from my ankle to the inside of my knee. My instinct was to pull away, but she'd smartly planned ahead. The fingers curled around my ankle weren't letting me go anywhere. She pressed another kiss against my inner ankle, a little higher than the first.

The single slit of my costume stopped high on my upper right thigh. Julia reached forward so the bottom edge of the scissors rested against my naked upper thigh. We seemed to hold a collective breath when she made the first incision. The cheap polyester-blend material practically melted under the scissors' blades, a testament to their sharpness.

She continued to cut away at the bedazzled dress. I hissed when the bottom of the blades passed over the front panel of my underwear and touched my bare abdomen. It reminded me of swimming in a bikini at my parents' cabin on Lake Armstrong. The temperature of the water was always fine until it hit my stomach.

Julia's dark eyes clouded with concern. "Are you okay?"

I clenched my teeth. "Yeah. The metal's cold."

"Poor baby," she clucked.

She stopped, but only to crawl higher up on the mattress so she could continue with her task. I reached for her, but she swatted my hands away. The scissors were returned to the bedside table, and delicate but sure fingers gripped my wrists and pinned them into the mattress. I'd once asked her not to take it easy on me in bed, and she'd remained faithful to that promise.

Her mouth was warm against the side of my neck. "This isn't a race, my dear," she roughly whispered. "We've no place to be. And if I'm remembering correctly, you seem to enjoy it when I take my time."

I hadn't mounted a protest against the pacing of her endeavors, but she must have suspected I was becoming antsy.

The scissors reappeared in her hand. She leaned over my body to press butterfly light kisses on the exposed skin just above my underwear. The scissors traveled higher still. She continued to cut and kiss up the center of my body. She dipped her tongue into my belly button and licked a line up the center of my twitching abdomen.

The cutting paused and Julia arched a quizzical eyebrow when she discovered I hadn't been wearing a bra underneath the dress. I shrugged in response to her nonverbal judgment. The costume had built-in cups and my modest-sized breasts didn't require much support.

The dress continued to cut away from my body like glittery wrapping paper. When the scissors skated against my collarbone to complete the job, an unsavory thought popped into my head: Kennedy Petersik had been carved up like this on the autopsy table. I saw the ugly, jagged stitches up the center of chest. The star-shaped entry wound in her stomach had looked just like the star-shaped wound in the back of Amir's head. I'd made him turn around. I hadn't been able to look him in the eyes.

A lump formed in my throat, nearly choking me. I shut my eyes tight. *Not now, brain,* I berated myself. *Please, don't ruin this.*

"These will have to go, too," I heard Julia hum. She hadn't noticed my distraction. Before I could react, she'd slid the open blade under the elastic leg band of my cotton underwear and cut.

My eyes flew open and the star-shaped hole disappeared. "Hey! I actually liked those!"

Julia smirked. "I'll take you lingerie shopping."

"Will you try on things for me?" I asked.

"If you behave, maybe we can share a fitting room," she mused.

My mouth watered at the possibilities.

Julia had only cut away one side of the underwear. She took her time with the second leg. She opened the scissors' blades and ran the bottom blade along the length of my thigh. My upper thigh muscles involuntarily twitched. The blade snuck under the remaining leg band. Instead of one, long, even incision, she snipped away at my underwear in short, precise cuts.

The muscles in my abdomen jumped each time she opened and closed the blades. The scissors' hard metal underside glided across my pelvis and slid past my hip bone.

When she was finished, Julia stood back to admire her handiwork. My costume, and my underwear, had been completely dismantled. Scraps of bedazzled fabric littered the duvet cover. I was a little bewildered, but mostly turned on.

"Now that I've unwrapped my present," Julia mused, "it's time for me to enjoy her."

She ran her tongue up my body, starting at my pubic bone and ending at the hollow in my throat. My nipples pebbled in her capable hands.

Julia hovered above and showed me her teeth. "Keep your eyes open, darling. I want you watching me."

She retreated back down my body, kissing a wet trail down the center of my body. I held myself up on my elbows so I could watch every kiss, every nip, every movement of her pink tongue. My eyes nearly closed when she sank her teeth into the tender flesh of my inner thigh, but I somehow managed to keep my eyes locked with hers.

Julia positioned herself between my twitching thighs. She barely touched me with her tongue. I felt the heat and the moisture from her warm breath against my shaved skin. Her tongue was delicate and light as she licked up and down my slick center. A thin line of her saliva and my arousal connected the tip of her tongue to my pussy lips. I groaned at the erotic sight.

I couldn't stop the movement of my lower body. I rolled my hips and flexed my backside to lift me up and down. Julia did nothing to stop me, but she maintained her distance, denying me the direct contact that I so desperately desired.

My hips jerked toward the ceiling, and I choked out a sharp gasp when she finally made contact with my aching clit. She circled a finger around and around the fleshy nub, drawing out more liquid from my seeping slit.

The tip of her middle finger disappeared between my swollen lips. I clawed at the bedsheets to keep from tugging on her hair. Her finger plunged deeper. She withdrew the single digit and replaced it with two. I felt her start to quicken her pace. It was all too much, too soon.

The destruction of my dress had been somewhat practical but also torturous foreplay. I was a raw recruit again with a hairpin trigger. I didn't want to cum so soon.

I somehow found my voice. "Slow and deep," I instructed. "Keep doing that."

Julia didn't protest or deny me what I wanted or how I wanted it. She settled between my thighs and continued to penetrate me with slow, even thrusts. Contented groans and sighs slipped past my parted lips. I wiggled on the mattress to help set the pressure and pace while Julia patiently stroked her fingers in and out of my tightening sex.

"I need your mouth," I groaned. "Please."

I cried out louder when she obediently sucked my clit into her mouth. I felt the orgasm tingling in my core. It took root in my most sensitive nerve endings and spread like tentacles across my lower body. I pulsed, I ached everywhere.

I gripped the top of Julia's head so she had no place to go. My back arched, my eyes shut, and my mouth opened wider. I felt the rush wash over me, all the way down to my curling toes.

I finally released my hold of Julia's head and breathed out. My body seemed to sink deeper into the mattress with each exhalation. I stared at the ceiling while my breathing returned to normal.

The white plaster ceiling was smooth, with no visible cracks, and yet a star-shaped hole floated before my eyes. The star-shaped hole in the back of his head. I'd made him get on his knees. I'd pulled the trigger, and he'd fallen forward into a pile of dirty sand and concrete—the only thing left of what used to be our safe house.

Julia's voice pulled me back. "Where did you just go?"

I couldn't lie. Not to her. "Afghanistan."

The muscles in her jaw flexed, but she didn't say a word. Instead, she rested her head on my collarbone and wiggled closer. Her arm and leg draped across my body.

"Has that ever happened before? During sex?" Her voice was quiet.

"No."

"Are you getting worse?"

I wanted to deny the question out of hand. "I don't know. Maybe I'm just overly tired or stressed."

"Do you know what triggered you?"

I thought her questions were incredibly brave. Put in her position, I didn't know if I would have been able to confront my condition head-on. It was easier to ignore it and hope it would go away. That's how I'd gotten myself in trouble in the first place though.

"The scissors," I answered truthfully. "They reminded me of something."

Julia shifted in bed again so she could look directly at me. She rested her chin on my chest. Her raven hair fell across her forehead and into her eyes. "Maybe you should talk to Dr. Warren about the virtual reality treatment?"

"Maybe," I deflected.

It hardly seemed the time or place to be having this conversation. I didn't want to talk about it now. I didn't want to talk about it ever.

"When's your next appointment?" she asked.

"I don't know," I dismissed. "I've got it written down."

"Cassidy," she censured. "This is important."

"I know it is," I returned. "But it's not your job to fix me, okay? And if this is too much for you, nothing says you have to stay. You don't owe me anything."

I expected Julia to snap back at me with the same heat as I'd given her. Instead, I felt her body go rigid. She didn't speak to me; she stiffly separated herself from my side and climbed out of bed. I watched her pad silently to the en suite bathroom. She turned on the bathroom light and shut the door behind her.

I sat up in bed and rested my head in my hands. "Fuck," I muttered under my breath.

I peeled off what remained of my ridiculous Halloween costume. The long sleeves had gotten stuck to my arms. The non-breathable material had never been intended for this kind of activity. Scattered pieces of sequined fabric were strewn across the bed. I tried to collect all the bits and pieces, but I was sure we'd still be finding glittery blue thread on the carpet and in the bed until next Halloween.

I looked around at the empty room. Julia's bedroom was a disaster. Half of her wardrobe spilled out of her closet from her fruitless search for a last-minute Halloween costume. I felt disgusted with myself. Julia was always so tidy and so neat. I'd done this to her; I'd made everything a mess.

I grabbed a t-shirt from the floor and pulled it over my head to at least partially cover my nakedness. I climbed out of bed and knocked lightly on the bathroom door.

"Julia?" I waited for the response I knew wouldn't come. "I'm sorry. I didn't mean to take my frustrations out on you. I know you were only trying to help."

I hated apologizing through a door.

I wet my lips. "Julia," I called to her. "I killed a man."

The bathroom door swung open with Julia on the other side. She hadn't locked the door, but I hadn't tried the doorknob.

"I killed a man," I repeated the horrible truth. "I shot him in the back of the head. And they gave me a medal and called me a hero."

She didn't say a word. She didn't try to fix me or tell me everything was going to be okay. Her arms wrapped around me and she pulled my head down to her shoulder. I fell apart. Hot tears dripped down my cheeks. If not for the solidness and stability of her body, I would have crumbled to the floor.

I felt as broken and as torn up as that damn princess costume.

CHAPTER SEVENTEEN

The wind rustled through the trees, a variable kaleidoscope of reds, yellows, and oranges that would remain for a few more weeks until the leaves fell and were carted away in wheelbarrows and yard waste bags. Fall in Minnesota was special, but fleeting. A good, strong wind storm could rip the color from the trees within a few hours, leaving behind the skeleton of oak and maple trees until spring eventually rolled around.

I supposed I was a bit of an oddity in my ambivalence about the season. I didn't stock up on pumpkin spice everything. I didn't go leaf peeping or apple picking or carve up pumpkins. Those kinds of traditions had bypassed my family entirely. But I did appreciate being able to wear flannel multiple times a week without feeling too butch.

Julia sat across the table from me at our favorite brunch place. I would have previously rolled my eyes at the word 'brunch,' and especially at the idea of having a favorite spot, but love makes you do unnatural things.

My attention was divided between the menu in my hands and the woman across the table. She wore a light cardigan, open at the neck and shoulders with a matching patterned camisole. A delicate silver chain hung around her neck, drawing attention to her defined clavicle. I hadn't known Julia in cold weather yet. I worried the skirts might go away or that she might button up her blouses more, or worse yet, that she might start wearing turtlenecks.

I watched her over the top of my menu as her gaze lifted from her own to follow a man in his mid-thirties as he walked by our table. He and I were similarly dressed in button-up flannel, leather ankle boots, and tight skinny jeans. I frowned when I noticed how her eyes lingered a little too long on the passing man.

"Did you just check out that guy's butt?" I exclaimed.

I watched Julia go stiff. "That's the most ridiculous thing I've ever heard—and you've been known to say some ridiculous things."

"I saw that double-take, babe. I'm a trained observer."

"If you really must know," she sniffed, "I was checking out his baby."

"Oh." Only when I spun around to look at the man a second time did I notice the newborn in a backpack-like carrier. I hadn't even registered there being a baby present.

"Charlotte's daughter is already seven," Julia sighed dejectedly. "It made me feel old. And … I think I've begun to tick."

"Tick?" I spun back around to my original seated position.

"Like a clock?" she clarified. "A biological clock."

"Oh." I let Julia's words sink in a little deeper. "Ohhhh."

She ran her hands over her face. "I used to feel *nothing* when I saw children. No—I take that back—I used to feel *relieved* that I didn't have one. And now …" She trailed off.

"And now you want one?" I guessed.

"I don't know!" Her voice pitched higher than her usual smoky register. "But I do know that I'm not getting any younger and neither are my eggs."

It was like walking on unsteady ground, looking out for landmines. I didn't know what to say. This was totally new territory for me—for her too, I imagined. But it certainly wasn't the kind of conversation I'd pictured us having before brunch.

She wet her lips. "You're freaking out, aren't you?"

"No!" I insisted. "I'm not freaking out. I'm not *not* freaking out," I qualified, "I'm just kind of taking it all in."

"It's new to me, too. I didn't exactly expect it."

"So you want to have a baby?"

"No. No. No," she shook her head. "The timing is all wrong."

"How so?"

"Because." She toyed with the stem of her champagne glass. "Melissa Ferdet called me the other day."

"Oh?" I hoped my face wasn't doing weird things.

"The firm where she works, Grisham and Stein, is creating a new position. They're looking to give back to the community and take on more pro bono cases. Melissa thinks I should apply for the job."

"She does."

Julia's mouth ticked down. "I know she's not your favorite person."

"I don't know her." My first impressions had not been favorable, but all I had was a brief, peripheral conversation and a few of Julia's stories. "Are you considering it?"

She sighed. "I don't know. There's a lot of things to consider."

"Like?"

"Like, you."

"I know I'm a jealous ass sometimes," I breezed, "but that shouldn't stop you from applying. I'll get over it eventually."

"It's more about the hours," she corrected. "You know that the work I do is very time consuming. If I went to work for Grisham and Stein, my days would get even longer."

"And we wouldn't see each other as much," I said, catching on.

She bit her lower lip in an uncharacteristic show of uncertainty. "What do you think I should do?"

I didn't have an answer. "It's not my decision to make."

"I know that," she countered. "But if you were me ..."

"I'm *not* you, Julia," I continued to deny. "What do *you* want to do? What's going to make you happy?"

A corner of her expressive mouth rose. "Retire early and run away with you?"

I exhaled. "Sounds good to me."

I reached for my mimosa while maintaining my eye contact. I overestimated my hand-eye coordination, however. The tips of my fingers nudged the fluted glass just hard enough to knock it over. The glass didn't break, but the bubbly orange liquid spilled across the tabletop and flowed menacingly in Julia's direction.

I leapt from my chair, nearly knocking the table over, and grabbed the cloth napkin that had been lying across my lap. I rushed to Julia's side of the table and threw down my napkin like a dam to stop the flood. I stopped most, but not all of the liquid. The remainder splashed over the side of the table and onto Julia's lap.

I heard her slight intake of air as my beverage hit her thighs. Luckily, her outfit wasn't dry-clean only.

I grabbed a napkin from a nearby table and dropped to my knees. I dabbed with purpose at the extra liquid that had collected on her lap.

"Darling," she quietly laughed. "It's fine."

"You shouldn't need a tarp to have a drink with me," I complained.

I looked up when her hands settled on top of mine. Julia stared down at me and smiled.

There was a smile Julia reserved only for me. She typically grew annoyed with most people—myself included—but I was also the only person to whom she shared that particular smile.

A frivolous, unexpected thought popped into my head: *I could propose to her down from here.*

My frantic hands stilled, but my heart seemed to pound a little heavier. I watched her caramel eyes shift in her head. She looked … scared.

Her mouth barely moved. "I'll be right back."

She scooted back in her chair and rose from the table. I watched her retreat towards the back of the restaurant, presumably in the direction of the restrooms.

"Stupid, stupid," I sighed to myself. I got off of my knees and flopped back down in my chair on the opposite side of the table.

With Julia gone, I reached into my jacket pocket and pulled out my phone. I intended on distracting myself by checking on the score of my fantasy football team, but a text message from Stanley was waiting for me when I unlocked my phone. His words distracted me from logging into my fantasy football app.

Julia caught me with my phone out when she returned to the table. "I thought we agreed no phones at the table, dear."

"I know," I acknowledged, not looking up. "I'm sorry."

I continued to stare at Stanley's text. It didn't make any sense.

"Is everything okay?" Julia asked when I ignored her words and failed to put my phone away.

"It's work."

"What's the matter?" she pressed.

I distractedly apologized again. "I'm sorry. I've got to make a call."

I abruptly stood and left Julia at the table with an annoyed, but perplexed look on her face.

I hadn't had the phone number stored in my cell for long, but I'd figured it was important to keep his number close considering how twisted his panties had become the last time I left him out of the loop. Now I was the one on the outside.

I waited until I was outside of the restaurant and in a semi-private location before pulling up his number.

"What the fuck, man?" I growled when Detective Ryan answered my call. "Stanley just texted me that you picked up Landon Tauer."

"I didn't have a choice," he defended. "The D.A.'s office has been getting bombarded with calls about us letting him walk. It's like the Petersik family are robo-callers or something."

"We let him walk because we've got nothing on him."

"What about the gun?"

"What about it? Landon said he gave it to Kennedy for protection. We've got no concrete evidence. It's all circumstantial hearsay!" I began to pace back and forth in front of the restaurant. "That's not gonna hold up in court."

"We got our guy."

"No. We got *a* guy," I emphasized. "What about the beer can we found? That all but proves that his story about Michael Bloom's death is true."

It was quite possible that the land had been used for target practice in the years between the graduation party and when we'd inspected the land, but it seemed like too much of a coincidence to have found the can.

"Landon could have been the one who shot Bloom, not Kennedy," Ryan pointed out. "He could have pulled the trigger both times, Miller. He's a smart kid; getting Kennedy to call from a landline," he cited as example.

I ran my fingers through my hair. "We need Kennedy's journals. I know her mom doesn't want us reading them, but we've waited as long as we can. We need to get a search warrant for the Petersiks' house so we can confiscate those diaries."

"Let me worry about that; it's supposed to be your day off," Ryan said. "I'll see you at work tomorrow. Try to enjoy the rest of your day off."

"Yeah, thanks," I returned sourly. I stabbed my finger against the phone screen to end the call.

"When you didn't come back," I heard Julia's carefully clipped tone, "I got worried."

I whipped my head in the direction of her voice. She'd noiselessly approached me. Her purse hung over her shoulder. I wondered if she'd already paid our bill or if she just hadn't wanted to leave her bag unattended at the table.

"I'm sorry," I exhaled.

"Stop with the apologies already, Cassidy," she frowned. Her tone curled with annoyance. "Just tell me what's going on."

"This is totally selfish of me to ask. I need you to defend Landon Tauer."

She looked at me quizzically. "The suspect in your double murder case?"

"Yes," I confirmed. "He didn't do it. And the public defender assigned to him is probably going to be some snot-nosed kid straight out of law school."

"Why are you so convinced he didn't kill that girl?"

"Don't you ever get a gut feeling with a client?" I asked. "Like, you can just tell that they're innocent?"

"Sometimes, sure. But I put in the same amount of effort, regardless of if I think the person committed the crime or not."

"He didn't do it," I said with conviction. "There's absolutely no motive."

"What about love?" Julia posed.

"Love?" I echoed.

"Women fear being murdered by their dates; men fear ridicule. What if this boy professed his love to Kennedy? What if he killed her after she rejected him?" she proposed. "The headlines are filled with young men doing far worse after being slighted by a girl."

"I don't have any proof," I admitted. "Nothing to convince a court of law, at least. But I don't have any proof that he did it, either. All we have is a gun that's registered to his dad. There's no prints, no blood, no DNA, no clothing fragments. Nothing puts him in that car with her."

Julia looked thoughtful. "I'm surprised the D.A. is pushing the case forward. They typically like slam dunk cases."

"It's definitely not one of those. Kennedy's parents have been riding the D.A.'s office pretty hard. And if they can connect Landon to my cold case, that's two crimes for the price of one."

I also suspected that Chase Trask's parents had been pushing the District Attorney for a swift conviction to clear up any suspicion that their son had somehow been involved.

I could see her hesitate. "Is this retribution for Halloween?" she asked.

"Please, Julia," I implored. "This is what you do. Landon is the exact reason why you became a public defender. Just a working-class kid who has had a string of bad luck. The system is going to chew him up if we don't do something to stop it."

She sighed. I almost had her convinced.

"He's only being charged with Kennedy's death right now," I noted. "But if he's found guilty, you can bet they'll find a way to pin the other death on him as well."

Julia's shoulders dropped. "Fine. Yes. I'll defend this boy."

I grabbed her by the hips and pressed an overly aggressive kiss to her painted mouth. She initially stiffened, but eventually melted into the embrace. When our mouths parted, she remained close. Her fingers gripped the front of my flannel shirt.

She pressed a gentle kiss to my mouth. "Landon Tauer is extremely lucky to have you in his corner."

CHAPTER EIGHTEEN

Boxes filled with spiral-bound notebooks were waiting for me on my desk when I returned to work the next day. I found a yellow sticky note from Detective Ryan at the top of the stack: *Don't say I never got you anything.*

Sarah, Stanley, and I worked around the clock to decipher Kennedy Petersik's looping handwriting. We scanned through junior high anxieties about acne and body image, first crushes and first dates, the excitement of getting a scholarship to Pius, the nervousness about fitting in. Stanley even had a few guest appearances in the journal as her mentor to help her through that first uncomfortable year of high school.

Collectively, they provided a window into a young woman's life and her desire to belong, but the entries ended months before her high school graduation. After her excitement about being accepted into college at St. Olaf, the writing had abruptly stopped. I'd been so hopeful that the journals would open up the case for us, but instead they were yet another dead end.

More troubling, the trial against Landon Tauer seemed to be moving in hyper-drive. He'd remained in police custody until his court hearing, and once he'd entered a plea of Not Guilty, jury selection had almost immediately taken place. The Sixth Amendment to the Constitution guarantees the right to a speedy trial, but this seemed without precedent. The timing of the trial could work in Landon's favor, however. With a quick start, it gave the State less time to put together its case.

Because Landon's bail had been set so high—the D.A.'s office had convinced the judge during the bail hearing that Landon was a flight risk—Julia had to convene with her client in his holding cell at the county jail across the street from the district court house.

I wasn't able to accompany her during these meetings. It wouldn't have been professional or ethical for one of the detectives assigned to the Petersik case to be present in those preparatory meetings. Instead, I waited across the street in front of the twenty-four story Hennepin County Government Center with a cup of coffee in each hand.

I jumped up from my concrete bench when I spotted Julia exiting the county jail. The weather had started to take a turn toward winter temperatures, so a dark blue trench coat covered her pencil skirt and blouse. Her long, lean legs stuck out from the bottom of the jacket to fill respectably high heels that clicked against the pavement as she crossed the busy intersection to meet me.

Julia welcomed my presence with a kiss to my cheek before accepting one of the proffered coffee cups.

"How's Landon doing?" I asked.

"Nervous, but that's to be expected."

I waited patiently while Julia rubbed away the lipsticked evidence of her kiss from my cheek.

Her painted mouth somehow always matched her outfit, yet I was certain she only owned one shade of lipstick. I couldn't pull off wearing more makeup beyond a layer of mascara on my upper lids. Any time I tried, I only ended up looking like a clown.

"Are you still considering not letting him take the witness stand?" I asked.

She'd filled me in on few details and strategies she intended to follow over shared takeout in her office. I occupied a precarious position; by day I was gathering evidence for the State. At night, I was a sounding board for Julia as she prepared to go to trial.

"It's very unusual these days to allow your client to be grilled in such a high-profile case," she told me. "Landon is emotional. I'm sure you've seen it. And that can only hurt him in the eyes of a jury."

"You don't think a jury would sympathize with him?" I questioned.

"Just the opposite," she opined. "If he's too emotional, too lovesick over Kennedy's death, the prosecution could twist that as evidence that he was prone to fits of passion that might have resulted in him killing Kennedy if she rejected him. And if he's too stoical about her death, then he's a sociopath."

I cringed at the final words. "Damned if he does, damned if he doesn't."

Julia nodded. "Precisely." She took a few more sips of her coffee before discarding the cardboard cup into a nearby garbage can.

Julia stood beside me and stared up at the skyscraper that housed the county courthouse. "It's almost show time," she announced.

"Are you sure having me in there isn't going to be a distraction?" I momentarily worried.

Julia arched an eyebrow. "You're not planning on theatrics, are you?"

"No, of course not," I readily dismissed. "But I'm, like, on the opposing team."

"I see it much differently than you do, dear. I see you as neutral. You do the leg work, you find the clues, you gather the facts. It's up to the prosecution and the defense to prove that the evidence you've assembled proves what our respective side is arguing."

She grabbed my arm and we started up the steps to the twin government towers. "You're like ... a prep cook," she continued with her analogy. "You set everything out, get all of the ingredients ready. And it's my job as the *chef de cuisine* to do something with those ingredients."

It was in my nature to argue differently or at least show a heavy dose of skepticism, but Julia's confidence in her statement had me saving my reservations to myself.

"Trust me, dear," she said, patting my arm. "I'm very good at what I do."

Julia breezed into the front lobby of the district court building like she'd done it a thousand times before. I stood a few feet behind to admire the vastness of the glass atrium and the large center fountain that could have doubled as an Olympic-sized pool. In the background, a metal detector periodically beeped with the entrance of each new visitor.

"Good morning, Rodrigo," Julia greeted the police officer in charge of the metal detector and bag check. She removed her jacket and tossed her leather satchel onto the conveyor belt.

I didn't know the cop, but he could have been about my age. His face broke into a broad, boyish smile when he saw my girlfriend.

"Julia! It's been a minute." He leaned against the side of the free-standing metal detector.

"I know," she returned his smile. "I keep settling out of court lately. It's terrible."

"It's only terrible because your smile hasn't been around," he returned.

I watched Julia's bag go through the x-ray machine without his notice. She could have been smuggling drugs and explosives into the building and no one would have stopped her.

Julia laughed affably at his compliment and retrieved her unexamined bag from the end of the conveyor belt.

Rodrigo's smile vanished when he looked at me, next in line. His features returned to the flat boredom of doing and saying the same things over and over again.

"Personal belongings on the conveyor belt. Make sure there's nothing in your pockets. No cell phones, food, or drink admitted."

I tossed my bag that contained my wallet and badge onto the conveyer belt. My pockets were empty as I walked through the metal detector, but I knew it wouldn't make a difference. I still beeped.

"Anything in your pockets, ma'am? Any large jewelry or belt buckles?" Rodrigo asked in an emotionless drone.

"Schrapnel."

"Say that again?" he asked.

"There's metal fragments from a dirty bomb lodged in my back," I explained. "Better get your magic wand."

The bored look on Rodrigo's face was replaced with interest as he grabbed the black and yellow handheld metal detector and rounded the conveyor belt to meet me on the other side.

I raised my arms above my head without having to be asked.

Rodrigo waved the wand in front of my torso and down the front of my legs. It remained silent until he reached my back. He pulled the wand back and forth; it clicked and beeped like I was radioactive each time it passed my back.

"Are you gonna have to strip search me?" I meant the question as a joke, but I couldn't deny the acrid notes that crept into my tone.

"Rodrigo, Detective Miller is with me," Julia chimed in. "I can vouch for her."

"Detective?" Between Julia's approval, my job title, and the metal in my back, Rodrigo's head looked ready to spin off into space. Plus, a line had begun to form behind me of others waiting to gain entrance to the government building. I almost felt sorry for him. Almost.

I grabbed my bag from the end of the conveyor belt and took Julia's hand in mine. I gave her arm a slight tug until her hip collided with mine. Her face drew just close enough with the movement for me to kiss her soundly in the lips.

I heard Julia's intake of air. "Detective," she murmured against my mouth.

I knew I'd hear complaints about PDAs in her place of work or how I'd smudged her perfectly applied lipstick.

"Come on, Hero," she sighed instead. When she didn't drop my hand, but instead only held it tighter, my insides crowed in victory.

+ + +

I had had the opportunity to observe Julia in a courtroom on three previous occasions. The first as City Attorney when a bar owner in Embarrass had alleged that David Addams had unfairly targeted his bar. The second as a defense lawyer on her father's behalf, and the third when she and her father had fought over custody of her mother. I'd been in awe—hypnotized each time—regardless of my skin in the game or the trials' outcomes.

Just as I couldn't conceive of being anything other than a police officer, I similarly couldn't imagine Julia without a courtroom. The environment suited her nearly as well as her grey pencil skirt and buttoned-up blouse. She stalked purposefully and in control at the front of the courtroom. Thin carpeting silenced her high heels, but my brain supplied its own soundtrack. Her voice, cool and confident, curled around the space. Her carriage, erect and defiant, captured the undivided attention of everyone in the room—judge and jury included.

The curve of her backside beneath the grey pencil skirt was nearly enough to distract my attention from Julia's opening statement.

"Your Honor. Members of the jury," she began. "Over the next few days, the State is going to tell you all about a young woman named Kennedy Petersik. Devoted daughter. Loving big sister. Top of her class at a prestigious private high school. Academic scholarship at St. Olaf College. Popular. Pretty. Kind."

Julia paused to wet her painted lips. "But this trial isn't about Kennedy Petersik. This trial is about my client, Landon Tauer. So you may be asking yourself, 'Why would the State spend so much time and energy building up the character and likeability of Miss Petersik?' And the answer is terribly simple. The State doesn't have a case. They have what amounts to flimsy and circumstantial evidence which they'll try to manipulate to accuse my client of an unthinkable act—the murder of an innocent woman."

Julia rounded the podium and approached the jurors' box. "The State is going to make you feel sorry for Kennedy. They're going to play on your human decency. They're going to convince you what a tragedy it is that a young, promising life was lost. And they're not wrong." Julia's tone softened in sincerity. "It *is* a tragedy that Kennedy is no longer with us."

After a pregnant pause, Julia continued. "Over the next few days, it's okay to feel sad about Kennedy Petersik's death. It's natural. It's decent. But what I ask you to do is separate those emotions from the facts. The State has very few, which is why they'll want you only thinking about Kennedy. We have a gun registered to my client's father—a gun that he gave to Kennedy at her bequest. Landon's DNA was not in Kennedy's car. No blood. No clothing fragments. And no signs of struggle. Nothing suggests that Landon is responsible for Kennedy's death. But that's not my job. The State has to convince you—beyond a reasonable doubt—that Landon Tauer killed his childhood friend. The motive? Who knows," she shrugged with a dramatic flair. "I guess we'll discover together whatever flimsy excuse the State has fabricated for you."

I exhaled the breath I hadn't realized I'd been holding. I should have felt uncomfortable that Julia was essentially bad mouthing my bosses, but I only felt entranced.

Celeste Rivers was the first expert witness to be called to the stand. Typically she would have been called as a witness for the State to explain some esoteric data or crime lab discoveries, but this case was different. There was no physical evidence to consider. This absence made her the perfect witness for the Defense.

The pretty crime lab tech wore a light grey pantsuit to court that day. Her hair was pulled back in her usual bun. She looked at ease in the witness box; it made me wonder how often she found herself in that position.

"Ms. Rivers," Julia began her questioning, "do you recognize this laptop?"

She set a slim, silver laptop on the elevated ledge of the witness stand.

Celeste gave the computer a cursory glance before responding. "Yes. It was recovered from Kennedy Petersik's dorm room at St. Olaf College."

"And can you tell us what you discovered on the laptop?" Julia asked.

"No."

Julia feigned surprise. "No?"

"I can't tell you because there was nothing on the laptop—it had been wiped clean. Restored to the default factory settings. We tried to recover the data, but my best guess is it had been remotely wiped."

"What reasons would a young woman have to erase the contents of her computer?" Julia inquired. "Certainly a laptop is essential for academic success these days: essays, lecture notes, e-mail."

"Objection!" The Assistant D.A. assigned to the case stood up. I didn't know the woman. Typically I dealt with Assistant District Attorney Jeremy Rudolph. Rudolph was a balding black man with a great barrel chest. He was in charge of the Special Prosecutions Unit under the District of Minnesota's Criminal Division, which focused on long-term, time intensive investigations. He would have been the prosecutor standing behind the walnut table if Landon had been charged with Michael Bloom's death. In his place, this Assistant D.A. was a small, mousey woman. She looked sloppy in comparison to Julia's impeccable wardrobe. I was starting to appreciate why clothes were so important to the work she did.

"This is speculation," the Assistant D.A. protested. "There's no evidence that Kennedy Petersik was the one who erased the laptop."

Julia inclined her head. "I'll rephrase, Your Honor. What reason would a *person* have to erase the contents of this computer?"

Celeste shrugged. "There was something on the laptop they didn't want anyone else to see."

"In your expert forensics opinion, Ms. Rivers," Julia continued her line of questioning, "does this suggest pre-meditated self-harm or something a murderer might do post-crime?"

Celeste sat a little straighter in her chair and leaned closer to the microphone in front of her. "I would say this is indicative of someone cleaning up loose ends. However, whoever erased the laptop would have also needed access to Ms. Petersik's phone, which has a lock code that wasn't set up for face recognition or a thumb print. They would have needed her four-number security code."

"Who do you think wiped the laptop?" Julia questioned.

"Unless we're dealing with someone who can hack cell phones, I'd have to say Kennedy Petersik was responsible."

"Objection, Your Honor!" the Assistant DA huffed. "This is all speculation! The State recognizes Ms. Rivers as an expert in forensic science, but even this is beyond her purview. Nothing in the science indicates Ms. Petersik was responsible."

"Sustained," the stern-faced judge remarked. "The witness's response will be struck from the record and the jury will disregard Ms. River's statement."

Julia's features were schooled as she moved on with her line of questioning. "You mentioned Ms. Petersik's phone. What was your office able to extract in the way of evidence from her cell phone?"

"Her phone was wiped, too," Celeste revealed. "We were able to restart to factory settings, but all of her text transcripts, stored voicemails, etcetera, were destroyed. Whoever did this, they probably erased everything all at the same time."

"Your Honor!" The Assistant D.A. shouted to be heard. Her lungs were getting quite the workout and the trial had barely begun. "We'd like to petition that Ms. Petersik's phone records be purged from the evidence docket. There's no evidence that the cell phone was actually with her on the day of her murder. If the defendant, who lives next door to the victim, was in possession of the phone, the cell records would not be able to tell us that."

Celeste Rivers appeared to be getting flustered, as if she herself was on trial. "Forensic evidence is the foundation of justice," she spoke up. She lifted her proud chin. "It doesn't lie on stand. It doesn't conveniently forget or suddenly remember what it saw."

"Your Honor," Julia cut in, "if the State is so eager to suppress the only tangible evidence this case has produced, I'm very eager and curious to know how they plan on presenting their case." She turned to the Assistant D.A. and spoke to her directly. "Will we be presenting character witnesses all day or do you actually have proof that Mr. Tauer killed Kennedy Petersik?" She spun on her heels to once again face the presiding judge. "To be honest, Your Honor, in my entire career as both a city prosecutor and now as a public defender, I've never seen such a flimsily supported case. I'm honestly shocked we're even standing in this courtroom today."

Sensing he was starting to lose control of his courtroom, the judge lightly struck his gavel. "Motion to suppress Ms. Petersik's cell phone records is denied. Ms. Desjardin, you may continue with your witness."

Julia flashed the judge a dazzling smile. "Thank you, Your Honor."

I might have been imagining it, but he seemed to smile back.

CHAPTER NINETEEN

I whistled to myself in the basement of the Fourth Precinct. Once Landon had been arrested, Homicide had moved back upstairs and left us alone. I was thankful to have our space back again, but not about the reason. As much as I wanted to be a fly on the wall, I wasn't going to be able to attend every day of the courtroom drama. I still had a job to attend to. Even though the District Attorney's office believed they'd found the person responsible for Kennedy Petersik's death, we police didn't sit around on our laurels and wait for the jury to make a decision. We continued to search for new clues, new leads, that might alter the trajectory of the current court case. I was confident, however, that with Julia at his side, Landon Tauer would receive a fair trial.

I'd thought myself alone, but my whistling attracted the attention of my immediate supervisor in Cold Case, Captain Forrester.

He stuck his head out of his office like a prairie dog out of its hole. "Miller!" he barked. "My office! Now!"

I rarely had a reason to be in my supervisor's office. It wasn't a complaint, however. His office gave me the creeps. Stuffed woodland animals peered down at me from their respective shelves with their lifeless, black beady eyes. Captain Forrester was an avid taxidermist who spent more time dusting his office critters than solving crimes. It was obvious he was biding his time until retirement when he could collect his pension, and he didn't care who knew.

He glared at me from behind his desk, and I wondered what I'd done wrong. "Do you like being a police officer?"

My features pinched. "Of course. It's the reason I get out of bed every morning."

"They why are you so determined to shoot yourself in the goddamn foot?"

"What do you mean, Captain?"

"You've got a good gig here." He spoke slowly to me as if explaining something to a child. "Decent pay. Good benefits. A pension when you retire."

I shook my head. I still wasn't following Captain Forrester's line of questioning.

"Julia Desjardin." He said her name like it left a bad taste in her mouth. "I hear she's defending our suspect in the double homicide."

I didn't correct him that Landon Tauer was only being charged for one murder. I also didn't correct him on his choice of pronoun since *he'd* had nothing to do with the case. I couldn't speak; I felt too sick to respond.

No one could have known that I had been the one to ask Julia to represent Landon Tauer. Only Julia and I knew that detail. Landon's family didn't have the money for fancy, independent counsel. To an outsider, anyone would have believed she'd randomly been assigned to the case by the public defender's office.

"You're roommates, right?"

"She's-she's my girlfriend," I corrected.

Where was Forrester getting this intel?

"Listen. I don't care how you get your rocks off. But if you're serious about a career with the Minneapolis Police Department, you might wanna be more careful about who knows you're sleeping with a criminal defense lawyer."

"She's a public defender."

"I don't care how you spell it—she's a lawyer," he countered. "And you're *supposed* to be a cop."

I sat up straighter in my chair. "I don't think Landon Tauer is guilty, sir. If you look at the evidence we've been able to collect—."

"Well it's a good thing we're not paying you to think," Forrester cut me off with a snarl. "Now get out of my face."

I stood in the hallway outside of Captain Forrester's office, shaking with rage. My heart was lodged in my throat. I clenched and unclenched my fists at my side debating going right back into his office and telling Forrester where he could shove this job.

But before I could become a contestant on *Who Wants to be Unemployed*, my colleague from Homicide skipped down the stairs.

"Miller—there you are," Jason Ryan called out. "I've been looking for you." He paused long enough to look me in the face. "What's wrong?"

"Nothing," I quickly lied.

It was obvious I was annoyed at the very least, but Ryan smartly ignored my lie. He held up an official-looking piece of paper. "I got the judge to sign a search warrant. Let's go check out the Tauer house."

+ + +

"Lemme know if you find any nudie magazines," Ryan told me. "I'll handle them so they don't offend your delicate sensibilities."

I wrinkled my nose. "You wish."

Ryan and I rummaged through Landon Tauer's bedroom in his parents' basement. Ryan had been in such a rush to arrest Landon's father and then Landon himself that he'd never bothered to get a search warrant for the Tauer's house. I was there to find evidence to incriminate Landon in Kennedy's death, but after my conversation with Captain Forrester, my heart wasn't in it.

I contemplated texting Julia to tell her about the confrontation, but I decided to keep it to myself for the moment. She would be upset with me for keeping my supervisor's words of warning to myself, but I worried she might give up on Landon if she thought my job security was in jeopardy. I knew what we were doing was a conflict of interest, but I couldn't sit idle while the System tried to pin a murder on a young man without a shred of evidence. For me, being a cop was about keeping the peace, not trying to find a convenient scapegoat.

I sifted through a stack of opened mail that had accumulated on Landon's desk.

"Isn't that a federal offense?" Ryan remarked.

"Not if it's already opened. But I know you're chomping at the bit to make another arrest," I said, not hiding the bitterness in my tone, "so go ahead."

Ryan looked like he wanted to make a comment—perhaps another statement about my menstrual cycle—but he kept his words to himself. We'd spent enough time together that he could tell I was annoyed by something besides himself for once.

"Well, shit," I muttered.

"Find something?"

I unfolded a piece of paper. "Yeah. A life insurance certificate."

Ryan tried to peer over my shoulder to see what I'd discovered. "Our guy took out a life insurance policy?"

"No." I blinked in disbelief. "Kennedy Petersik did. And it looks like the sole beneficiary is her sister, Kayla."

+ + +

Julia dropped a manila envelope on the table in front of Landon Tauer. The presiding judge had granted her a brief recess in the trial so she could contemplate newly discovered evidence. Landon sat in his County Jail jumpsuit. The dark circles under his eyes clued me in to how he was enjoying life behind bars so far.

I stood in the corner of the interrogation room. I typically wouldn't have been allowed to observe a private conversation between a public defender and her client, but my job was to babysit the evidence that Ryan and I had found in Landon's room. I'd somehow convinced Ryan not to take the envelope and its contents directly to the crime lab. I wasn't convinced that if it was presented to the District Attorney that it would ever see the light of day again.

"Why did Kennedy mail this to you?" Julia asked.

Landon didn't touch the envelope, but he already knew its contents. "It came a few days after the police found her body. I know I should have told someone—maybe her parents, but the note inside told me to wait until after the life insurance check cleared."

"Landon, they think you killed their daughter!" I tried not to explode. "Is this really the hill you want to die on?"

"Isn't this your job?" he challenged. "Find new evidence and exonerate innocent people?"

"*This* is the evidence!" I exclaimed. "There's no reason for you to be in here! Besides, how are you planning on giving this letter to her parents if you're in prison?"

Landon's eyes opened a little wider. "I-I didn't think about that part."

"I'm going to present this information to the judge," Julia decided. "This certificate alone should exonerate you."

"Please don't," Landon pled. "Kayla won't get the money if the insurance company thinks it was a suicide."

Julia leveled her stare on her client: "Landon. What aren't you telling us?"

The young man took a deep breath. "Kayla's not Kennedy's sister; she's her daughter."

+ + +

Ryan and I sat with the Petersiks at their dining room table. Black coffee cooled in ceramic cups. A coffee cake went untouched on a patterned serving tray. Kayla Petersik bounced up and down on Mr. Petersik's knee. She blew spit bubbles and babbled without care. The life insurance certificate sat in the center of the table.

Mrs. Petersik touched her fingertips against the edge of the paper stock. She touched it delicately as though she expected it to crumble. "Landon knew?"

I nodded. "Kennedy told him about Kayla when she asked him for the gun. He had no idea what she really intended on doing with it though. He genuinely thought she was trying to protect herself—not protect her daughter's future. He didn't put the pieces together until he received the life insurance certificate and her letter in the mail. And by then, it was too late. She was already dead."

Mrs. Petersik stood from the dining room table. She didn't say a word, but I sensed that she wanted me to follow her. She floated down the hallway until she came to a closed door that I knew belonged to Kennedy's bedroom.

She opened the door and walked to Kennedy's desk. She opened up the top drawer and pulled out a notebook. I'd assumed I'd seen every one of Kennedy's diaries, but apparently Mrs. Petersik had specifically kept this one from us.

She hesitated before handing it to me—her daughter's private musings that she'd purposefully hidden from the police.

I looked to her for some kind of instruction, but her face remained impassive. I sat down on the edge of Kennedy's childhood bed, opened the notebook to the first page, and began to read.

My throat tightened as I scanned over the feminine, looped handwriting that had become so familiar. It was all there. It wasn't exactly a suicide note, but it was page after page of Kennedy's intimate thoughts and fears and worries. The multiple pregnancy kits that all indicated the same thing. The internal debate about telling her parents or not. The anguish over terminating the pregnancy or seeing the pregnancy to term. Her decision to break up with Chase and keep the pregnancy a secret from him so as to not complicate his future. Deferring college for a year so no one would know she'd ever been pregnant. A prisoner in her parents' home when she'd started to show. The heartache of deciding between giving up the child for adoption or trying to raise it on her own. But never having to make that decision because her parents were going to pretend that their granddaughter was their daughter.

I closed the journal and its painful truths. "This is why you didn't want us reading her journals."

Mrs. Petersik looked as though in a trance. "I didn't want them to know. I didn't want them to think less of her."

"Who is them?" I asked.

"All of them. Everyone. She was such a good girl. A dream daughter. She was always so careful; she never made mistakes. But then …but then …"

"Your miracle baby," I finished for her.

"Detective, are you from around here?"

"I grew up in St. Cloud."

She nodded solemnly. "Then you know how judgmental people can be. They call it Minnesota Nice, but only because people aren't mean to your face. No, we save all of that nonsense for when company goes home."

Mrs. Petersik worried her hands in front of her body. "Kennedy told us about the pregnancy just before graduation. We told her the decision was up to her. We didn't want to force her to have an abortion, but we also couldn't stand by while she ruined her life. With Kayla, she never would have been able to go to St. Olaf, and she'd worked so hard to make that happen."

She sighed wearily and sat beside me on the small bed. "Oh that, girl. She couldn't put the baby up for adoption. After carrying that child around for nine months, she couldn't just erase her from her life."

"So you offered to raise Kayla as your own?" I supplied.

A peculiar smile appeared on her face. "That was actually Frank's idea. I had no idea how much he'd been wanting another child; he'd never spoken about it before." She flattened her hands on her lap. "We thought we'd found a happy medium. Kennedy got to see Kayla when she was home on breaks, but then she could concentrate on her studies when she was back at school. Until I read her journal, I had no idea how this double life was tearing her apart."

"Do you think it could have been postpartum depression?"

Mrs. Petersik made a noise like a hiccup. "You know, when I was pregnant with Kennedy, we didn't have a word for that. We just called it the Baby Blues."

Her features suddenly crumbled. "It was there the whole time. I've read through these journals so many times, but I couldn't admit it to myself. Landon didn't kill my baby; *I* killed Kennedy," she choked up. "I made her feel so ashamed. I made her keep Kayla a secret. I told her to just go on with her life—to pretend like she'd never created a life. That burden. That secret. That shame. It killed my daughter."

Landon Tauer would go free. Mrs. Petersik probably could have been charged with obstruction, but I wouldn't be making another arrest. Her offense wasn't all that criminal, but it didn't matter anymore. She'd already constructed her own personal prison.

Case closed.

CHAPTER TWENTY

"Are you done with that?" Stanley Harris looked down at me expectantly. I sat at my desk in the Cold Case office in the basement of the Fourth Precinct of the Minneapolis Police Department.

I separated the sports section and the comics from the daily paper for myself and handed the rest to Stanley. He carefully folded the newspaper in half and tucked it under his arm.

"If anyone calls …" he trailed off as he walked out the office door.

"I know, I know," I chuckled after him. "You're not on the can."

In light of newly discovered evidence, Julia had arranged for all charges against Landon Tauer to be dropped. He could have still been charged with involuntary manslaughter or at least evidence tampering, but it appeared as though the D.A.'s office no longer wanted anything to do with the case. Sarah would contact Michael Bloom's parents to let them know what had happened to their son, and two pending criminal cases would be cleared from the boards.

After Landon's release from jail and the Petersik family's acceptance of what had happened to their daughter, the rhythm of our work days in Cold Case had returned to normal. We waited for tips that might allow us to take a second look at an unsolved crime, we kept an eye on active investigations that might be tangentially connected to a case that had gone cold. We looked for the long shots. But at least now I felt like we had a few more allies in the Homicide Division and the Crime Lab. It wasn't just Stanley, Sarah, and me against the world.

My cell phone, which I typically stored out of sight in my office desk, buzzed to life and rattled around the inside of the metal desk drawer. I pulled the phone from its cubby. An uneasy feeling settled in my stomach when I glanced at my caller ID.

I hadn't spoken to David Addams, my former colleague in the Embarrass police force since Julia had lost legal custody of her ailing mother. It might have been inappropriate, but I had asked David to keep an eye on her parents and to let me know if anything happened to her mother that Julia might be able to draw on to wrestle away guardianship from her estranged father.

Addams could have been calling to catch up or to give me hell about something, but my instincts told me this wasn't a friendly call. My phone only seemed to ring when there was bad news to report. I had expected the worst when my mom had called a few weeks prior, but my gut told me somehow that David Addams wasn't calling me from the Mall of America.

"Hello?" I answered the call.

"Miller, hey. It's Addams. Uh, David Addams," he said unsure. "From Embarrass." His voice was quiet and somewhat muffled. I wondered about the phone connection. Embarrass' cellular reliability could be, well, unreliable.

"Hey, buddy," I replied, trying to maintain a positive attitude despite the uncomfortable twisting in my stomach. "What's up?"

"Listen, I don't know if you and Julia Desjardin are still a thing or not, and I probably shouldn't be doing this, but I wanted to give you a heads up." He paused, as though bracing himself. "Julia's dad was found dead in his home."

My throat constricted with the unexpected news. "What? How?" I managed to choke out.

"It, like, just happened—or, we just found out," he continued in that same hushed tone. "The nurse who comes in periodically to check on Mrs. Desjardin found him. And Cassidy, it's too early to tell, but I don't think he died of natural causes."

I gripped my phone tighter. "Jesus. Is Mrs. Desjardin alright?"

"Yeah. Luckily they had the nurse service checking in on her, otherwise who knows how long it would have been until someone found him."

"Are you thinking he was murdered?" I grimaced.

"I can't really talk about it right now," he seemed to whisper. "I'm probably breaking all kinds of cop ethics and laws right now by calling you. And you may have heard, but we no longer have a hot-shot city prosecutor who can defend me."

Another question entered my head. My stomach doubled in knots. "Does Julia know?"

"The Chief just called her," he confirmed. "It why I'm calling; I thought you might appreciate a little heads up so you weren't totally blindsided. Julia's not exactly … easy."

"Yeah. Fuck," I exhaled. "Thanks, Addams."

"Sure thing. Tell Julia I'm sorry, yeah? Her dad was a giant douchebag for scamming the city, but …" He trailed off, like he didn't know what else to say.

I didn't know what else to say either or how to finish his thought. So instead I thanked him again for the information and hung up.

My hands shook as I pressed the button on my phone to call Julia. I let it ring a few times before hanging up and trying again. I was on my third attempt when Stanley strolled through the office door with the morning paper still neatly tucked under his arm.

"Stanley, I've got to go," I announced. I grabbed my jacket off the back of my chair.

Stanley inspected me with interest. "Is everything okay?"

"No."

I knew he was expecting me to elaborate, but this wasn't my news to share. My priority was getting to Julia, not gossiping with my co-worker.

+ + +

Julia's black Mercedes wasn't in the parking lot adjacent to the public defender office, and it wasn't in her parking spot at the apartment. It hadn't been at the bar where we'd first met either. Beyond those three spaces, I didn't know where she might be.

An uneasy feeling took residence in my stomach as I walked towards her office building. I'd asked her to marry me, and yet I didn't know her go-to spots when she was upset. In Embarrass it had been her family's cottage by a lake, but in the Twin Cities, I was directionless.

I'd never visited her office so early in the day. Typically I only came over after hours when she and maybe Alice, the office manager, were the only ones left. I walked in to a whirlwind of activity. The lobby area was filled with clients or potential clients, I didn't know which. The typical stale coffee scent had been replaced by the aroma of freshly roasted coffee beans.

Alice stood at the reception desk as the gatekeeper of the chaos. At that moment she had the office phone pressed to her ear. I wanted to be patient and wait for her to hang up with whomever she was talking to, but I felt like a ticking bomb. I had to find Julia.

"Alice—hey," I tried to cut in.

She held up a single finger to stop me, and I had no choice but to wait for her to finish.

"Yes, I understand that," she said to whomever was on the phone. "But we have a bit of a waitlist for Ms. Desjardin at the moment." She grinned, but it was more like a grimace, to let me know she saw me still waiting on her.

"No, I don't think the judge will delay your trial until she's free. Yes, I'm sorry, too. But our offices provide quality defense from any of our many other—." She stopped as she was cut off by the person on the phone. "No? Okay, well I can appreciate your position. Best of luck."

"Hi, Cassidy. Sorry," Alice breathed as she hung up the phone. "It's a bit of a zoo today. News coverage of your girl's court victory has really boosted our profile."

I forced a smile to my lips. "Is she in?"

"No. She left a little while ago."

"Oh." I scratched my neck. "Did she—did she say where she was going?" I didn't want to let on that anything was wrong. Julia was highly private and I wasn't sure if she'd shared the news of her father's unexpected death with her office assistant. It wasn't my place to do so in her stead.

"She—." Alice stopped and bit her lip. It was clear she knew something, but was withholding information. I admired her dedication and loyalty to Julia, but now was not the time for a stalemate.

The office phone began to ring again. Alice's eyes darted from the phone to my face and back to the ringing phone again.

"I'm worried about her, Alice. There's been an emergency, and she's not answering her phone. Any information you have." I wasn't above begging.

Sensing I wasn't going to give up, Alice caved. "She might be at Jake's?" she offered.

"Jake's?" My voice strained on the syllable. She'd never mentioned anyone by that name before. Just another thing to add to the growing list of things I didn't know about the woman I wanted to marry.

Alice answered the office phone and cradled it between her ear and her shoulder. "It's a neighborhood bar. It's a total dive."

It didn't sound at all like the kind of establishment where Julia might frequent, but I'd run out of leads. "Thanks for the tip."

A neon red sign hanging on the outside of the building announced the name of the bar. The cream brick structure looked as though it had been there for centuries; the faded remnants of old advertisements were barely visible on the exterior. It was early—too early even for day drinking—so I was surprised the front door opened when I tugged on the handle.

My nostrils flared upon entering the bar. The air was tainted with cigarette smoke despite the city-wide anti-smoking ordinances. I stood just within the doorway and scanned the empty bar. I spied a solo bartender, washing glassware behind the bar, but the tables and stools were vacant. It definitely didn't look like the kind of place Julia Desjardin would willingly frequent, but her black Mercedes was parked on the street out front.

The crisp crack of billiard balls alerted me to the back corner of the bar. A woman in an impeccably tailored suit began to rack the pool balls. Her beautiful face was deep in concentration as she organized the multi-colored solids and stripes into the holding triangle.

I quietly stalked through the bar, maneuvering past tables and chairs as I made my way to the pool tables in the back. "Why aren't you answering your phone?"

Julia's eyes lifted from the green felt to meet my stare. She'd always had the best poker face. Her features were impassive, her eyes flicking to my face.

"I must have forgotten it at the office."

She resumed arranging the billiard balls before retrieving a pool stick from a stand against the wall.

I watched her lean over the table and take aim. Her stick connected with the white cue ball, which collided with the tightly arranged colored balls, which ricocheted across the billiard table.

"How are you?" I didn't know how to approach the situation. Julia and her father had a complicated history.

She didn't ask me how I'd found her, but that wasn't important. I would always find her. She also didn't ask how I'd learned that her father was dead. But those were all questions for another day.

She slowly righted herself. "Do you play?" she posed, ignoring my question with one of her own.

I shrugged. "Not very well."

The next-door neighbors had had a pool table in their basement that I'd gotten to play on when they invited my family over to watch Vikings games. But that had been two decades ago.

She handed me her pool stick. "Your shot."

My fingers curved around the contours of the pool cue. I grabbed a cube of blue chalk and applied it to the end of the stick. I wasn't going to demand that she confront her emotions. If she wanted to delay reality for a while, I was content to hang in that limbo with her.

I walked around the table and lined up my opening shot. I felt the heat of Julia's body press against the back of my thighs and backside. Her soft breasts pressed against my back as she curled her body over mine. I stiffened momentarily at her proximity and flicked my eyes in the direction of the bartender who appeared disinterested in our activities.

"Advice." Her warm breath tickled the back of my ear. "Shoot through the white ball."

When I didn't take the shot, her arm wrapped around my midsection and her hand traveled lower. She ran her fingers along the front zipper of my dress pants. She cupped me and the heel of her palm pressed against my clit through my dress pants and underwear.

My eyes shuttered as a wave of arousal flooded over me. I felt the lump forming in my throat. The bar was empty with the exception of the bartender, but I still wasn't an exhibitionist. But I also couldn't help how my body responded to hers.

Only the realization of her flicking open the top button of my pants had me crashing back to reality. Her hand was probably hidden from sight, shielded by our bodies and the pool table, but we were still in public.

"Not here," I said in a low tone. "Not like this."

Julia ignored my quiet warning. Her insistent hand found the space necessary to slide under the front of my underwear. The tips of her outstretched fingers sought out my clit, gave me a rough rub, and continued on to the collecting dampness between my thighs.

My legs wobbled as her fingers bisected my pussy. The pool cue fell from my hands and clattered noisily against the sides of the green-felted table. Julia pressed her face between my shoulder blades and her hand stilled between my legs. I didn't know what was happening until I felt her body rocking silently against mine.

She was crying.

Gently, I fished her hand out of my underwear. She put up no resistance this time. I quickly re-buttoned the top of my pants and turned to face her.

"Elliott," Julia called out in a cool, clear voice. "Could you give us a minute?"

I didn't know to whom she was speaking, but I assumed it was the bartender, since we were the only people in the bar.

I looked to her with too many unanswered questions. Who was Elliott? Why was she at this bar? How did she have such control over her emotions?

Julia leaned against the pool table, slightly sitting on its edge. "Elliott's a former client of mine," she revealed, answering one of my unspoken questions. "His family owns the bar. It's close to my office, so I come here sometimes to think."

I nodded, but kept quiet. She had much more talking and explaining to do.

Julia tilted her chin and stared up at the ceiling. I heard her long exhale. "I have to go back. There's so much to do. The funeral to plan. His assets to settle. My mother—." The words caught in her throat. "My mother—." She tried again without success.

I grabbed onto her hand. "I know."

Her father had been her mother's legal caretaker. With his passing, that responsibility now fell to her. I could only imagine the tumultuous thoughts ricocheting around in her head and how they might be affecting her heart.

I held her hand more tightly. "It's going to be okay." I had no idea if it actually was. "You don't have to take this on alone. You said it yourself—I'm due a vacation, right?" I tried to make light of the situation since the alternative terrified me.

I didn't know if it was my words or if it was the reality of the situation that finally broke her. The walls she'd so carefully constructed and maintained began to crumble. The erectness of her posture slumped. Her shoulders curved forward. Tears tumbled down her pale cheeks faster than she could wipe away.

"Cassidy." My name sounded like a strangled cry coming from her lips. "My dad is dead."

I'd only ever heard her refer to William Desjardin with the formal 'father.' I nearly collapsed myself at her word choice. She looked so lost and little and young. Words failed me, so I pulled her to me and her face went to my shoulder.

Her body seemed to fold in on itself, like she couldn't bear to take up any space. Her pain was contained, however; she swallowed down any verbal evidence of remorse. I pressed my lips to the side of her head and remained there until she eventually pulled away.

Julia wiped under her eyes even though her makeup had magically stayed in place. "How did you know?" she asked.

Her question lacked specifics, so I answered them all.

"David Addams called me. I went to your office to find you; Alice thought you might be here."

She nodded, lips tight. I could tell she hated that so many people already knew. It was probably, literally, front page news by now. Embarrass wasn't a place for secrets.

"I should apologize for trying to fuck you on a pool table," she said, slipping into a more formal tone. Her shoulders straightened and she flicked at her raven hair. "I'm not practiced at these kinds of things."

I slowly shook my head. "I don't think anyone is."

I watched with great remorse as those fortress walls began to reassemble around her. For a brief moment they had started to wobble and fall, but that weakness had only been temporary. She tugged at the bottom hem of her suit jacket and rearranged the collar of her blouse as if checking on her body armor. Even her lipstick was still in its place.

I hadn't wanted or expected her to be a blubbering mess, but I also knew firsthand the damage that holding in so many unchecked emotions could do. But I couldn't force her to grieve. I couldn't even make her tell me how she felt. No one could make Julia do anything she didn't want to do; she would deal with her father's death on her own terms.

EPILOGUE

William Desjardin was dead. I'd said the statement over and over again in my head. I was familiar with death, but that didn't mean I was at ease with it. The sudden permanency of it would be forever startling. You would never see that person again, never get to talk to them or ask them questions. They'd never tell you another joke or share another secret. They were just gone. One minute my buddies were laughing and celebrating after a successful directive, the next, they'd been obliterated by an undetected IED as if they'd never existed in the first place.

My parents hadn't raised me to be religious, and the concept of an afterlife had never caught on during any of my tours abroad. Plenty of Marines carried religious paraphernalia with them—a holy book, a rosary, a picture of their god—but just as many carried a lucky rabbit's foot or some other good-luck charm. I considered them all the same.

Julia's suitcase was packed in the trunk of her Mercedes. I'd watched her fill the luggage with meticulously folded blouses and pencil skirts. The more outfits she packed, the more I wondered if she planned on coming back. The postal mail had been put on hold. She'd asked a neighbor to keep an eye on the apartment and to water her houseplants in her absence.

I'd been surprised she hadn't put up more of a fight when I insisted that I come along with her to Embarrass. I didn't own proper luggage, so she'd let me borrow one of her suitcases.

I'd informed Captain Forrester that there'd been a family emergency. Stanley and Sarah would hold down the fort while I was away. I kept the details sparse.

Julia's Mercedes idled at a stoplight. Embarrass, Minnesota was just over three hours away, a straight shot north on I-35.

Talk radio played quietly in the background. Julia's hand rested lightly on the automatic shifter in the center console. I put my hand on top of hers and squeezed.

I was in it. I was there for her. She may not have been ready for marriage or babies or whatever that next step looked like for us, but I wanted her to know that I was there for her—for better or for worse. And I hoped that for the time being, that would be enough.

ABOUT THE AUTHOR

Eliza Lentzski is the author of lesbian fiction, romance, and erotica including the best-selling *Winter Jacket* and *Don't Call Me Hero* series, and the forthcoming novel, *The Woman in 3B* (Spring 2020). She publishes urban fantasy and paranormal romance under the penname E.L. Blaisdell. Although a historian by day, Eliza is passionate about fiction. She was born and raised in the upper Midwest, which is often the setting for her novels. She currently lives in Boston with her wife and their cat, Charley.

Follow her on Twitter and Instagram, @ElizaLentzski, and Like her on Facebook (http://www.facebook.com/elizalentzski) for updates and exclusive previews of future original releases.

http://www.elizalentzski.com

Printed in Poland
by Amazon Fulfillment
Poland Sp. z o.o., Wrocław

50904441R00127